A VOW TO KEEP

Other Books by Susan Evans McCloud

A Vow to Keep

Susan Evans McCloud

Deseret Book Company
Salt Lake City, Utah

©1989 Susan Evans McCloud

First printing February 1989

Library of Congress Cataloging-in-Publication Data

McCloud, Susan Evans.
    A vow to keep.

    1. Title.
PS3563.A26176V6   1989   813'.54   88-31056
ISBN 0-87579-180-8

New horizons should go to those
with tomorrow in their eyes:
This one is for Heather Jean
and Michael Wayne Huff

GRAHAM FAMILY

Oscar and Suzanne [Miller] Graham died February 1856

PERCY
Went to: Benjamin & Claire Gillman
(Their children: Belinda, Ellen, Mary)

LOUISA
Went to: Frank & Edith Bascom
Married: Victor Maughan

STANLEY
Went to: Squire Geoffrey Beal

LAURA
Went to: Aunt Judith Douglas (Scotland)
Married: Jack Armstrong of Selkirk

RANDALL
Went to: Aunt Judith Douglas

ROSE
Went to: Dr. Preston Davies & May (his daughter)
May married John Thomas

PART I

1

*I*t was a night for dying. A cold wind was wailing, with the cries of lost souls in its voice, brittle rain in its breath. The sky churned with thick, black clouds — the sky trembled with blackness and cast its vast shade upon the land that lay huddled below.

The bedroom was cold. Percy thought it was cold, though a fire was burning. He didn't like the smell of it, either. His father was there, sitting hunched, half-swallowed in shadow. He never looked up. There was one candle burning. Percy took it and walked with care to the bedside, and looked on her face, and knew that his mother was dying.

He bent down by her head. She opened her eyes and her lips moved, but he could hear nothing. She smiled, and for a moment the sickness and pain were not there, and her large brown eyes grew luminous, bright as a girl's, and her features were gentle and beautiful. Then, with a moan, she fell back against the limp pillow and lay gasping for breath, a wasted and dying woman.

She groped for his hand. He gave it to her and she clung to it with thin, talonlike fingers.

"My children —"

Percy heard her. "I'll care for them, Mother. Don't fret."

She opened her eyes and looked at him. "Don't lose my children," she said. "Out in the cold — my babies — my Rosie —"

There were tears in her eyes. He opened his mouth to reply, but his chin began trembling and the words would not form on his lips.

"Mother, Mother, don't cry!" He bent to touch her. Her skin was hot. He wiped a wet streak from her cheek.

"Would you like Rosie? Would you like to see Rosie?"

She nodded her head. Her chest rose and fell, struggling to draw in the precious air.

Percy ran from the room. He would gather them all. It was time. When he stood Rosie before her she opened her wide eyes and looked on the child. But there wasn't much left of her but that deep gaze which seemed to take them all in: sturdy Louisa, thirteen now, doing the cooking and cleaning, keeping the household together; himself, a young man of fourteen, nearly grown, feeling grown suddenly in a way that was hollow and uncomfortable; Stanley, newly twelve, a scrapper who could care for himself; Laura, eleven, a sweet, obedient girl; Randall, eight, a good boy, a pet of them all; and Rose, little Rosie, the baby, seven years old, Mama's gift child.

Love is like a lovely rose, the world's delight — so Mama often said, kissing her. She lay there looking out at the fair face of love until her blue eyes went blind and their father came out from somewhere in the shadows and closed them. Still the children stood there until Stanley said, rather too loudly, "She's dead." And Louisa, with tears in her voice, said, "Her soul's gone to heaven."

"Is it flying up to heaven right now?" Laura asked. Percy nodded his head. Rosie tore from his hands, which had sheltered her gently, and ran past the bed to the window that let in the darkness. She pressed her nose to the glass.

"How will she make it? It's much too fierce, Percy. Just look at the rain. And the wind—I can hear the mean, angry wind, Percy—"

He pulled her away. He felt weary and strangely ageless. "Come, Rose, back to bed. That's a good girl. If you catch a chill you'll never get better."

There were four of them sick: Laura, Rose, Randall, and the woman who now lay past sickness, past health, perhaps even past love. It was a dismal night. Randall went back to his bed in a stupor. *I don't think he knows. I don't think it even got through to him*, Percy thought, tucking the boy in. He went out to where Louisa was waiting.

She smiled at him thinly. "Oh, well. It was bound to happen. We knew it." She drew her shawl tightly across her shoulders. Her face was too thin. She and their father had both been sick, though they seemed now on the mend. But she was working too hard, much too hard.

"Where is Stanley?" Stanley could be helping more than he did; he always had to be prodded.

"I won't get the plague," he had said last week, tauntingly, "because I'm too bad. And Percy won't get it because he's too good."

The plague. They knew the word, the proper medical term for the sickness: *diphtheria*. It wasn't a pretty word; it sat hard on the tongue. It wasn't a pretty way to die, either: a putrid evil in the nose and throat, violent coughing, poison spreading throughout the body, the awful smell, then the swelling of the throat, the choking, the panic, the vain struggle for air, sweet air —

"You'd best see to Father." Stanley came from behind, jarring Percy from his dark thoughts.

"What's the matter?" he asked.

"He's back in the corner, just sitting there, shivering —"

"Leave him to his grief!" Louisa cried with a passion that startled Percy.

"It isn't right, him sitting there, staring like she did, all glassy-eyed. He ought to rouse himself. Heaven knows what he'll come to. Percy?"

"Yes, I'll go round. I'll check in on him."

"And then off to bed with you. There's naught to do here, naught we can do till morning." Louisa turned with a sigh, taking her own advice, hurrying down the long, shadow-filled hall.

Percy moved the other way, back toward their parents' room. He stood in the hall. The door was shut. He was loath to go in there, to see her again. And what in the world could he say to his father? What difference could he make?

He took a step, two steps, three: he was past it. Then suddenly he turned, found the handle, and twisted it; the door didn't move.

It had been bolted tight from the inside. So be it. The man had the right. There was nothing any human could do for him tonight.

Percy stepped back with a terrible shudder, and groped his way down the hall toward the room that he shared with Stanley, toward a warm bed and the oblivion, the safety of sleep.

When the sun rose next morning it showed the face of a fair, clear day. Though the breeze was still cold, there was the first hint of spring in the air, the false spring that entices. Percy felt it. It seemed to mock him. There was little sign here of the ravages of last night's storm: a few twigs scattered, bent grasses at the edge of the yard, standing puddles. Nothing much to take notice of. And those who were alive went on living, though the sick in their beds took no notice—they had their own work to do, their own struggles to occupy them.

"Thank heaven for the church!" Those were the first words Percy heard from Louisa when she set his breakfast before him. "Have you been in there?" She indicated by the nod of her head what she meant, though her meaning was already obvious.

"No," Percy said.

"Father's still in there. Hasn't come out yet. Stanley banged on the door a bit ago, but there wasn't a sound." A gentle sadness moved across Percy's spirit, like a cloud over sun.

"The vicar's wife called in," Louisa continued. "She was civil enough. Said she'd take care of all the arrangements." She leaned close. "Of course, she asked after him. I wish he would come out."

This isn't like him, Percy thought. *Nothing lays him low.*

He thought of the men who worked under his father, the factory men, the men who kept the brick kilns hot and roaring. On such a day as today his father ought to be whistling off to work with his lunch pail tucked under his arm, off to Stourbridge by eight, to be back just past seven for a good stout and his dinner—

That's all different now. It will always be different with Mother gone from him.

Percy and Stanley worked, too, in the brass foundry down on

the east end. The work there was hard, but the hours that Birmingham businesses kept were fair ones, and Percy had done much fudging of late, taking care of the house. And because of his father's position not much had been said.

He was glad this morning of work to keep his hands busy. He didn't envy Louisa, who had to face a houseful of sick children and the ladies of the parish as well. He knew they would be dressing his mother for burial, laying her out, and he didn't want to think about it, much less be here, be any part of it, see what was happening. He went off to his work with what he believed, what he hoped, were a man's strengths within his young breast.

*T*hey buried her the following day, a gray afternoon when the heavens wept with her motherless children. They all walked in a line, all save Randall, who could not leave his bed. They walked with heads high, eyes tearless, past the curious, pity-eyed faces that watched them. They entered the church by the north porch, past the three pilgrim crosses from medieval days, through the long nave held in place by tall pillars, to the high chancel arch, where they stopped to say farewell to their mother.

Percy lifted Rose up over the coffin, loath to look down himself at the frozen face, framed now in white. But at last he did look. Her face seemed much paler, her cheeks sunken in, her hair curled in unnatural waves over her forehead and ears. He recognized the gown they had dressed her in—an old faded white that had seen better days. Percy remembered her wearing it on special occasions, saying with embarrassed good humor, "Yes, I know it's grown tight. Stretches in all the wrong places now. That's what six babies will do." Strange how it hung on her today, limp and formless. Was she that formless inside? That thin and formless?

They sat with their father all along the front bench. There were no other relatives in the party, for there were none to be had. Only one maiden great-aunt on their mother's side, and she lived away up on the borders of Scotland, too far to come even for her niece, Suzanne. Suzanne Miller Graham, born in Warwick, 1821, died February 7, 1856, in the city of Birmingham, England, age thirty-five. Survived by her husband Oscar Graham and her six children . . . Vicar Evans droned on. He had known Suzanne as a young woman, as a bride, as a wife, as a mother who did well her duty—all the proper things said. "She is at rest now." Eleven-year-old Laura cried loud as the rain that dripped like a drumbeat in Percy's ear. Rose was silent and pale. She rested her head on Louisa's shoulder.

> The lily has a smooth stalk,
> Will never hurt your hand;
> But the rose upon her briar
> Is lady of the land—

"The Lord giveth, and the Lord taketh away;"

> There's sweetness in an apple tree,
> And profit in the corn;
> But lady of all beauty
> Is a rose upon a thorn—

"Blessed be the name of the Lord."

> When with moss and honey
> She tips her bending briar,
> And half unfolds her glowing heart,
> She sets the world on fire.

Percy could hear her voice chanting the sweet words. Her voice had been a pleasure, light and untroubled, part of her beauty; now silenced, now broken, now gone with her, gone to a better place, leaving them here.

The new grave appeared narrow and shallow: so little ground, so scanty a place to find rest in. The rain wet the spot with its tears. Percy crushed a rose and scattered the silken petals over where she would lay her head. He gave another to Rosie. When the box was in place he helped her sprinkle it at the head of the coffin. *Breathe in their fragrance, Mother, please. You can breathe now. Smell the roses, smell them in remembrance of your Rosie and me.*

Rosie cried in his arms, and he buried his face against the damp scent of her long hair to hide his own tears.

*   *   *

They walked in single file down the long lane that led from the church to their house. They could hear the peal of the six bells from the bell tower ringing out the clear notes of a hymn, then the tolling, the clangorous tolling. Percy counted the times: thirty-five for the years of her life. Five, six, seven ... the same age as Rosie; eleven, twelve ... sixteen, seventeen ... Percy knew she had married when she was just seventeen. What had she been like as a girl? Full of laughter and mischief, he knew that much; she still liked to tease. And she had been educated, being a clergyman's daughter. She had taught all her children to read, even Randall and Rose. Twenty, twenty-one ... she had been twenty-one when he was born. Only a girl still. He stubbed his toe on a large stone and stumbled, and decided to stop counting. *She will never again stub her toe on a stone, she will not walk this way, she will not sew with the parish ladies, she will not bake new bread, or sing songs to Rosie, or—*

They had reached their own house, quiet and unlit. They filed up the stone path. Their father waited until all were inside before he bolted the door. He took off his greatcoat and hung it on the peg beside their mother's plaid shawl. He helped Laura and Rose with their wraps. He never said a word. He sat down to table and ate the cold pie Louisa served him and drank her hot tea with never a complaint about the lack of his ale. It was always to bother Percy that his father did not have a tall mug of ale to drink on that day.

They sat back from the meal, stomachs filled, but not satisfied. Oscar Graham coughed, a slight, nervous gesture, unlike him.

"I am wearied," he said. "I believe I shall go to bed, daughter." He rose and kissed Louisa's cheek; then he kissed little Laura, who still had tears in her eyes.

"I'll go see if Randall has finished his plate yet." Louisa slipped from the room, her handkerchief pressed to her eyes.

Oscar nodded to Stanley.

"Good night, Father," Stanley answered.

He looked at Percy. "Will you have prayers with them, lad?"

"Certainly, Father." Percy's voice had a frog in it.

His father's big arms enfolded Rosie, swallowed her, nearly. "My fair rosebud, good night."

He murmured the words so that Percy scarcely heard them. She kissed his freshly shaved cheek and ran her fingers along his broad forehead.

He went up to his bed. He moved heavily, but then, he was a big man, and weary, he'd said. He took to his bed on the day he buried his wife, and he never rose from it again.

It took him three days to die, just three days. When Dr. Davies came in he met with Percy alone in the parlor and shook his head.

"He never got better, lad."

"Yes, he was better! When Randall got ill, and then little Rosie, and Mother was so bad—"

The doctor touched Percy's shoulder. "That's what I'm tellin' you, lad. He only pretended, he willed himself, somehow—for her sake, I'm sure—"

"So, what are you telling me?"

"I'm telling you he's past help now." The doctor shrugged his shoulders, and the gesture had compassion in it, but the habit of resignation as well. Oscar had been his loved friend. "We can ease his suffering some, help with the dying—"

Percy turned from his eyes, whose dispassionate clarity stripped his soul to their gaze. He had nowhere to turn, no one to turn to in this terrible moment.

Not until later that night, when the others were in bed and they were alone, did he weaken and confide his terrible knowledge to Louisa. She only nodded her head.

"I knew as much," she said, and her voice held no expression. Only her eyes mirrored her pain. "It's I who've had the care of him, Percy. The signs are all there. Same as with—her." She couldn't say the word *Mother*. "I'm glad that you know. Now the burden's no longer on my shoulders."

They made it through one more day. Oscar struggled and fought with the enemy, angry perhaps at the tactics death used, but he knew he would die. He was not a woman, he was not a mother—there was no calling together, no weeping, no last words. The next afternoon sometime, alone, he let go and gave in. Death took him, and that was the end of it. No fanfare. Not even nature seemed to notice his passing. The clock ticked on, people kept to their chores, to their business. It was an ordinary day.

When Percy came in from work Louisa told him. But he already knew, before the words were out—he knew from her eyes. Stanley was with him. He looked up at Percy. "We're orphans now, right?"

That was Stanley's way, forthright to the point of rudeness.

"Shut up, Stanley," he said, surprised at the response that escaped him.

"We are," Stanley countered, sticking his chin out and shoving his hands deep inside his pants pockets. "We're orphans, the lot of us, whether you choose to face it or not, Percy Graham."

Stanley stomped out of the room. He would grieve alone; if he cried you could be sure that no one would see him. Louisa leaned against the wall with a sigh. Stanley's words had deflated what little strength she had left.

"I haven't told the girls yet." She turned up her eyes. Percy could read their appeal.

"I'll tell them," he said.

"We could tell them together." She reached for his hand, then suddenly her face was buried in his coarse coat. It muffled her tears. "What will become of us, Percy?" she choked. He had no answer for her.

"We're a family. We'll always be a family."

The words were a cry in the dark. They held no faith, and they gave her no comfort.

*L*aura was given to tears; she was tender-hearted. She flung herself against Louisa and sobbed. It was a terrible thing.

Rose sat in silence for a while, then said quietly, "He's with Mother now, isn't he?"

"Yes." *She's a strange one*, Percy thought, watching her. "Yes, Rose, he is."

"Well, I'm glad then. He was so wretched without her." Her chin trembled a little. "Though we're the unhappy ones now. I don't want to go on living without Mama, Percy."

Still the tears would not come, only this awful, quiet suffering.

They made a bed on the sofa and carried Randall in to it. There was a need they all felt, a need to be together. Randall listened, but his mind was weak still.

"I can't believe it," he said over and over. "I can't believe it. Not Father. So strong, he was always so broad-shouldered. I can't believe it. Not him."

Stanley paced the room; he could not sit still through this.

"We'll go on like before." It was a tentative statement; Percy could hear his own doubt.

"They won't let us."

Percy ignored Louisa's warning. "We're a family still. Remember what *she* always said: 'A happy family is simply an earlier heaven.' "

"But Mama's in heaven right now. And we're not a family without her—"

"Yes, Rosie, we are! She wouldn't want to hear you say such a thing. We're hers, aren't we, still?"

"And she can watch over us. Angels can do that, Percy."

"Yes, Laura, yes. It will be difficult, but we'll be all right. We can make it, you'll see."

So they encouraged and cheered one another. So the dark hours wore on, until the little ones slept in exhaustion and Stanley stomped out his pain, and Louisa dropped in her tracks. But for Percy sleep would not come. He sat alone in the dark. He was the oldest; he had promised his mother. What was it she had said? *Out in the cold—don't lose my children—my babies—*

He shuddered to think of it. He had promised her! But now that his father was gone, he felt so powerless, so utterly powerless, and so afraid.

He slept at last with his face on the desk where his father's accounts lay. He awoke with his neck stiff and sore and bad dreams in his head.

They went on as though nothing had happened. What else could they do? Sit down and stop trying? Give up?

The day they buried their father the vicar's wife spoke to them. "You are brave children," she said. "Do not fear. We shall find good, happy homes for each one of you."

She put down the potatoes and bread she had brought, wagging a long, gloved finger at them. "No charity house for you, heavens, no—good homes. Your mother would expect as much." She patted Rose's bright head. "I would fear to face her having done less for you."

When she was gone, the room seemed to cup her words, the silence to echo them.

"What does she mean?" Laura was young enough to be able to eat still, despite her concern. Percy toyed with his food.

"She means what she said, ninny." Stanley was livid. He upset his stool as he rose angrily from the table. The clatter it made was like the breaking of sticks, like a gunshot.

"She means to divide us, to sell us like livestock to the highest bidder, to line us up as though—"

"Stop it, Stanley. Stop it right now, I say!" Percy stood and his eyes locked with Stanley's, and his brother backed down. And no more was said for the present while they choked down their food, each entertaining his own fears and dark thoughts.

Early the next afternoon, while Percy was still cleaning up from the work day and supper was cooking, the company solicitor, Mr. Wakefield, came calling. Louisa invited him into the parlor to wait for Percy.

This is it, Percy thought. *This is the moment. I'll be given hard facts now. Heaven help me accept them.*

He walked into the room. Anthony Wakefield stood and extended his hand. He was civil, even cordial. "It is Percy, I believe?"

"Yes, sir." *Let's get past this.*

"I believe you resemble your mother."

Yes, yes. I want no part of these pleasantries.

"Tolerable weather we're having for February, though I suppose it's near March, nearer than I'd realized."

Mr. Wakefield was perched on the edge of his chair. Percy saw quite suddenly: *This is difficult for him. He doesn't relish this task. He doesn't quite know how to get at it.* For some reason this calmed him down. To his own amazement he heard himself approach the subject first. "Mrs. Evans says she will find good homes for my brothers and sisters. But we hoped to stay here."

He saw the lines of the solicitor's face twitch and then tighten. With a sense of doom Percy went on.

"I know nothing of my father's affairs, sir—"

"Of course, lad, you don't." Mr. Wakefield glanced about him, as though the walls might have ears, or as though he expected to see Oscar Graham watching him from one of the corners.

"Your father was a good man. He did well for a man of his means. He provided—" a cough here into his handkerchief— "he provided well for a family the size of your own, in these times."

Percy was growing restless again. He leaned forward. "Go on, sir," he urged. "Please."

"To sum it up then, your father had some savings—and this money can be used to compensate those who will take it upon themselves to provide homes and livings for yourself and your brothers and sisters—"

Percy rose from his chair. "Have you already spoken with Mrs. Evans, sir?"

"Aye, and the vicar as well. 'Tis the proper order in such matters."

"What of this house, sir?"

"Yes. I am sorry to put an end to your hopes, but the fact is, lad, 'tis a company house you live in, company owned. There is no way, no possible way you could stay here."

Percy sat down again. He felt weak in his head and stunned, as if he'd just had a blow. Even his limbs felt weak, as though packed not with muscle, but with flax. *How stupid of me! I should have known. If I'd thought, I'd have known. Have I been blocking it all out on purpose?*

"I understand. The new superintendent will have to live — here."

Mr. Wakefield nodded with obvious relief. "We'll give you time, lad. We've no mind to — as long as you need."

Percy nodded. "Of course we shall — well — thank you, sir, that's most kind of you."

"No, son, not at all. 'Tis the least we could do for your father's sake."

Yes, do for him. Do for your mother: she'd expect as much. What about us? What about our feelings? Father is gone now, and so is she. We're the inconvenient remnants of two good people, and your conscience dictates that you deal with us as you would call fairly, but not for our sakes — for the sakes of two people who are dead! Look at us! We exist! We have feelings and needs of our own!

Anthony Wakefield stood at the door. Percy blinked, struggling to clear his head, pull his thoughts back.

"If you have any questions, any questions at all, feel free to contact me. Please."

Percy walked to the door. "What was it you said, sir, concerning the furniture, the things in the house?"

Mr. Wakefield peered at him closely and formed his words with more care. "Some of it stays with the house, that which is company owned only. What belonged to your father will be divided fairly, at Mrs. Evans's discretion, between the families — "

slight stress on the word *families* — "the families who choose to adopt you."

Choose? Choose to adopt us? And what of our choice?

There were no choices for them. Percy knew that. He knew they would go wherever the mercy of others took them.

"We could all run away." It was a solution suggested by Laura.

"I've thought about that," Stanley admitted. "But if *I* went, I'd go on my own."

"Don't be foolish. Don't do it. At least give the future a chance," Percy urged. "You can always bolt, Stanley. Don't do it yet."

The days came and went. The mill wheels of all change grind slowly. Randall grew stronger. He could stay out of bed now. They took life one day at a time, holding their breaths against each new tomorrow.

Then one day it came, as silently, as unceremoniously as death. The woman stood at the door with a carpetbag on her arm. Percy recognized her, just barely, by some sense of instinct.

"Aunt Judith," he said. She pushed past him and he saw that Mrs. Evans was with her and was coming in, too.

"Your Great-aunt Judith, Judith Douglas," he introduced her to the little ones. She had them stand in a line and looked them up and down, just as Stanley had predicted.

"Tell me your ages again."

"Would you like height and weight as well, ma'am?" Stanley growled at her.

"Don't be impertinent, young man. Your mother would not like to see such behavior. She trained you better, I'm sure."

That silenced him, though not for the reason she expected. Percy stood to the side, watching the strange, quiet drama. *This cannot be real. This cannot be happening to us.*

"I thought your own aunt should have first choice." Mrs. Evans interrupted the silence with her self-righteous statement. "I wrote her myself. There are others in the wings waiting—I've been doing my work." She smiled over them. In her own way she meant well, but she made Percy's skin crawl.

"Your aunt has most graciously said she would take two of

you." Mrs. Evans thrust out her head, like an old tortoise testing the weather.

"I can't afford one," Judith mumbled, "but family is family."

Oh, Father, why? Why did your brothers go to sea and both perish? Why have you no cousins, no aunts, no rich uncles hidden off in the highlands? Why is this crusty old woman the only thing left us, and beyond that despair?

"I'll make my decision after dinner," Aunt Judith announced. "It has long been my rule to do nothing important on an empty stomach. Well, Louisa, let's see how you cook."

CHAPTER

4

*I*t became a joke of sorts between them afterward that Louisa was saved by the fact that she burned the biscuits and scorched the gravy. She was nervous that night, and justifiably. But Laura, lonely and sick for attention, played up to the old aunt. And that cast her lot. Just before bedtime Aunt Judith gave her pronouncement.

"I'll take the middle child, Laura. She's a good worker, pleasantly framed, and inclined to obedience, I've noticed."

Laura beamed at the praise.

Perhaps, Percy thought, *If you treat her kindly, love and coddle her just a little . . .*

"What of your other?" he asked.

"I've not quite decided." Aunt Judith fidgeted where she stood. "I ought to have a girl and a boy, to be fair in this. And I ought to take him." She pointed a long, gnarled finger at Stanley, who drew visibly back. "But he's trouble, if ever I saw it, and I'll not bide with that."

She peered around her, her eyes narrow slits in the plane of her face.

"That leaves Randall, and he's a good boy," Laura prompted.

"Too pinch-faced, too young."

Laura tugged at her sleeve with some confidence. "I'd like him to come. He'll be no trouble, ma'am. I can take care of him, really I can. Look," she added, "Randall's built big, like Father. You must give him time. He'll be healthy and strong when he grows up."

Aunt Judith thought about that. She was parsimonious and

19

somewhat shriveled, but she could judge a good bargain when she saw one. She made him stand up for her, answer some questions. Then she nodded her thin, lace-capped head with vigor. "I shall take him," she said.

That was that.

"Now, my dears, I suggest we all retire to our beds. Laura and Randall can pack in the morning while I settle affairs with your vicar and his lovely wife." She yawned delicately and went off to her room.

The children waited. They gave her time, they even took turns standing guard at the door until Randall assured them that she snored like a sailor and could be heard clear down the hall.

They gathered in the parlor. Louisa carried her hanky, but her pale eyes were dry.

"This is our last night together," Percy said, looking round him. The words were not real. They stood for nothing that he could conceive of.

"We must be brave," Louisa said.

"Do you think you can be happy with the old bat?" Stanley growled.

Laura prickled a bit. "As happy with her as with any old stranger. They say the borders are fair; green rolling country with sheep. She keeps sheep. She has a collie, she said."

"You'll learn a Scot's accent, heaven help you," Stanley snorted.

He's been rejected himself. As Percy watched him a stab of panic swept over him. *Will it ever be thus? Draw in your prickles, Stanley boy, for your own sake, or who will want you, but some soured slave driver who will try to break your fine spirit—*

Percy could feel himself sweat, feel a heat in his head like a sickness. *"Don't lose my babies,"* she said. *I've lost two of them, Mother, already. And where am I headed from here? I have no way to hold onto them. Mother!*

They were all looking at him. *That's right. I had something to tell them. What was it?*

"Will you fetch Father's greatcoat for me, Stanley?"

"Yes, Percy." His face was solemn, but his green eyes were curious. He took the large coat from its hook and seemed to drag more than carry it to Percy. He let it drop onto his knees. Percy's legs and feet disappeared in its thick folds.

"Thank you, Stanley," he said.

He lifted it up so they all could look at it. "We're still a family," he said. "We come from a long line of noble ancestors. This coat you all know. Even Rose knows the story of her great-grandfather Robert, who wore this coat in the Seven Years' War and won a medal from the king for his bravery."

Rosie nodded her head. Her eyes were bright with new wonder.

"And where did your own grandfather wear this coat?" He nodded to Randall, who leaned forward eagerly.

"He wore it in battle against Napoleon, and again in the American War in the year 1812."

"And he distinguished himself," Louisa added. "See the decorations sewn here? And the medals?" She moved to touch the material, to smooth the rough nap with her hand.

"Our father was given this coat by his father, and he wore it well. He wore it the night the brick works caught fire and he went inside and carried eleven men out to safety before collapsing himself."

"But he didn't get burned. The coat saved him." Laura spoke the words with sure pride. "Show us the spot where the fire burned holes, Percy."

He turned the coat around. They drew in their breaths as he stuck his fingers through the black holes.

"He wore it again on the night Mother gave birth to Rose." This was their favorite tale. He could almost hear them sigh and settle in for the listening.

"It was a cold, stormy night with snow coming down, a real blizzard. The baby was coming, too, and Mother said, 'I don't need the doctor, I've had babies before.' But something was wrong. After hours of struggling, the baby still wouldn't come. Mother was in pain, and she grew afraid now. How could anyone get through the storm? Father put on his tall, hobbed boots and the greatcoat and started out. After just a few yards icicles grew on his mustache and his hands and feet went all numb. But he struggled forward, though the swirling snow blinded him. Mostly he felt his way from landmark to landmark: the schoolyard oak, the broken post by the priory, the old boarded well by the innside, and so on and on. When he came within feet of the doctor's he heard a strange sound. Not a moan, but a pitiful whimper. It raised the hairs on his head. He looked about him, half expecting a ghost to swoop down through the snow."

Percy could hear his father; he told the tale better. He embellished it, too, by the way he would pause and raise a black eyebrow in question, his pipe poised by his mouth. Or he would clamp the lighted pipe tight in his teeth and lean suddenly forward, drawing his bushy black eyebrows into one long, quivering line.

"He stood there shaking a moment."

"With the cold," Laura added, "not fear." There were chuckles at that.

"Then with his hand extended forward to help guide him he walked back into the storm, still thinking on ghosts and spirits. He heard the strange wail again, and at the same time his hand touched warm flesh, and the flesh shuddered and quivered and seemed to leap out from under his touch. He jumped aside with a cry."

"Poor Father. It was only old Turnip," Rosie laughed, "who was as frightened as he."

"So he discovered, to his relief," Percy continued. "The doctor's horse stood beside the overturned cart and his unconscious master. Father drew the doctor up into his arms and carried him into the house. He had upset his cart in the storm and he surely would have died there, frozen to death in the cold, if Father hadn't happened along.

" 'You are God-sent, Oscar,' Dr. Davies said.

"Father poured him some good strong Scotch whiskey. 'If I lead you on Turnip, can you make it to my house?' he asked.

" 'Get me my bag! It must be somewhere out there in that cursed snow. Suzanne shall have her doctor tonight if it's the last thing we do!'

"They made it back safely, but when they arrived they discovered that the doctor had broken his arm in the fall. So the doctor sat, a plump, helpless general calling out orders, with a mug of hot ale in his good hand, while Father did all the work. And that's how Dr. Davies was saved and our Rosie was born."

A sigh of pleasure escaped Laura's lips. "How I like that story!"

"Well, don't you forget it up there in Scotland. Tell it to your own children some day, don't let them forget that they have a grandfather named Oscar Graham."

Laura nodded, her eyes wide and serious.

"Where will the rest of us go?" It was a question no one had dared ask yet. Stanley asked it, of course.

"I don't know, I don't think we'll go far. But it doesn't matter. We're—"

"Don't say we're a family! We'll not be a family, not ever again." Stanley began pacing once more. It wore on Percy's nerves, but he bit back his reproach.

"I am the oldest, and I swear, one day, no matter how far they take us, no matter what they do to us, no matter where I may go—"

The room settled to silence; they listened with their spirits, not merely their minds.

"I promise that when I grow to be a man I'll search till I find you, each one of you. I'll bring us all back together. We'll be a family again."

It sounded solemn; it sounded impossible; it was what they wanted to hear. Percy nodded to Louisa and she drew the kitchen scissors out from the pocket of her skirt. Percy held up the greatcoat.

"There are enough buttons here." He took the scissors from Louisa and snipped off the first one. "One for each of us." He placed it very solemnly into Laura's white palm. "To remember. To keep until I find you." Laura closed her hand tight and the little fist trembled in her lap where it lay.

"One for you," Percy said, handing the next button to Randall. "Can you hang onto it? Through thick and through thin?"

"You can count on me, Percy."

Percy gave the next button to Stanley. He took it with feigned reluctance, but he didn't protest, and tears he could not hold back stood in his green eyes.

"One for Louisa and one for myself." Percy worked at the

thread. "Pieces of our history," he said, half to himself, "something to bind us together."

Rosie leaned forward. "Here's yours, darling. That's right, hold it tight."

"She'll lose it."

"I won't lose it, Stanley."

"She's too little."

"I'm not! I'm seven now, Stanley, and I know how to hide away treasures and not let them get lost."

She'll make it, Rosie will. It's important enough to her, even though she's so young. Percy held out the coat, which felt strangely denuded. "Put it back on the peg." It had to hang there by his mother's plaid shawl. It wouldn't be right, otherwise.

"It's late and you all need your sleep, but there's one more thing to do." This was the hardest for Percy. "Let's all kneel in prayer." He had promised his father, he dare not omit it. And they surely could use whatever aid Providence might choose to send them.

They knelt on the rug in an uneven circle, the girls holding hands, Stanley's arms crossed on his chest. *I must be mouthpiece*, Percy thought. *What a hard lot this is.*

He closed his eyes and drew in a deep breath. When he started to speak he was surprised at the flow of words that came from him. No, not from him. He felt they moved *through* him somehow, for he was not their source.

The night was mild, the stars bright in the sky. The air carried the smell of rain, but a spring rain. There was nothing to disturb the sweet spirit that filled the small room. The children drank in Percy's words. Stanley opened one eye to make sure it was still his brother who spoke them. And Laura, her gaze misted by tears, swore most solemnly for the rest of her life that when she opened her eyes once she saw her mother standing just over the fireplace, her feet resting on air. Not an angel who looked like her mother, but the mother she loved, dressed in white, with the beauty of her girlhood upon her and a strange, luminous glow on her face.

5

*P*ercy dawdled the next morning, not anxious to leave while Aunt Judith still lingered. He was more than curious to see what she would do, what she would take when she left. Yet she still surprised him by coming downstairs with two tightly packed hampers and a trunk whose bulging lid had been tied down with strong twine.

"Has the cart come round yet?" she asked, disposing of any other civilities.

"No."

"Well, Vicar Evans said he would arrange for it. I hope those two children will not keep me waiting."

"They are both packed and awaiting *your* pleasure. And what have you in there?"

Aunt Judith's quick, birdlike eyes grew narrow. "My share, son, my share." She reached and patted one of the hampers. "Family things, to be sure. Things you would not wish to fall into the hands of   strangers." She spoke the word as though it were something impolite, a shade below proper.

The hands of strangers, indeed. We shall fall into the hands of strangers, have you not thought of that?

She was eyeing him still. "Louisa helped me select them." She drew herself up, for his eyes had not softened. "Now look here, young man. You must bear this like a good Christian. We are all in God's hands. When he chooses to visit us with sorrow or pain, we must bend to his will, and bear all with a Christlike meekness."

You've the vicar in you, Percy thought. *Like your brother. Did*

*you snatch all of the clergyman's sense of things for yourself? I'd
not be surprised.*

He looked past her and with a slight bow turned and left the
room. Stanley's more volatile, impulsive nature hid Percy's own
faults, he knew. His sense of responsibility at being the oldest
generally helped to tone down his stubborn temper, his streak
of pride. But he was having great trouble with both today.

By the back porch a cart headed by a patient dray horse was
pulled up. A man elbowed past Percy and balanced his burden:
Father's large desk with the roll top and the pigeonhole cubbies
and pull-out drawers. Percy put a hand on it. "Where are you
going with that?"

"Move along, young fellow." Percy had not heard his aunt
come up behind him. "The desk will be Randall's someday. So
you see, it is far better with me than another."

His mother's oak wardrobe came next, then the small turn-
top table, mother-of-pearl inlaid. Aunt Judith had an eye for the
best. When it came to his mother's rocker, when they carted that
out, too, Percy could bear no more.

> Love me, I love you,
> Love me, my baby;
> Sing it high, sing it low;
> Sing it as may be.

She had sung lullabies every night since Percy could first
remember. Rocking Randall, then Rose, sometimes rocking himself when his head or throat were sore, folding her light arms
around him. The fragrance of herbs on her apron, the lavender
scent to her skin. And the sweet, even sound of her singing:

> Mother's arms under you,
> Her eyes above you,
> Sing it high, sing it low,
> Love me, I love you.

He went to find Laura. "Come and kiss me good-bye. I'm off
to the foundry. Morning's most gone now—"

She threw herself into his arms.

"You promised, Laura. Don't cry!"

"I can't help it!"

He held her and looked past her at Randall. The poor little tyke. Thin as a reed he was still. The journey would tire him—and what after that?

"You must be a brave girl for Randall's sake, sweetheart," he whispered into Laura's ear. "He's not much past a child yet, but you know how he'd feel if he cried."

He could sense her struggling. She reached for her hanky and blew her nose once or twice. "All right, Percy. I'll do it for Randall—and I'll do it for you."

More tears spilling. This was nearly past bearing! Percy gently lifted her arms and disengaged himself from her hold. "I must kiss Randall, too."

Randall heard and stuck his hand out, man-fashion, but Percy gathered him close.

"I'll have my last touch of you, Randall," he growled, "even if it makes us both bawl like babies."

It nearly did. "God go with you," he said, then he fled from the room. He found his way to the front door where no one would see him. Once out in the street he could thrust his hands down into his pockets and clench his fists hard, and allow a few tears to bathe the burning sting from his eyes.

It did not grow easier. Once their peace was broken, the changes came thick and fast. Mrs. Evans marched a stream of prospective parents through the house, her mouth set; she was one who would not shirk her duty. They seemed a poor bunch at best. Stanley coined names for them: *Mr. Turnip Face*, who looked like Dr. Davies's old horse; *Mrs. Cotton-bottom, Mrs. Persimmon, Miss Lemon Rind*. To make a game of it, even a grim game, helped a little.

Of course, Louisa went next. She was the most marketable of them all, as Stanley put it.

"If they sold us as slaves she'd fetch a tidy sum," he teased, but the tease had his usual sting in it. Frank and Edith Bascom were not friends, but they were members of the same congregation. Percy had seen them often before. They weren't people who excited much note. They were in middle age with no children of their own; their three sickly sons had all died. He worked in one of the glass factories and she ran a small, rather dirty bakery. Such a dull pair to consign their bright Louisa to!

"They'll work Louisa to death."

"I'll hear none of your dire prophecies, Stanley," Percy bit back at him. "Hold your tongue."

Mrs. Evans made all the arrangements. Louisa packed up her things. She grew very quiet, and that smote Percy's heart worse than ravings and tears.

"I'll be fine," she assured him. "You can come visit me."

"Of course I shall come!"

Only her eyes revealed what she was feeling. Percy read there a loneliness and a fear that alarmed him.

When the Bascoms came for "their girl," Mrs. Evans led them through the rooms and helped them select certain items.

"There'll be naught for you and me to take along but the chamber pot," Stanley complained. Percy agreed. All the rooms had great holes in them, empty spaces sometimes marked against wallpaper where a table had stood, or a highboy, or the old horsehair sofa. It gave an odd, hodgepodge effect.

Louisa left at noon. "I've cooked a big pot of soup," she said, "and there's bread in the cupboard." She showed Percy where everything was. He didn't try to assure her that they'd do just fine without her. Between them words would not do. They didn't need words. But Rosie required some coaxing.

"I'm not really going away," Louisa soothed. "You shall come visit me in a few days with Percy."

That helped some, but Rose knew. She knew with the instinctive awareness of children what would really take place.

That same afternoon a woman came asking after Rosie. Mrs. Evans showed her the child. Everything about her was both faded and severe: her tightly wound hair, her pale eyes, her worn dress, her thin, skin-tight hands, the line of her mouth that scarcely moved when she spoke to Mrs. Evans or asked questions of Rosie.

She never once smiled. After she had left, Mrs. Evans popped her hatted head back in, beaming.

"I believe Mrs. Simpson wants the child, Percy. She needs to speak to her husband and—"

"Well, she cannot have her! Ma'am."

The startled eyes blinked a few times.

"You must do better than that one, Mrs. Evans. I'd never rest, I could never face Mother if I gave her little Rose to a person like that."

The rebuke behind Percy's words silenced her. "Well then, we'll keep looking," she said, and went out with her mouth pursed in the resolute shape Percy had come to know so well.

Percy slept poorly that night. The next morning at a fair, early hour he looked out the back window where the long road from the country wound its way into town, to see a rider approaching, kicking up a good portion of dust. Rose had taken to shadowing Percy when he was home, and now she clung to his shirttails, peeping out like some strange, half-wild thing.

"Have they come to take me? Are they coming to take me away, Percy?"

"No, baby, no." The pain that was part of him now constricted into a hard lump in his throat. He swallowed, but that made no difference. *Yesterday frightened her more than I knew.*

As the rider drew closer Percy could see that the billows of dust were being caused not by the horse, but by a small coach that followed. There was a loud pounding at the front door and he ran to attend it. He opened to the vicar's wife, who was inside and clutching him before he quite recognized her.

"It is a wonder, Percy. We are so honored. Where is your brother?" She looked wildly around.

"He's out in the back, ma'am, tending to—"

"Well, get him! We've no time to spare."

"What *is* it, Mrs. Evans?"

She could see that he meant to stand his ground, have his answer. So she took a deep breath and tried to control herself.

"Squire Beal wants to take your brother! He's on his way here right now. Geoffrey Beal himself."

"Why?"

"What do you mean, *why*? What difference does that make?"

"It might make some difference to Stanley."

"Nonsense, he's landed gentry, a wealthy man. Your brother will have advantages he's never dreamed of. He is a fortunate boy."

"I don't believe that can be assumed, Mrs. Evans. From what I recollect, Squire Beal has never liked children much. Is he even married himself?"

"He is not married. He was married once, years ago, but the poor young thing died. Perhaps now, as he is growing older, he has become lonely—"

"I doubt it."

"Young man!"

Percy could see that he was truly disturbing her. But something was disturbing him, too: a feeling, a fear he couldn't put words to. "There's something behind this," he said. "He has some reason of his own."

"We all have reasons of our own that stand behind all our actions."

Percy knew that was so.

She came a step or two closer. He could see the indecision, the struggle on her face as she approached him.

"We will not do better for Stanley. You know—he is very defensive—perhaps it is partly his age. He turns people away—every one who has considered him."

Percy also knew this was so.

By the time Squire Beal's coach pulled up to their post Percy and Mrs. Evans were ready. They had Stanley inside, scrubbed and combed and looking presentable. And properly subdued.

"Do you know Squire Beal?" Percy had asked him.

"Aye, I remember him well. From Fair Days and country ridings. He's a soggy old bore."

And then some, Percy thought.

"That's all right. What better is there for me? I'll take the old bloke on. I can give him a run for his money, eh, Percy?"

The usual bravado. Percy just wished he knew how much fear stood behind it. Squire Beal's coachman announced him and when he strode into the room Mrs. Evans properly curtsied.

"So this is the lad. How old are you, boy?"

"Twelve, sir." Stanley stepped forward.

The squire looked him over with a cold, practiced eye. "He's a fine-looking boy, Mrs. Evans."

"Yes, he is."

"Strongly built. No obvious defects." He stood back on his heels and folded his hands across his brocaded belly. "Are you willing to go with me — what's your name?"

"My name is Stanley, sir."

"Stanley."

"Yes, sir. I'll come along if you want me."

Squire Beal attempted a smile. He knew Mrs. Evans was watching him. But the result was not good.

"I believe we can make something satisfactory out of this."

Something satisfactory? For whom?

"Very well, then. John will bring your belongings. You may come in the coach right now with me."

Stanley looked over at Percy. Their eyes met. Something in Stanley's face warned him. There were to be no good-byes then. They were boys, nearly men, though Stanley looked so young, so forlorn, standing with his hands thrust into his pockets and his eyes bright with tears. How would they have managed to say good-bye, anyway?

Percy watched him drive off. A far cloud passed in front of the sun, and the morning took on a gray cast. Percy couldn't help taking it for a bad omen. And yet later that day, after he had worked a short shift at the foundry and come back again and collected Rose from the neighbor woman who watched her, there came a knock at the door.

It was not Mrs. Evans he opened it to, but strangers, a man and woman he had never set eyes on before. They were a good-looking couple. He had sandy-red hair and broad shoulders; she was petite, with gentle blue eyes and fair skin. They introduced themselves as Benjamin and Claire Gillman. They were new in the town. He had been a farmer down Worcester way, but he had injured his back and therefore fell on hard times and lost the farm, so now he worked in the jeweler's trade here; it was all he could do.

"He's a supervisor already," Mrs. Gillman said proudly, "and the work of his hands has a certain turn to it, a look you can't miss. People ask for it now."

Percy knew that Birmingham was known as the "city of a thousand trades"; his father had made him feel proud of that. He was aware that over one hundred different trades found their homes here. It seemed his father had at some time mentioned that the jewelry trade had expanded ten times over in the last fifteen years.

Percy felt a smile at his lips; he invited them in. Claire Gillman sat on the one good parlor chair and the men pulled up stools. They talked politely of this and that. The Gillmans had three little girls. At first Percy's heart jumped: *They want another.* But then he knew. It wasn't Rosie they watched and asked questions of. Of course: an injured back, three little girls, no menfolk.

"We wouldn't work you hard, lad. That isn't our way."

For some reason Percy believed the man.

Claire Gillman drew a deep breath. "We'll be honest with you, lad. We can't afford hired help. And Benjamin needs someone to assist with the heavy chores." She paused slightly. "We did have a son—or we would have had. Died as a baby. How old are you?"

"Fourteen."

She nodded and her eyes grew bright. "He would have been nearly your age. As my husband said, we would not overwork you. You would be like our son. We don't belong to your congregation, but we are God-fearing folk. And we would never abuse or mistreat you."

Percy looked into her eyes. He saw deeply. He knew he could trust her. In her gaze he read—*love.* It nearly unnerved him.

He sent Rose off to play, then told them plainly that he would come with them, but not until Rosie was gone, not until he had found a good home for her. Benjamin Gillman nodded his head. Claire's eyes clouded.

"I wish we could take her, I truly do. But we've no room and scant money, and one more mouth to feed—"

She looked away from Percy's gaze, which held an appeal he could not disguise.

After they left, Percy sat by the window. He felt deflated and strangely listless. The room faded, grew dark. But he did not rise to find a candle and light it. This was no longer home. All the things that spelled home were gone from here, even the loved outward things, the trappings of living a family gathered that reflected themselves: their tastes, their occupations, their pleasures.

"I have no home." He said the words out loud, and they seemed to him like a death knell. *I must work, I must breathe, I must eat, I must somehow go on. I must find a place for my Rosie—and I must let her go. And I must somehow keep living, without mother or father or heart or home.*

I do not know these people. They are not of our faith, Percy."
Mrs. Evans fairly bristled.

"It appears you've done your work well. They've heard of
you and your houseful of orphans."

"I shall have Vicar Evans do a thorough—"

"No, please. Please, ma'am, save him the trouble. I've decided
to accept their offer."

"Percy, are you quite sure?"

"Quite sure, ma'am."

She looked about her, a little disoriented.

"That leaves only Rosie," he said for her. *You're down to one
now. What will you do to fill your time when you've disposed of
the lot of us?*

"Rosie. Yes."

"What about you? You and the vicar? Have you thought about
taking her?"

Jane Evans jumped visibly. "Yes, we have. We have given it
honest consideration. But you see, we have children of our own.
There are many without, there are those—"

Percy turned, mildly disgusted, away from her words. *Rose
can do better than you!* So his heart defended, but his mind was
afraid. *I must secure kindness for her, a chance to be happy. She
must have at least that!*

Two days passed. Percy found himself praying; it helped drive
away his dark fears. The longer they went, the harder it would

be to let go of the child. The harder it would be for Rosie to leave him.

There were just the two of them now. She helped him cook, she dried the dishes with one of Louisa's big aprons tied round her. They fed the animals together, those that were left. The Squire had taken their pony and their fine milk cow. The wealthy, well-intentioned Squire.

He tucked her in bed every night. He listened to her nighttime prayers, he read her the stories that he still remembered his mother reading when he was a child. Twice more he turned down Mrs. Evans and the people she brought: old half-blind Sally who had a husband who beat her; everybody knew that. It was a nightmare to even think of her touching his Rose. And Mrs. Sawyer, who was big as a barn and had eight children already, but had her eye on the highboy in the dining room and the carriage in the barn.

He was wearing Mrs. Evans's patience thin, and he knew it. He had no idea what he would do if someone didn't show up, someone who half fit his expectations. Then out of the clear blue, with no sort of warning, the miracle came. A commonplace miracle that had been right around the corner, just under their noses, one might say, the whole time.

The doctor was there when Percy came home from work. He was playing with Rose, sitting on the floor with her bandaging dolls and giving pills to the cats.

He looked up. Rosie looked up. And Percy knew.

"The doctor is sad," Rosie said, "because his wife died and left him, like Mother."

Percy knelt on his haunches and untangled a gray kitten from a long slice of gauze bandage.

"And May, his daughter, is sad because her husband went to heaven and left her, too."

"Is there anything at all we can do to help them?" Percy's throat felt dry, and his voice sounded more sad than he had meant it to.

"I think so, Percy. He wants me to come and be his little girl."

Percy felt Dr. Davies's big hand settle down on his shoulder.

"I'd have come before, lad, but I didn't think you'd be interested in an old codger like me. Then May told me the trouble you'd had—she talked to Louisa, you see."

"We've had some rare ones come through." Percy smiled, but he knew the expression didn't come out that way.

"May has had a hard time since Andrew died. She will make Rosie a fine, gentle mother."

"I know that, doctor, I know."

"The child will brighten both our lives."

Percy drew Rosie to him. "Are you packed, then, and ready?"

"Yes, May helped me. She'll be coming back in just a few minutes. Don't cry, Percy."

"I won't."

"What is this? The whole lot of you playing still? Isn't anyone hungry?"

"I am!" Rosie jumped up and went to the fair-haired young woman, who bent and gave her a kiss.

May is a jewel. May is more than I'd asked for. She is the answer to my prayers.

"Run and get that big basket for the kittens, Rosie. Hurry."

Rose skipped off to obey.

"Thank heaven for you, May," Percy said. She put her arms around him, just briefly, for she saw his great struggle.

"Percy, has the child anything of her mother's to take along? Something pretty and personal?"

Why didn't I think of that? Percy shook his head. "No. But there is a special locket, the one Mother wore since before I can remember. I think it was her mother's before her."

"Get it for Rosie, will you please? She should have it."

Percy raced for her room, hoping, praying the locket would be there still. The large bureau was gone, as was the small dressing table Mother sat down at to comb out her hair. His heart seemed to stop in his chest. *It's not here. It can't possibly be here. There's no place left for it to be.*

He walked around the bare room, fighting a feeling of desolation. The old wardrobe stood bare, nothing left but a few odds and ends, old worn pieces of clothing. He ran his hand idly along them. And as he dropped it, his fingers brushed against something. He stuck his whole head inside. He didn't believe what his eyes tried to tell him. Hanging there on a nail, hidden against the rough, unstained wood, was his mother's locket. He lifted it carefully. *Love is like a rose, the joy of all the earth.* He touched the delicate gold chain gently. *Thank you, Mother, for leaving it hidden here for your Rosie.*

He walked down the stairs to where May and the doctor were waiting. *She'll be all right. I think your Rosie will be all right, Mother.*

He took Rosie aside and held the locket before her. "Do you know what this is?"

She nodded solemnly. "Yes, Mother's locket. She wore it to church and to the socials, and sometimes on Fair Days."

"Well, Rosie dear, now it is yours."

She drew her breath in and reached out to touch it.

"May and I both agree that you should keep it to remind you of Mother. Take good care of it, Rosie. May will help you do that."

He fastened it around her small neck, lifting her heavy curls out of the way.

"Be a good girl, my Rose, and be happy." He kissed her just once. He wanted fiercely to add: *Don't forget me!*

He took her back in to May.

"I get to help the doctor feed Turnip tonight." She reached up for May's hand. Percy had seldom seen the child this excited.

"Come sup with us," May said, placing her other hand with a slight, soft pressure on his arm.

"I don't think so. I'm not very hungry." He tried to return her kind smile. "I couldn't do this again."

She nodded. "I understand."

They went gently. But that didn't make it less painful. Percy paced the still house, wondering if Stanley was pacing the Squire's large, elegant rooms. Louisa was probably putting supper on the table right now; she really was a good cook. Laura and Randall. He wasn't able to picture what their days might be like. He only hoped Laura could keep Aunt Judith charmed just a little, and that Randall would grow well and strong quickly.

It was the last parting. *I've lost them all, Mother.* The last little death. *Thank heaven for that.*

Or so Percy thought as he sat in the silence alone, staring out at the night.

*T*he Gillmans were kind; they went out of their way to be kind, but their house still wasn't home. Their ways were not Percy's ways and there was not a thing here that was familiar and known.

Percy still worked at the foundry, but only the short shift. The rest of the time he spent doing basic household chores: splitting wood, hauling water, emptying the coal stoves, caring for the animals. They treated him well. Claire Gillman cooked good food, and she was not stingy. He had a small room of his own on the attic floor; he was grateful for that. The three little girls, Belinda, Ellen, and Mary, were shy with him; they hung back, but they watched him with care. It would take Percy a while to warm up to them as well; they stirred too much pain. He saw Rose, only Rose, when he looked at them, and he wanted none other but her.

He had made one last round of the house the morning he left. There were things he took, too, happy to bring something to the Gillmans besides merely himself. But there wasn't much: a few kitchen utensils, his father's tools, a worn harness and saddle, an odd table and chair. He looked at the pegs on the wall. Louisa had taken their mother's plaid shawl; the long rack looked forlorn somehow without it. Only his own threadbare jacket hung at one end, his father's greatcoat at the other. He lifted it down. *This was meant to be mine. It might come in handy for me.*

He noticed in the corner where the shadows obscured it his father's old walking stick. It was a fine piece, made of strong bird's-eye maple topped with a carved lion's head. Percy reached for it eagerly, running his hands along the smooth, reassuring

39

wood. This was more than he'd hoped for. He was content to have this much that spoke home to him.

Perhaps that was why he put up no struggle when Mrs. Evans approached him.

"Tell me, Percy," she said, "could you find it in your heart to give the small buggy to the vicar?"

He blinked at her. "Is it still here, then?" he asked, wondering suddenly if she had not arranged that to be so. He knew she had taken small things, little pieces she especially admired.

"It would be a fitting gesture, I think."

Percy knew that the vicar had no nice buggy to drive to the church in. A man of his station would surely covet such a convenience.

Mrs. Evans stood still, with her hands clasped in front of her. Her thin mouth was pursed in that resolute line Percy had looked on so often, but her eyes were unsure.

"Certainly the vicar deserves a fine buggy more than this obscure, common couple who is taking me in."

It may have been unkind, but he wanted to make her squirm just a little.

"I will not give it to him."

Mrs. Evans twitched visibly.

"If it really is mine to give, ma'am, then I give it to you. It is you who has done all the arranging, the bother, the work." He struggled to keep his eyes looking wide and innocent. "If you choose to share it with him, that is certainly not my affair, ma'am."

She didn't know what to say. "I thank you, Percy. You are a fine boy and on the way, I believe, to becoming a fine gentleman. Like your father," she added.

Of all the things she arranged and gave and took from him, that was the one thing that mattered. He forgave her much on the strength of those three words.

He took life one day at a time. There was still much to learn, new little ways to discover. The days seemed long, but each day some of the awkwardness faded. His first surprise came Sunday morning when Benjamin Gillman shook him awake.

"I let you sleep a little late, lad. But it's time for meeting now."

"Of course." Percy sat up groggily. Benjamin cleared his throat and looked down at the covers. "Will you come along, lad?"

"Yes, I'll come. We're a churchgoing family."

"No, I'm not meaning that. I know you are." Mr. Gillman was obviously uncomfortable.

"What is it then?"

"We go to the Church of the Latter-day Saints. Have you heard of them? Mormons?"

Perhaps. Vaguely. He rubbed his eyes. "Not really."

"Well. Good. Will you come? Claire and I decided if you're to be a part of the family, you might as well know that we take our religion most seriously. Will you consider it, Percy? You'll find it different from what you're used to."

Percy nodded. "I will." *You've given me no reason to do anything else.*

But he wasn't prepared for the real differences Benjamin Gillman alluded to. He felt awkward at first, ill at ease. The pattern of things seemed too casual, too intimate, if that was the word. But there was something else that he liked, that eluded him. He felt it again and again. When they all sang the hymns, though they were the same hymns he'd sung since his childhood, they sounded different somehow. And the sermons — delivered by *laymen*. There was no vicar here. He had heard the word *president* and the word *bishop*. One of the men seemed to preside over the meeting, but so many took part. There was no definite form he could put his finger on. But the feeling that came drew him past the alarming differences, drew him time after time. He would have to think on this feeling he got here.

When the meeting was done many people came up to greet him. They seemed so sincere, so genuinely interested in his welfare. Much more than polite, much, much more than stiff and proper. He could not understand. But he went away with the feeling wrapped around him, like a warm, downy coat, and it took hours, even days, to fade from him.

Meanwhile he worked, he learned his new place, and he tried to be patient. Three days into the week, after supper, Claire

Gillman called him aside and said in her own kindly way, "I've noticed several times, Percy, you've stumbled over what you should call us. You're a boy nearly grown. We'll never be mother and father to you; I wouldn't want to ask that. But Mrs. Gillman, or ma'am?" She laughed pleasantly. "I don't fancy that. In the Church we call each other brother or sister. Do you think that would do?"

Percy considered a moment. He liked it. It was one of the things he had noticed on Sunday. Sometimes in the Church of England a parishioner would be referred to as Brother this-or-that. But not in the same sort of way, and not all of the time. It became an endearment the way Mormons used it.

"Yes, I'd like that," he agreed.

She nearly hugged him. That was one more thing settled.

The following night there was a knock at the door and Percy watched two young men enter. They were strangers to him, one not much older than himself, the other closer to thirty. Sister Gillman seemed to know them both well. They took off their topcoats and hats; they appeared to be settling in. Percy noticed that they both carried Bibles and other thick books as well.

"Percy, come meet these gentlemen." Sister Gillman seemed a little nervous, but excited at the same time.

"Elder Joseph Jenkins and Elder Thomas Jones," she introduced them.

Both men elders! An elder in Percy's mind was an older, respected man of the community who sat in counsel over parish affairs.

"These men are missionaries. They're the ones who brought the gospel to us." Sister Gillman's smile nearly beamed. "They've come to talk to you."

"Talk to me?"

"Teach you the gospel." Elder Jenkins gave great weight to the pronouncement. Percy must have shied back.

Sister Gillman said more gently, "Teach you Mormonism, Percy."

"What if I don't want to know?" The words escaped him before he half thought them.

"Since you'll be living with us, part of our family, you must give it a try, Percy." The words were a plea. If they had come out in the form of command, or even recommendation, things might have turned out very differently. But entreaty was there. Percy remembered the Sunday feeling.

"All right, I'll listen," he said. "Give them a fair try."

That was all they needed, but Percy didn't know that. Three and a half hours and a large slice of cake later, Brother Gillman chased them both out the door. Percy sincerely believed that was the only way the two would have left. Otherwise they'd have talked through till the morning. His head was swimming with new ideas, new doctrine, the strange history of the young man named Joseph Smith who had seen God the Father and an angel, who held the priesthood—what a strange word that was—who had translated this book Percy now held in his hands called the Book of Mormon.

"Read it and pray over it," Elder Jenkins had said, "then you'll know for yourself."

What a singular thing! A new religion based on new revelation. God still dealing with man. Something about it made sense to Percy. Something about it felt right.

He took the book with him up to his room. He stretched out on the bed. He meant only to leaf through the pages a little. But he did not close his eyes until the small square of his window grew light with the morning.

He stumbled through the long day with his thoughts on the things he'd been reading. He could not wait to get back.

After washing up, after gulping down a hasty dinner, he excused himself and went to his room. The Gillmans said not a word. He was unaware of their breathless watching. He was immersed in this world: the world of Nephi, the world of Moroni, the world of prophets and kings, wars and contentions, and mighty conversions. It set his head going around. He spent his days thinking about it, his nights living in it.

When the Sabbath day came he went to meeting again at the Allison Street chapel, and this time he asked questions. The missionaries were there. They answered his questions, but so did half a dozen odd others. Everyone seemed to know, seemed to thoroughly grasp the staggering doctrine, the knowledge this new religion contained. Percy couldn't help being impressed. This was bread, this was meat; this was the staff of life to these people.

He continued to read. When he had finished the Book of Mormon he read every tract, every printed word he could find about Mormonism. And that was no small amount. Through Claire's efforts he borrowed from various members copies of the *Millennial Star*, which was published twice monthly, and the *Journal of Discourses*, a sixteen-page periodical that came out of Liverpool twice monthly as well. In their pages he could explore proselyting work, offices in the priesthood, restoration of keys, and family organization and temple work.

This was the sun bursting through shadow, the calm after storm, the morning that breaks when night's darkness has faded and fled.

An eternal family, marriage through the eternities, children sealed to father and mother—all things he had dreamed of, yet never dared hope for. This spoke to his heart with a purity that swept through his spirit; he knew it was truth.

He had much to ponder, and the days now went swiftly. It seemed he had too much to do, too many things to claim the precious hours he now wanted to spend in a pursuit men called study: a thing Percy had been a stranger to before. He could remember his father reading from the Bible on Sunday evenings, but not every week. Perhaps in bad weather, perhaps on special occasions. His mother had read. She had read everything she could lay her hands on: she had read while she worked, while she baked; she would get up early and go to bed late just to be able to read. Percy felt the same way now; he could not get enough. Sometimes in the late evenings, while Brother Gillman sat with his newspaper and Sister Gillman her sewing, Percy would sit with his pamphlets and scriptures. Then one night a chance comment drew him back into reality, as though someone had snapped his fingers, or had taken him by the shoulders and given him a rough shake.

"The arrogant old skinflint, so he's going to do it." Benjamin Gillman didn't sound pleased.

"What is it?" Claire asked.

He looked up from the newspaper he had been reading.

"Says here that old Squire Beal plans to sit for the House of Commons next term."

"Fancy that."

"I don't, Claire." He read on for a moment. "Why, Percy, look here at this. There's mention of your brother, of your family, right here."

Percy laid down his book and reached for the paper. He could feel a tightness inside, almost a dread to read what might be written. He searched for the place. The words leaped out at him:

> *In addition to Squire Beal's impressive*
> *civic record, he is in some parts known*
> *for his philanthropic leanings. We refer*
> *especially to his recent adoption of one*
> *of the orphan children of Oscar and*
> *Suzanne Graham lately of . . .*

So there had been a reason! Percy remembered his conversation with Mrs. Evans. He had been right to suspect the old fraud.

He's got a mean streak, that one.

Where did he remember those words from? He closed his eyes. Squire Beal at a picnic—no, it was winter. A Christmas lighting celebration? Perhaps. It was his father who said it, turning to his mother. He could see them both now!

He's a bit of a hypocrite, Beal. I've heard he's a bad employer, cruel to his men. Not much of the milk of human kindness in his veins, even at this season.

An image of Stanley's face rose before Percy's eyes. *I'll take the old bloke on. I can give him a run for his money, eh, Percy?*

Dear heaven, what had he done? Why hadn't he remembered before he let the Squire take Stanley? There was little he could hope to do now. Anger and fear, remorse and loneliness mingled inside him, souring his spirit, sapping the confidence he had felt these past days.

I am Percy Graham. I am not a Gillman. I'm not a Latter-day Saint.

He excused himself and went up to his room—small and cold, but it offered him privacy. How he wished he could cry, throw himself on the bed and cry like a child. What a luxury, that. Nothing else could ease this terrible pain building in him.

He didn't read the Book of Mormon that night, nor the next, nor the next. If Claire Gillman noticed any difference in him, she held her peace. And she prayed. He didn't know she was praying until many years later when she told him quite by accident.

The next Sunday came. Percy had taken to measuring his new life from Sunday to Sunday. He went to church as before. If he seemed a little withdrawn, no one noticed. The people were as kind as they ever had been. Elder Jones approached him with an air of real eagerness.

"Look what I've got for you." He held up a thick pamphlet. The words of the title read: Pearl of Great Price. Percy felt an excitement run through his veins. He reached out for it.

"Thank you," he said, "I'll start reading it today."

And he did. He sat upstairs after supper and read until the light left the window. Then he lit a lamp and read on past time, past reckoning. President Franklin Richards had compiled many gems of great price in this volume: ancient scriptures that told of Adam teaching the gospel, of Enoch and his vision of Zion, of the purpose and creation of this world, of our pre-earthly existence as described by Abraham. It was nearly too much for his mind to take hold of. And yet he read on. He read portions of Joseph Smith's own history, his account of himself, and pieces from some of his revelations concerning the restoration. Percy could not make himself stop. Near the end were thirteen brief statements identified as the Articles of Faith. He read through them once, twice, a third time. His mind seemed to clear, and the plainness of them seemed evident. At the end of the tract was printed a poem by a British convert, John Jaques, written not far from here at Stratford-upon-Avon. Percy glanced at the words, then found himself speaking them softly, out loud to himself:

> Oh say, what is truth? 'Tis the fairest gem
> That the riches of worlds can produce,
> And priceless the value of truth will be when
> The proud monarch's costliest diadem
> Is counted but dross and refuse.

The sound of his voice grew louder, more sure.

Then say, what is truth? 'Tis the last and the first,
For the limits of time it steps o'er.
Tho' the heavens depart and the earth's fountains burst,
Truth, the sum of existence, will weather the worst,
Eternal, unchanged evermore.

He stopped. The silence was singing. He dropped down to his knees. Read it and pray over it, Elder Jenkins had said. Then you'll know for yourself.

Joseph Smith—the Book of Mormon—truth unchanging; Percy needed to know, he really needed to know for himself. He stayed down on his knees a long time. He said things from his heart that he had not known were there; he bared that heart before God. He kept nothing concealed or unspoken, and he asked with a faith he had been a stranger to before the death of his parents and this knowledge of Mormonism.

When he rose from his knees, when he stood again on his stiff, shaky legs, he was a different young man. He had felt spirit answer his spirit; some power had quickened his mind and sent a pure light streaming all through his body. He had no place left for doubt. He felt like a child who had been lost, who had been struggling to find his way, weary and heartsore, stumbling through mists, pain, and darkness. And then, as though suddenly turning a corner and finding it there, he had come upon this bright knowledge that something in his spirit remembered and recognized: he had been lost, and now he was home.

Percy moved through the next day with a glow he could still feel surrounding him. He wondered: *Why me? Why has this happiness reached out to touch me, and why have I embraced it so quickly?* He could see no reason. He poured out his gratitude and gladness to God, that Heavenly Father who could see all reasons that his unborn tomorrows yet held in their hands.

8

Benjamin and Claire Gillman had joined the Mormon church before they came to Birmingham, six years before, while he was still an independent farmer. But even then they had wanted to immigrate to Zion. Now that he knew a trade, Benjamin was an even more valuable candidate. They had saved what they could, but saving was a long and difficult process, particularly in the midst of trials. By this spring of 1856 the end was at least within sight. Two years at the most, one year at the least, they could board ship and join the Saints who had gathered to Zion!

Percy knew nothing of this. Percy had not the vaguest idea that these grandiose plans for the future existed. When he opened the front door, he opened the door to a mighty whirlwind that took him in its teeth and shook him like a terrier shakes a rat.

He was the only one home. The Gillmans had gone visiting with their three little girls, and he had stayed home to read, to enjoy the solitude which was such a rare pleasure. The man at the door looked vaguely familiar to him, that was all. He introduced himself as Brother Day. He was area president, he lived over in Coventry, and he had some good news, some wonderful news for Brother and Sister Gillman.

Percy could tell that he had. He was fairly bubbling over with it. He kept checking his watch, taking it in and out of his pocket, then craning his neck toward the window.

"I must be on my way. I've other business to attend to this evening thirty miles north of here."

Finally he stopped pacing and fussing and made a decision. "Look, I'd like to tell them myself, I'd very much like to be the first one to tell them, but that isn't to be. They must contact Brother Mumbsy first thing in the morning, so they must have the news now. I must tell you, young man, in their stead." He drew himself up. "Benjamin's cousin in Utah put in a request that the PEF help them, and at the same time the missionaries nominated the Gillmans as particularly worthy members to be considered for emigration assistance. So, there you are."

"There I am what, sir?" Percy understood none of this.

"They have been chosen and approved. The Perpetual Emigration Fund will assist them. I believe a space has been found."

"Found where, Brother Day?"

This was the crux of the good news. "Aboard ship! They will be leaving in May, sometime in May, I believe."

"Leaving?"

"Leaving for Zion, my son."

Percy's face must have mirrored the surprised shock he was feeling. Brother Day clasped him around the shoulders, misreading his expression.

"Yes, it is marvelous news. I wish I could see their faces when you tell them, Percy." He was suddenly half out the door. "Don't forget: Brother Mumbsy's office tomorrow morning. They'll learn all the facts there."

He pumped Percy's hand, beamed a moment longer, then was gone from the room. Percy found his way to a chair and sat down. What did this news mean for him? Certainly he couldn't stay with the Gillmans now—go with them—to Zion!

When they came in two hours later, the girls were tired and excited and needed calming down, getting ready for bed. Percy hung back. He didn't know how to tell them. He helped feed the girls their bread and milk while Sister Gillman bustled about and Brother Gillman slipped laughingly out to the shed to avoid them all. Percy helped all he could, moving with such speed and efficiency that he drew Claire's attention.

"What's gotten into you, lad?"

He looked up, appeal in his eyes. "I have something to tell you."

She thought it might be bad news. "Well, let's get these little rascals in bed. I'll manage now. You go out and drag Benjamin back here."

When that was accomplished they sat, the three of them, in the front parlor. There was no other way than to jump right in with both feet.

"Brother Day was here earlier."

"Brother Day? What could he want?" Claire wondered.

Percy looked into their eyes and read no deception, no hiding. This really was a surprise.

"He said the Perpetual Emigration Fund—" Percy had written the words down after Brother Day left so he would not forget them—"has agreed to aid you. I don't know what that means. But you're going to Zion."

Claire leaned forward. "We're going to Zion!" she repeated.

"Yes, somehow they're helping you go. You don't have to wait however long you'd been planning on waiting. There's a ship leaving in May."

"A ship leaving in May?"

"And you're supposed to be on it."

"There must be some mistake." Benjamin rose and walked to the mantel. He wouldn't give in to his hope, to the clear reality of the words Percy had spoken. "There must be some mistake."

"You must see Brother Mumbsy tomorrow."

Claire leaned forward again. Percy feared she might tumble right over. "He's the agent," she said. "He's the agent in charge of emigration, Benjamin."

They looked at each other. "I know." Benjamin ran his hand through his thick, coarse hair. "It just couldn't be."

"I think it is." Percy startled them both. "Brother Day seemed quite sure. He wanted to be here to tell you himself. He wanted to see—" *See your joy.* There was such obvious ecstasy creeping into their warm eyes, playing at their mouths, teasing the doubt from their voices.

"I'll not sleep this night." Benjamin spoke the words with the force of a dirge. "I'll not sleep till I know of a certain."

Claire nodded her head. It would be a long night for them both.

Percy went up to bed. He had his own stake in this, but they were too worked up to think of him now. He had an entire workday to make it through before he would come back and know, know what this meant in regard to his future. He had a feeling inside that the complications of today would reach out and touch him more than he knew, more than he could imagine right now in his ignorance. He slept poorly, too, and woke with a sense of excitement that stayed with him all day.

It had been true, then. He read that in Claire's face when he walked in the door.

She sat him down. She explained all the details. They would leave May 10th, sail from Liverpool on the *Adventurer*, come to port in New York, and from there travel by rail to a place called Council Bluffs, Iowa. At that place or a point in Nebraska they would be outfitted for the long journey by handcart—over a thousand miles long—to the city of the Saints.

She spoke words, just a jumble of words. Percy had no pictures to fit them, no images at all to bring them into reality.

"We have some little money saved, more than most, apparently, who'll be going. They want us to use it to help outfit ourselves for the last leg of the journey West. The major portion we borrow from the Fund we can pay back after reaching the Valley, after we get settled there. And the money will be used and reused to help others come over."

It seemed a very good plan. These Mormons were paragons of organization. Percy already knew that.

"There isn't much time," he said.

"No, there isn't!"

"Are you happy? Have you no fears, no reservations?"

Claire considered his question, giving it fair answer. "I have fears, I'll admit. But many thousands have crossed over safely, so why not us, too? And I want to go, with all my heart, Percy."

"Why? England's your home. You would leave just like that! Never see her again?"

"It's not as hasty as it seems to you, Percy; we've been planning for years. Ever since we first joined the Church. And we've been praying. We know that it's right. But it will be most hasty for you."

Percy's heart stood still. "Hasty for me?"

Claire drew her breath in. "We booked space for you, Percy. We are hoping you'll come."

He could say nothing. He sat staring at her. She moved to sit by his side.

"I know it comes as a shock to you, Percy. It wasn't meant to be so. If it had been as we'd planned, you'd have had time to know for yourself."

"What do you mean by that?"

"Well, I mean join the Church, gain your own testimony, feel the desire to gather to Zion—" She looked at his face and threw up her hands. "Perhaps this has ruined it all, and then I shall never forgive myself!"

She walked to the window. Percy thought she might start to weep.

"Ruined what, Sister Gillman?"

She did not turn to face him. "Your chances for happiness."

He was more confused than before. "What chances for happiness?"

Claire took the risk and turned around. "I wasn't always a Mormon, you know. I was converted, like you—" She walked closer and held his gaze. "You are converted—you can't say that you aren't. But I *know* what you are just starting to feel, that your only real chances for happiness lie here, within Mormonism. If this scares you away..." She paused again, upset by her own words.

"It wasn't meant to come this fast, to overwhelm you." She sighed. "But perhaps even this has a purpose in it that we can't see."

She sat down; she seemed drained. Percy reached out and took her hand without thinking. She seemed to welcome the touch.

"Don't worry, Sister Gillman." What more could he say? "I'll admit I—" No, he didn't want to admit anything yet. "Give me time, just a little time."

She squeezed his hand. "Surely. I'd best go start the potatoes."

She left the room, but Percy sat where he was, sat long minutes in thought.

"I believe I'll take a walk before supper," he called. He could feel the taut silence when she failed to reply. "I'll be back, Sister Gillman, don't worry."

He walked out and away from the town toward open country; it wasn't too far. He walked swiftly and the effort felt good, the fresh air cleared his head. He thought about going to see Louisa, but she would be working and have difficulty getting the freedom to talk with him. And what could she say? She could be no help in this. No one could. Percy knew that. It was his own decision to make.

He'd never felt more alone. He slowed his pace some and drew in the clean smell of green, growing things. *Spring in England—is there anything like it? How could I possibly leave? And for what? This dream isn't my dream. What is Zion to me?*

He walked a bit further. There were trees now, growing thick, with a slim path worn between. He took the path. The silence reached out to touch him, the fragrance, the peace. It brought to his mind the Sunday feeling that had first drawn him to listen, to read the new books. He thought of the night he had spent on his knees, of the things he now knew. *I am not the same person I was two brief months ago.* The realization was painful. It seemed to increase his sense of aloneness. *First the death of both of my parents—who could remain unchanged through something like that? The breaking up, the loss of my family, and now this—this new religion that has opened my heart, this new knowledge . . .*

He found a large stump high enough to sit down on. He knew he couldn't ignore what had happened around him, what had happened within him. *Mother, what would you do?* The question came unbidden, but it came from his heart. *What would you have me do?*

The silence was dumb, no whispered answer came to him through the new leaves' rustlings, no voice on the breeze. But a calm—unexpected and sweet—settled over his spirit, and he knelt by the tree stump and prayed before walking back to the house.

When he came in the door he could feel more than hear Claire's relieved sigh. She threw him a grateful glance. They all sat to the table and ate, listening to the little girls' chatter, occupied by it. After the dishes were cleared and the girls tucked in bed, Percy said, "Can we talk?"

Benjamin, who had been watching him, nodded. There was an awkwardness between them that had not been there before. Sitting all together with the two of them staring at him, Percy didn't feel ready. He said as much.

"I'm not ready to talk now. I need to think yet awhile."

He could read their eyes saying: *You haven't much time.*

"Could I ask a few questions?"

"Anything you'd like."

"Was this journey to Zion in your minds when you decided to—take me in?"

Claire glanced at Benjamin. Her look said: *Let's tell him the truth.*

Benjamin must have concurred. "Yes, it was," he replied very quietly. "It was on our minds. We knew a man's strength would be needed—a strength I don't have. But we had thought: someday. Sometime in the future. Not—surely not now." His kind, honest eyes blinked across at Percy.

"It wasn't just that." Claire, too, spoke quietly, and her voice held emotion she had to work to control. "It wasn't as though we had been out looking for someone," she said, "not at all. We were just going about our business as usual. Then—it was a small thing, really, I took a wrong turn, going to a market one of the sisters had recommended, I took a wrong turn and came out by your old church—right in front of it, really, and your vicar was just going in, and I asked him the way."

She took a deep breath. Percy leaned forward, listening. "He was really quite kind," she continued. "He gave me the instructions I needed, then he handed me a piece of paper. 'Would you be interested?' he asked.

"I took it. I read the advertisement, for so it looked: *Wanted: Homes for six orphan children. Come from good local family. Names and ages listed below.*

She half smiled at Percy. "I must have looked strange or hesitated, for he reached out his hand as if to take it back again and I said quickly, 'Oh no, thank you, sir, let me keep it. We may have an interest in this.' He nodded slowly, said something polite, and then went on his way. For some reason I had a feeling—"

She broke off suddenly. "I don't know, Benjamin, maybe I ought not to continue—"

"No, don't stop now! Please!" Percy had half risen out of his chair. Claire, seeing his response, seemed to calm down some, regain her confidence.

"All right," she said. "I came home, I showed the paper to Benjamin. I thought he might laugh, or think I had taken leave of my senses." She smiled: a vague, whimsical expression that rose from her lips to her cheeks and seemed to rest softly in her eyes. Percy knew she was remembering something. It made him feel slightly uncomfortable, left out.

"But instead he took the paper and sat down with it. 'Why did you accept this?' he asked. I tried to explain. He seemed to understand. He nodded and ran his finger down the lines of the paper. Then he moved it back up until it rested on your name."

"*Percy.* I said the word out loud."

Both of them jumped at Benjamin's unexpected interruption.

"Something in me said *him.* Something in me seemed to almost recognize your name. I said to Claire, 'We want him.' "

He lifted his head, drew Percy's gaze and held it. "I wasn't thinking of the work, lad, and that be the truth. Something just told me: *him.*"

Percy felt himself nodding, as if in some strange agreement.

"You know what happened then—what happened when we came to talk with you, what's happened since."

Percy ran his fingers across his scalp.

"I know you don't understand." Benjamin's voice was patient and gentle. "I don't understand it myself."

"It's been crazy from the start," Claire broke in. "Why, in some ways I didn't want a strange boy in my house. I didn't want to get involved—I didn't know what we'd get in for." She shrugged her shoulders. "You'll have to make your own sense out of it, Percy." She sighed, then laughed lightly. "I don't envy you the task."

She rose, as if on an impulse, glided close to his chair, then bent suddenly and kissed his forehead. "I hope you can make it,

I do. *And quickly!*" The last two words were a whisper. They had their desired effect. Percy laughed and shook his head at her. Benjamin smiled into her eyes. The heavy air lifted—the weight they had felt pressing on them.

"I've still got beasts to bed down." Percy rose and smiled shyly. "Thanks, both of you."

He went from the room out to the back hall to get his jacket. His greatcoat hung on a nail in a place of its own in the corner, out of everyone's way. He had worn it a time or two, on the cold nights that confused their way into spring. He touched the thick, roughened wool.

Two misfits, he thought to himself. But the words didn't feel right. They were, somehow, no longer accurate. He walked back to the barn. The dark path was already familiar to him. He didn't marvel at that. He merely went about his business with a sense of ease, almost a sense of happiness—although he would not have recognized it for that.

He did say his prayers before going to bed. He remembered that. He did ask about Zion and England and where the Lord might happen to want him. But he didn't expect any kind of a real, tangible answer. Yet his answer did come, and it came in the form of a dream. And to him that meant something. Percy was not a dreamer of dreams. What few dreams he could even remember were jumbled, unclear, making practically no sense at all, meaning nothing. But this dream . . .

He awoke in the morning with it clear in his head, every detail perfect and vivid and so very real that he blinked his eyes, almost surprised to find himself in the same dim attic room where he had last gone to bed.

In the dream he had stood upon some great height and looked down on a valley. This was not England; there were no mountains in England as high as he stood. And the valley that stretched out below him was a wide, barren wasteland: a desert. That word had come to him. Yet water was there: a winding river and a large stretch of lake at the valley's end. And he could hear singing, and the singing was joyful, and it made the air sweet. Everything in him longed for that valley. He felt joyful himself: young and strong and hopeful, and all that he longed for seemed to lie at his feet, and it was his greatest desire to be there, to descend the mountain, come home.

He awoke with that thought in his mind: *Home. When I find this valley I will find the home I have not had since my parents died.*

He told no one of his dream; he went off to work as usual. But the clarity of the vision stayed with him. That night he asked Claire, "What does Zion look like?"

She smiled. "I'm not certain," she said, "since I've never been there myself. But I've heard Salt Lake City sits in a large basin, a bowllike valley, enclosed by high mountains."

"And is it green and forested, like England?" Percy's voice sounded light, it seemed to echo inside his own head.

"Heavens no, dear. 'Tis a desert with nothing green in it but what the Saints have planted themselves."

Percy's mouth was dry and he swallowed to ease it. He felt a mounting excitement, as though he had just discovered some unknown treasure, some hidden thing that was beautiful to look on and of immeasurable worth.

He rose and spoke the six words: "Sister Gillman, I'm going to Zion." And from that moment on he never wavered or doubted or feared.

He did not tell her his dream; it didn't seem right to, somehow. It was *his* answer. It was all he had needed and more. The vision remained as fresh, as real as the world he moved through. On the strength of the dream he was able to do what he had to do — which he would not have been able to do alone.

CHAPTER
9

Percy had never before known what it meant to have too little time. There had never been anything pressing, no deadlines to life. Now this immovable date, May 10th, controlled all his actions, every step he took, every breath he drew. Only a matter of weeks. And new things seemed to crop up out of nowhere, things that had to be done, had to be dealt with before May 10th closed the door forever, letting nothing, however pressing and demanding, come through.

So, with some justification, he wasn't just putting it off. The list of things to do before sailing from Liverpool seemed to grow each day rather than diminish. He fell exhausted every night into a heavy, dreamless sleep. He seemed to run through the days with a sense of going around in circles, never quite in control. And yet, he must face them all sometime.

He eased himself into it. He sat down and wrote a long letter to Laura and another to Randall. He wrote as much as he could: all the common details of life since they'd left him, all the changes that had come, all the reasons — as far as he could explain them — for what he now planned to do, and all the endearments, the assurances he dared offer. It helped to spell it all out, to clarify it all in his own mind. But who should come next? Perhaps Louisa. Would she try to dissuade him? Maybe Stanley instead. Not his baby — he couldn't let himself even think about Rosie.

He went to visit Louisa. He found her up to her elbows in flour, her cheek smeared with the stuff. He knew she worked long hours in the bakery as well as taking care of most of the household chores. He didn't like to think about it. Mrs. Bascom glared at him.

"There's some of us has work to do," she sniveled.

He tried to ignore her. He spoke into the air, into the row of dusty beams stretched above him. "Louisa's coming with me. It's very important and it can't wait. I'll return her, ma'am, as soon as I'm able."

He took her hand and literally dragged her out with him. She wiped her other white hand along her apron.

"Percy—"

"Hush, come with me." He led her a little aside from the house, around a sharp corner to a spot where three lilac bushes stretched, all in the first bursting of faint purple bloom. He spread his jacket for her to sit down on.

She was more than curious now. There was an almost frightened look in her eyes. He took her thin hands in his. "I'm going away, Louisa," he said.

She did not understand. He looked down where a smear of red jelly stained her white apron. "It's something I have to do, and I know you won't understand it; I don't expect that you will. On May 10th the Gillmans sail for America, and I'm going along."

There was silence; he feared perhaps she had fainted and slowly lifted his eyes to see tears running down her pale cheeks. She snatched her hand away and wiped at her eyes with her apron corner.

"Do you know what you're doing, Percy?" Her tone of voice said: *I doubt that you do.*

"Do you think I would go lightly across the ocean, thousands of miles from my home, to a strange land I know nothing of, if I didn't feel I was sure?" He was nearly shouting, and he hadn't meant to.

"It's your own life," she said. "You must do what you must do." She rose to her feet. "I'd best be getting straight back."

He broke a sprig of the new lilac and worked it through her buttonhole and, although she protested, it won him a faint, half-warm smile.

"Don't look so miserable, Percy. I meant what I said. It is

your life. You'll do me no good hanging around here, and you know it. So take what comes to you."

"I'll be back."

She turned and laughed, and the sound was not pleasant. "If it helps you to think so—" She shrugged her thin shoulders.

"I promised!"

"Percy—"

"I did! Didn't you believe me, even back in the house that night?"

"Percy—" She stopped and faced him. "You mean well, I know. But to come back from clear over the ocean—it's just not likely to happen."

"It will happen. I will come back."

"All right, fine. I'll be glad. I'll be a proper married woman by then, with some money to give you a grand welcome and perhaps a small nephew for you to kiss and bring presents to."

"You'll see, Louisa."

"You're right, I'll see. Meantime, there's work to be done."

They walked on for a moment in silence. They were nearing the house and the yeasty smell of the bakery clung to Percy's nostrils, destroying the sweet flower scent.

"I'll see you again before you leave?"

Percy nodded. Louisa bent and kissed his cheek, a quick, birdlike motion. "Don't fret, Percy, don't fret. You're like Mother that way. She could fret up a storm and Father had the deuce of a time working her out of it."

She smiled; she was gone. He stood alone with the sour smell of the bakery clinging to him; he seemed to carry it with him, smell it all through the day.

He waited another day before calling on Stanley; he had to shore up his courage a little. He found his brother alone in the small coach house polishing the heavy silver and brass fittings on the fine coaches the Squire kept. Percy picked up a rag. "Go on, Stanley, I'll help while we talk."

"What've you come for?" Stanley looked over his shoulder.

"You've come for something, I'll bet. You're as nervous as a canary when the cat comes prowling."

That was something his mother had always said.

"You're right." Percy drew a deep breath. "I've come to tell you that I'm going to America with the Gillmans. We sail May 10th. From Liverpool."

Stanley said something that nearly made Percy blush.

"Watch your mouth! You never used to talk that way."

Stanley raised a dark eyebrow. "The Squire's learned me a thing or two." He went back to his work. "So you're running out on us. I didn't think you had it in you."

Percy held his own tongue.

"What's in it for you? What in the devil do they have there that England doesn't have?"

Percy smiled. *That's a good question, Stanley.*

"For one thing, they've got land. A man can own more land there than most Englishmen see in a lifetime."

"That's not why you're going."

"No, it's not."

"Well then, why?" Stanley had stopped polishing and was watching him closely. "It's that new religion, I know. You've gone clean out of your head because of it, Percy."

"Well, I wouldn't say that."

"If it weren't for Mormonism you wouldn't be going. Isn't that right?"

"That's right." Percy looked full at his brother, gazed into the dark, troubled eyes.

"Then I reckon I shall hate Mormonism—"

"Stanley!"

"Well, Percy, I do. It takes you away from me! What's in it for me to feel good about?"

The clear-sighted literalist! It made Percy shudder just watching the boy.

"I'll come back, Stanley."

His scoff said the same thing that Louisa had said. Percy felt the heat of his own temper rising.

"I don't care if you want me or not, if it matters nothing to you. I made a promise, and I plan to keep it. I'll be back here someday."

"Bully for you." Stanley moved to the door where the sunset, just fading, seemed to reach in with long golden fingers; the whole outdoors seemed to glow. Percy felt it, but Stanley, a storm cloud, stood impervious, stiff.

Is the Squire mistreating you? He had seen the cuts and bruises on Stanley's face, the cold fear in his eyes whenever the Squire's name was mentioned. Percy wanted to ask him, but he didn't quite dare. He was not only afraid of how Stanley might act, but of what Stanley might say, what unpleasant truths he might give the stamp of reality to with the spoken word. He didn't like this awful helplessness he felt whenever he was with Stanley.

"It's a good decision, I suppose. I'd do it in your place." Stanley was talking more to himself than to Percy. Then he turned with his sharp eyes slanted. "Are you up to it, huh? The adventure? I'm the one should be going."

"That's partly true."

"Partly true!" Stanley threw his brother a black look.

"There's more than adventure, you know. Responsibility— lots of backbreaking work—"

"More than is here, do you think?" Stanley kicked at a tall carriage wheel.

"Is it so bad then?" The words were out, softly. Stanley didn't respond, didn't meet Percy's eyes, but Percy could feel his sullen pain and frustration.

"Mayhap I'll stow away. Surprise all of you." He was back to the bantering he could handle so well, the brittle bantering that covered his soft spots.

"I'd like that," Percy said. "I'd like nothing better."

"Aw, you've had your fill of me. Everyone has." He turned away from the door. It was too dark for Percy to read what was in his face.

"Help me finish these blasted lamps," he said from the shadows, "and I'll walk you home."

"Will the Squire mind?"

Stanley snorted. "He's half-drunk already. He'll be out of his mind before I get back." He bent and rubbed with firm strokes the brass casings. "I can keep out of his way."

"Is he meaner, then, when he's drunk?"

"He's mean all of the time. I hope he wins the election. Then London can have him."

Percy bent to the task. "They deserve one another, I'd say."

"I'd drink to that—if I had some of the Squire's whiskey."

The brothers worked side by side. Percy thought: *It will never be like this with us again. He is already changed.* He didn't dare think about when he came back someday and what he might find.

Innocence came to his rescue, but at the same time it wounded him. He had spoken to May; May knew everything; May was his comfort. When he at last went to Rose, when he drew her aside and tried to explain, he didn't get very far. He could see his words running through her mind the way fine sand runs through open fingers. She couldn't contain it, save for the few soft pieces that clung to her.

"Percy, will you come back?"

"Yes," he said patiently, for the fourth or fifth time. "But by then you'll be grown, or nearly grown. A young lady and pretty— as pretty as May is, I'll bet."

She beamed at that; she already warmed to praise in that feminine way Percy thought must be inborn.

"Well, if I'm grown up like that, how will you know me?" She was distressed for the first time.

Percy lifted the oval of gold from her neck so that it lay in his hand, feeling slight and nearly weightless.

"Wear this always," he said. "Don't lose it—"

She shook her head solemnly.

"And when you are grown I shall come looking for the prettiest lady of all, and there you shall be with this gold locket around your neck, and that's how I shall know that it is my own little Rosie grown up."

She hugged him impulsively, hugged him so tight that the back of his neck ached.

"Don't forget me," he said, feeling foolish, but he had to say it.

She gazed back at him, as solemn suddenly as he was himself. "I can never forget you, Percy. I have you here, in my heart."

She placed her plump little hand over her smock at the place she thought her heart would be. "I'll wait for you, Percy."

He couldn't speak. She saw it and hugged him again.

"Don't cry, Percy."

"I won't, sweetheart."

He took the long way back to the Gillmans'; it helped to walk out the pain that made even his muscles and joints ache. He had believed this was over and done with. He'd gone through this before: saying good-bye, letting go, feeling something within himself die, or rather grow hard and go numb and seem to drop off, like some dead, useless limb, leaving him the less for the loss of it.

What am I doing? Is this madness? he wondered. Yet he could not deny what had happened that night on his knees, what his dream had foretold. Perhaps he was merely feeling spent and empty; he should have expected as much.

It is the price people pay for loving. So his mother had said in a mood as close to complaint as she ever came, said when someone was ill, when one of her children was hurt or upset over something, or misused by a classmate or friend. *Perhaps it was hard for her, too. Perhaps she felt things too deeply, the way I seem to feel them.*

Percy walked on. The dusk gathered and thickened, but for a few quiet moments he did not feel that he was walking alone.

In the midst of all this feverish activity the missionaries slipped Percy's baptism in. One of the most important events of his life, taken as more or less commonplace. How does one stamp such a day in a way to make it stand out, be somehow apart from the rest?

It was a regular warm, fair Sunday. After the morning meeting was concluded the major portion of the congregation traipsed down to the river with Percy, the missionaries, and the Gillman family, and stood watching, arms folded, heads bowed, as Elder Jenkins led the boy into the cool stream, spoke the sacred words, and lowered him gently into the waters of baptism.

Percy knew something had happened to him. Indeed, when the elders placed their hands on his head and, at Percy's request, Benjamin Gillman invoked the Holy Ghost to be the young man's companion, Percy felt a great thrill. He wasn't instantly better, he wasn't instantly changed, but he had been marked. He had again felt the spirit and responded in spirit, and that wove a strength, a quiet, subtle strength within him.

He also requested a hymn, the hymn that was printed in the Pearl of Great Price: "Oh Say, What Is Truth?" He listened to the voices rise on the still spring air, filled with faith, filled with hope. He felt the power of the words move clear through him with that same sense of light they had given him when he first read them. They made the moment special for him. He would ever after associate them with spring in England and his baptism day.

CHAPTER

10

*T*he time came. The days were too short to be counted now, lest panic set in. Preparing for a journey such as this was like preparing for death, in a way, Percy thought. One did all one could to get ready, put his life in order, tie all the loose ends neatly together—but when time cut him off, what was done was done, and what was undone would remain undone forever.

Percy schooled himself to not think, to not care, so that when the time came he had the strength to take that first step out of one life and into another.

And so it was. And so it felt all along. Even the trip to Liverpool seemed a momentous step, an adventure Percy would never have imagined nor hoped to obtain. To ride a train—what Stanley would think of this! To sit on a bench in a warm, closed com-partment and feel that magical power vibrating through him, around him, while it sped him along at a pace that ought to be making his head spin. And then to see that tall ship, the breadth and depth of her, somehow sitting upright in the water—sitting poised, uneasy, waiting, waiting to be released, to bow her head to the wind, to slice the water with her prow and push seaward.

Fate had chosen a good time for them to be travelers; Percy knew that was true. The government had just passed a new Pas-sengers' Act to improve conditions aboard emigrant ships. And the changes were being felt, especially in the area of diet on board. Beef, pork, potatoes, and peas were added to enhance the basic biscuits and oatmeal. The vessels were larger now, too, with two decks for berths rather than one. The Crimean War was still raging and many of England's jobless and poor, hoping to escape the hunger and chaos of breadlines, felt willing to take their chances in a new country rather than stick it out here.

But the Mormon emigrants were different. They were not deserting England, they were embracing a cause. They were giving up one loved home for another. A sweet sorrow pervaded the very air that surrounded them.

Percy liked life on board. The *Adventurer* crossed the ocean in fewer days than her slower, older sisters had done, and the fact that the ship would dock in New York rather than New Orleans chopped another two weeks off the trip. There was room enough to move, to draw breath in, there was decent fare, there was music—Percy loved the songs of Zion he was learning to sing, and the old English ballads that drew pictures of home and brought tears to his eyes. And there was work to keep his hands and mind busy. One of the things he was taught to do was to cut and sew canvas tents and heavy wagon covers, which they would need in plenty for the difficult overland journey to the city of the Saints. He liked the work, he could think what he wanted while his hands went along, even daydream and plan for the future. There were some teachers on board, and Percy availed himself of their services and in turn worked patiently with the three little Gillman girls, who were learning the rudiments of reading and ciphering.

He had never before realized or been able to appreciate how much his mother had taught her children, how far ahead they all were. He thought of Rosie; he couldn't help but think of her. Sometimes while he helped the young girls he would pretend one or another was Rosie—a foolish thing, but it helped. All the while he was instructing, comforting, tucking in bed, combing out long, golden hair—in all the things he was doing to help little Ellen or Mary, he imagined Rose.

Benjamin had a hard time. The stiff, narrow ship bunks were hard on his back. So was standing on deck. He had little chance for relief from the pain Percy knew he was hiding. Often he walked the dark decks when the rest of the ship rocked in slumber, walked with the roll and pitch of the ship until his tall, bulky shape learned to move in a unique rhythm with it. Percy walked with him sometimes: on a night when his own spirit felt restless, or when memories of home drove all rest and peace from his mind.

He would walk for a spell, but eventually he would be drawn to a spot in the bow as close to the forecastle as the crew would allow him. There, by the dim glow of the ship's lights, he watched the sea. It seemed a live thing that moved around and beneath them, a monster they rode who might heave up at any moment and discard them. That was the fathomless sea. But what of the waves that built and crested and lapped at their sides? Each wave had a life of its own and Percy, watching, was drawn into that moving life, mesmerized by it, by the distinct beauty of the movement and pattern of each wave in its turn. *We are much like that,* he thought. *England was the ocean that bore me, upon which I moved and made my own progress. Now I have found my way into the wide sea of Mormonism; I am a wave of that sea, as distinct in my patterns and powers as is each other Saint, yet partaking of the power of the whole, and in my way adding as well; consumed, yet distinct, with a beauty entirely mine.*

The thought repeated itself time after time. So he moved forward, swept with the current that knew where it was going when he did not.

So the great, strong sea bird carried them safely, the ocean endured them upon her back, and God and time brought them to this place which so many had known as the Promised Land. New York City. The very name drew excitement. This powerful land was still in its infancy, yet it belied tradition and history and stood as a haven of freedom, a touchstone for man—any man who was stumbling and seeking, any man who could dream. Percy felt it. *Am I really here?* He seemed to move in a daze. *Percy Graham, lately of Birmingham, England. Do I stand on this spot, do I really gaze at the lights of New York, that glittering city, which makes even London appear provincial?*

It seemed too strange to be true; too many sensations overloaded his senses. They were scarcely through the chaos of landing and customs when he found himself on a train—a train very different from the ones in England, but a train just the same that sped them across the trackless stretch of America, this great, spread-out land, to a place called Council Bluffs, Iowa.

Here the real work began. This place had originally been called Kanesville when the Mormons first fled from Nauvoo and found a temporary haven here. The emigrants began gathering supplies for the westward journey at this point. Percy's powers of organization were stretched when they handed him the seemingly endless list of "essentials," the least amount required for actual survival. He was himself city bred, used to factories and chimney smoke, milk carts, fish markets, a bustling yet cozy conglomeration of men and their trades, with all the products of those trades spread before him. There was nothing here. These people were primitive! And when he said as much he was laughed at and assured that it would only get worse.

He set himself to the task, not sure that he would ever complete it. Benjamin handled the finer points that required real workmanship, and his knowledge of foodstuffs and livestock came in handy as well. Together they muddled it out. The women meantime mended clothing, secured what they could to supplement that already worn by much traveling, knitted stockings, and preserved every scrap of food they could lay their hands on.

It was a busy time. June slipped away from them almost without their noticing, and the prairie summer set in, and Percy felt heat like he never had known. On every side people wilted: women finding what relief they could from sunbonnets and good feathered fans, men donning wide-brimmed hats and kerchiefs around their necks to help soak up the sweat. Percy loved it. Was he a hothouse flower? Perhaps kin to a desert cactus, some teased. He couldn't seem to get enough. They crossed the river to Florence, Nebraska, and the heat was worse there. *Wait till you hit real desert*, they were warned. But Percy continued to thrive. And he was beginning to like the wild, open spaces and the different sensations they drew from some deep reservoir within his own being.

Florence had been known as Winter Quarters in the earlier days. It was here they were outfitted with handcarts. They were some of the first to try this less expensive, more accessible means of travel. How narrow, how shallow the carts seemed! To carry one's whole life in such a contrivance! For the first time, perhaps, the impact of just what they were doing struck Percy. The blow stunned him into a wakefulness he knew he would be needing.

"Gird your loins, there are hard times ahead." He heard that time after time. Once he faced it squarely he felt a new surge of confidence. He took the past that he loved, the whole past that was his life and identity, and tucked it like a treasure into a safe, protected part of his being. He had to put it behind; he would need all his wits about him to handle the tasks at hand. And he welcomed those tasks, with all the dangers that supposedly shadowed them.

"That's because you're a man." So Claire told him when he confided his feelings. "It's a man's world here, that's certain."

She glanced to where Benjamin sat, bent over his workbench. Percy knew what she was thinking. A man with a handicap, however small, was looked down upon here. Not out of prejudice, but in the light of simple reality: he didn't quite measure up. He couldn't quite handle the imperatives that would ensure his own life and the lives of those who might be dependent on him.

And so Percy, though young, stepped into the foreground of the family. He knew he was needed. How Benjamin felt, what struggles he grappled with and overcame, Percy never knew. The man wasn't one to talk about what he was feeling, or to pity himself. He set his thin mouth into a hard line of acceptance, and he never complained. And he never envied or punished Percy when he saw the boy act in his place, accomplish things he could no longer do. Never—except once. And that once was to be understood.

If Benjamin went on uncomplaining, Claire made up for him, complaining her share, his, and then some besides. There were times Percy flared back at her when she heated his temper past the boiling point. When that happened she backed down with a smile.

"I'm a bear to live with, I know, Percy," she would apologize. And that would be that. It would clear the air between them. Once or twice she would add, by way of explanation or excuse, "It's not easy for me. I don't take to this country like you do."

They hadn't been on the trail long when Percy noticed some

unusual things about Claire. For one, she tired too fast. She stopped too often to mop her forehead and rest from pulling. She looked haggard and thin. Little things would set her off crying. She seemed to have lost all her color, and once or twice he caught her vomiting behind some bush, with her hanky to her mouth. Then an embarrassed color would rise to her cheeks and Percy would pull in her place. Now and then she would ride, but only at Benjamin's insistence. It finally got to the point where she was doing none of the pushing or pulling, none of the heavy hauling, and still she didn't get well. At last one night Percy spoke to Benjamin.

"What's wrong with Claire?" He had come to call them both by their first names; with time they had grown too intimate for *brother* and *sister* to suffice.

Benjamin grinned despite himself. "Heavens, boy, don't you know?"

Percy blushed at the older man's expression, but he was still in the dark. "No, I don't know, else I wouldn't be asking you."

Benjamin struggled to work the grin off his face. "It's really naught to make light of, I suppose. She's with child."

Percy gasped. He didn't care if Benjamin saw him. *So that's what's been wrong!* He thought of all the times she had dragged, had been sick. "Will she be all right?"

Benjamin's nod came with some reluctance. "She ought to be. Things seem normal enough. She's had four children, including the one that we lost, with no trouble to speak of."

"But isn't this too much for her? The walking, the sun, the cooking over a fire?"

"Well, none of it can be helped. She won't be the first woman to give birth in the wilderness. We'll just have to hope for the best."

Percy did more than hope for the best. He asked help from the Lord in his prayers. He thought it wasn't fair for a woman to suffer so. He saw now why Claire had complained, and he began to notice instead all the times that she held her tongue, all the times she made jokes out of hardships, all the times she endured, pale-faced and ill, with a smile on her face.

He helped her as much as he could. She always noticed, she

always thanked him. By this time it was plain, it was visible to anyone who looked for it. She had lost her slim waist. She let out her dresses to accommodate the new swell of the growing child.

"When is this baby due?" Percy asked her one night. It was the first thing he had said directly referring to the pregnancy or the child. She laughed like a girl.

"I'm not sure. I ought to know, I know I ought to." She shrugged her thin shoulders and sighed. "I was pregnant when I left England, but I didn't know it." She smiled a little shyly. "I figure come the new year, a new year's present for Benjamin."

Then it won't be born in the wilderness, at least, Percy thought. *I'll be grateful for that.*

"Will you—" He paused; he didn't know how to ask it. "Will you be sick the whole time?"

They had been twenty-one days on the trail. It was July 31st, a new month tomorrow. They still had weeks of travel ahead of them. The past days had seasoned them some. But to shake and be weak and vomit—

"I should get better," she said, though her quiet voice didn't ring with conviction. "Actually, it's much worse this time. I'm not sure why." A slight note of worry gave weight to her words. "Perhaps it's the climate, the food—"

"The sun," Percy added.

"The dust—"

"The buffalo chips!"

Soon they were laughing and that same girlish innocence altered her features.

"You look pretty," he said, holding his breath, not sure how she would receive it.

"Why, thank you, Percy," she breathed. "Coming from you, that's—"

She didn't finish. Had he embarrassed her, then?

"They call it the bloom of motherhood," she said softly. "I'm glad it's coming to me. It's a good sign."

"Are you worried, Claire?"

"No, not really." Again the flat, lackluster tone. "But I want this child. So does he—" She nodded toward the small, lantern-lit tent where Benjamin labored. "I want to give him a son, the son he lost."

This was the first time Percy had had such a close glimpse into the mysterious workings of womankind. He felt slightly awed and almost weakened with a feeling of tenderness.

"I hope you get what you want." He said the words softly, but his young voice was trembling.

"Thank you, Percy," she replied. "If God is as good to me as you are, I've got nothing to fear."

It was praise that was unexpected. He was glad for the dark to hide the pleasure that he was sure must have shown in his face.

11

*T*here was something new to be seen every day, things for a boy to discover. And despite the strenuous work and the hardships, Percy was but a boy, and there was a freedom here that he drank in and grew almost addicted to.

There were several milestones to go by: the Platte River, Fort Laramie, Independence Rock, Sweetwater. Now the distance left to travel was compressed into a small, shrunken figure: 263 miles, according to the Emigrants' Guide. When they had started out and Benjamin had shown Percy the number printed at the top of the first page, 1031 — 1031 miles from Winter Quarters to the city of the Great Salt Lake — it was as though someone had hit him and knocked all the air out of him. Great Britain, he knew, was at most six hundred miles from tip to tip, and that included both England and Scotland. This immense distance boggled his mind. How could people ever organize and get things done here? Whoever would dream of traveling a thousand miles over dangerous wilderness just so they might live in a different place? The American spirit. To him it seemed madness.

Yet, just the same, it was this spirit that drew him, intrigued him, seemed excitedly in tune with his own.

They reached South Pass — the summit, the magnificent dividing range between the waters of the Atlantic and the waters of the Pacific. It rose over seven thousand feet into a blue sky too piercing for clouds. Percy could stand and see into distance that he knew had no end. Like a pilgrim he felt he could wander for the rest of his life and that purple-gray distance would beckon him on, unattainable still.

They were just forty miles from Fort Bridger when a storm
caught them full force, a desert downpour that emptied the heavens into mud streams at their feet. It was a cold rain and, soaked
to the bones, people huddled and shivered. They camped early
along Green River and built roaring fires and tried to dry out
their clothes and dispel the chill gnawing at their bones. But the
storm blew up again at gale force and the fires sizzled, then went
sadly out. Some of the tents were blown over and the animals
were frightened. After the wind spent itself things calmed down
some, but the rain kept up steadily through the night.

Benjamin couldn't get Claire to stop shaking. At last they
bedded her down in the handcart with a canopy of canvas to shut
out the rain. Benjamin rubbed her cold feet and placed a hot
brick wrapped in flannel down under the blankets. Percy added
what he could, his greatcoat. He tucked the rough folds of it up
under her chin. It was less damp than the blankets. He waited
with Benjamin and watched her. Later in the night a premature
labor started, and before dawn came to open the sky her five-
months' son was born, breathed for a moment, then died in her
arms.

There was no dawn for them that morning; there was no light
they could see. The captain placed Claire in one of the company's
three wagons; she was still, deathly still: no words, no tears,
nothing behind her blank eyes.

Benjamin chose a low, sheltered spot near a small stand of
timber where the wind would not reach. But the grave could
look up through the arms of the branches at a stretch of blue
sky where high clouds and occasional eagles passed to say a hello.

Percy took a shovel and started the digging. The soil was
sandy and the bedrock pushed close here; he wouldn't be able
to go very deep. He bent to the task with all his pent-up anger,
which needed someplace to go. After a few minutes he felt a
rough hand grab his shoulder. He stumbled and turned.

"This is my work. Give way."

Percy blinked. Benjamin's eyes, rimmed with red, were as
wild as a mad bull's in the springtime. Percy replied not a word.
He handed the shovel to the older man and stood quickly aside.
He knew what each bend of the back, each shovelful cost him,

but it only seemed right. And perhaps the pain, the very feel of it, was the most cleansing remedy the man had at hand.

It wasn't as easy for Claire. She watched them bury her baby with a face that was dead of expression and eyes that were dry. They moved out, dragging mud that the high sun had not yet dried. There was nothing else they could do. She could not kneel, mourning, at a grave with a proper headstone on a grass-carpeted hill. She would never visit the grave, never see it again in her lifetime. She had buried her last hope for a son in a wild, unnamed spot, which would be claimed by the wolves and the elements.

They reached Bridger. There was some rest, some relief here. But nothing touched Claire. Bit by bit she was regaining her physical strength, but her spirit was frozen, suspended in some inner chamber that she would not disturb, would not allow anyone else to enter. She took care of the work, cared for the little girls without murmur, saw to Benjamin's needs. But she did it as if in a dream; she was not really there.

Benjamin waited; he was stolid and patient. Percy tried to be, too. He resented just a little the dampened atmosphere. They were nearing their goal. The pitch of excitement, of anticipation, was driving him mad. He wanted to jump and shout and put words to his dreams, but there was no place for that here.

"She'll come out of it," Benjamin assured him. "She just needs some more time."

Time propelled them from the site of Fort Bridger past Soda Springs, Sulphur Creek, the swift-running Bear River to the mouth of Cache Cave at the head of Echo Creek; sixty-six miles from home. They found the Red Fork of Weber River and caught trout in the stream. Percy cooked an especially plump one for Claire and took it to her. She ate every last bite. He thought he saw a spark, a tiny spark of something behind her shuttered eyes.

Pratt's Pass. Forty miles from the valley. They traveled along Kanyon creek, crossing it thirteen dizzied times, wading two rancid swamps before they began to ascend the high mountain, the highest of all they would cross, which stood just twenty-one miles from the valley. It felt high, it felt steep. Percy felt he had walked off two pair, maybe three pair of feet. He wondered if the ache in them would ever leave him.

He didn't plan anything. He didn't come up with a brilliant idea and try it out. He merely responded to some natural instinct.

When they reached the cold spring that stood beside Brown's Creek, scarcely a rod from the road, under a protected grove of black birch bushes, something inside him gave way. Perhaps it was partly because the birch bushes reminded him of those which had stretched clear along the north side of his house back in Birmingham, perhaps because he could see his mother moving among them and singing. He sat in the pale, cooling shade and felt weary and just a little bit frightened. He was suddenly within shouting distance of a new, unknown life and, for perhaps the first time, it felt as though he *had* walked a thousand miles, as though he were in the middle of nowhere, as though England and life as he'd known it were millions of lifetimes away.

Claire came up beside him and sat without speaking. She increased his bad humor somehow by just sitting there, staring before her with dull, lifeless eyes.

"This is a pretty spot," Percy ventured. "It reminds me of home."

She didn't answer. He felt no response from her. He could see Benjamin bent over one of Seth Johnson's cows who was ready to calve. He could see the three girls playing down by the wagon with the two Liscom girls, whose bright red pigtails made natural spotters. He saw the late sun, dappled like buttermilk, drop in large splotches through the lacework of bushes. He saw the flanks of the far mountains stretch gold under a sky of deep, burnished red. *She sees nothing*, he thought, *she cares nothing*.

"Listen, Claire." He took her by the shoulders and turned her to face him. "You just listen to me. What do you expect of us? We're human, too." He could feel his rising anger buzz in his head. "Benjamin — just how much more do you think he can take? He's hurting, too, you know, but who cares about that?"

He released his tight hold. She seemed to fall away from him. He stood and turned, so her empty eyes couldn't see his face.

"Maybe it's just me. Maybe he can keep going on and on by himself this way, but I can't, Claire." He didn't know that his voice held an anguish. He just stumbled on. "Maybe Benjamin's never been left before, Claire, but I have! I've been left by my father and my mother. Don't you leave me, too. Not here in the middle of nowhere, don't leave me, Claire!"

He took a few steps forward, still away from her. He was trembling. He felt like a fool. He could hear his own labored breathing, then a new sound came through. A small, broken sound, high and terrible: the sound of her tears.

He raced back, he had his strong arms around her, he felt her tears on his cheek.

"Can you forgive me? Forgive me?" She was saying the words over and over again.

He tightened his hold on her. "Claire," he said earnestly, "please don't cry so. We love you. I love you—" He stopped, aware of the words he had said. She had heard, too. She lifted her face. Through the tears her dark eyes were glowing.

"Yes, I love you," he said, reaching out to brush back a wet strand of her hair. "There's nothing to forgive—I've seen what you've been through, Claire."

She buried her face again, deep in his shoulder. "My baby . . . my baby son . . . " Was she saying that?

"Just don't leave us, Claire! Don't leave me! We all need you so badly. I'll be your son." He spoke low and close to her ear. "I know I'm not like a child to raise up all your own. But I'll be your son, Claire, the best that I can."

She heard the tears in his voice. She raised her head slowly and when her eyes found his it was joy meeting joy in a way that surprised them both. She shook her head, shook the tears from her eyes and tried to smile at him.

"You are so good to me, Percy," she said. "Your own mother — how proud she would be of you."

12

After six thousand miles of anticipation, could the Valley measure up? Could Great Salt Lake City in autumn hold its own as a dream that came true?

Percy knew that some of the British Saints struggled with disappointments, missing England's ways, England's trees, England's fields, England's autumn colors this time of year. Percy loved the place from the very beginning; it felt like home. His first sight of it had not been his first, but a repeat of his dream, so that he recognized all he was seeing and he knew he was home. The clean, unspoiled feel of the wilderness—he didn't know why, but it held a powerful attraction for him.

And they were lucky. Benjamin's cousin, Tom Gillman, had secured a small home, a two-room cabin with both a loft and a kitchen, where they could live. Benjamin moved them right in. And Tom had work for him to do; there was no despairing, no searching or begging for a means of support, a means of sustaining themselves.

Claire settled in. There was much she could turn her hand to here, and the results would all show: new curtains for windows and room dividers, new quilts for the beds. It was too late to plant, so Percy helped her harvest what others offered and she put up every scrap of fruit or vegetable that came her way. These were good, fruitful days for them all. Percy fenced off their plot of farmland, cared for the animals Benjamin bought and traded for, repaired and built tools, dug irrigation ditches in preparation for spring, repaired an old barn that had been offered them to winter their beasts. The work to be done never ceased. But it was good work, it was working for self—there were no dark, windowless factory rooms here, no harsh masters to answer to. From the very first day Percy tasted the freedom he knew what it meant, and valued it, and gave all he could with a grateful heart.

Perhaps that was why when the call came Percy felt to answer it. President Young from the pulpit at general conference issued a plea in behalf of the two handcart companies stuck out in the snow of the mountains. Three companies of Saints had come safely through, and perhaps because Percy had been part of those handcart men he felt a keen awareness of what the people in Brother Willie and Brother Martin's companies were suffering. How could he turn away? Perhaps, too, he was moved by the eloquence of the strong, bearded man who stood with the power and conviction of a prophet before him. To sit here in this place and listen to the words of a living prophet for the first time in his life, and not act upon them?

He spoke to Benjamin. "If I went as a teamster, could you get on for a while?"

Benjamin didn't even take time to consider. "Of course we could."

"Those are our people out there," Claire added. "You go in our name, too." And to prove what she said, when he left she stuffed into his surprised arms one of the new quilts she had just finished.

"Claire—" he began to protest.

"They need it more than we do. Now, take it and go quickly."

He knew how hard it was for her to give something she had paid for so dearly. She hugged him and kissed his cheek, and he went off on a borrowed horse to join the fifty other men, most of them young like himself, who would drive the rescue wagons. He was simply amazed at the goods he saw gathered to aid the distressed Saints. There was everything here from shoes, coats, shawls, dresses, shirts, caps, nightshirts, handkerchiefs, and neckties to bushels of onions, oats, flour, and even twelve precious pounds of dried meat.

They paired each inexperienced man like himself with a seasoned driver. Percy bent his neck to the wind as the team drew them up toward the winter mountains; the bare, exposed rock looked as cold to him as the snow that laced through it. The November cold bit into his skin and soon numbed it. But he raised the collar of the old greatcoat and bent his head to the force of it. *What a joy this is*, he couldn't help thinking, *to be riding off on such a mission with these marvelous men, feeling the warmth of their camaraderie, the support of their faith. Being an active, working Saint in the midst of the mountains.*

Such an attitude pulled him through the rough spots: fording half-frozen streams, but getting wet enough nevertheless to feel your pants and gloves stiffen into ice within minutes, to tear your own skin trying to remove them; to sit by a fire that raged all night, but never seem to thaw out and grow warm; to lose a boot to a raging torrent that suddenly gushed up through the ice and go the rest of the way with only a large swath of linsey cloth wrapped around your foot to keep out the cold. All this was real suffering, but when they reached the encampment and saw those poor souls Percy knew that he had not yet learned the true meaning of suffering.

His wagon was one of the first to arrive. He and the other strong young men who were there tried to dig graves for the dead, but the ground was too hard. The wrapped the bodies instead in blankets and put them into a pile, which they covered carefully with snow, and left them to their cold sleep.

They carried some of the men, as well as the women and children who could no longer walk on their frostbitten feet, and placed them tenderly into the wagons. Percy gave Claire's blanket to a mother and her new baby and covered two children with the warm folds of his father's old greatcoat and spoon-fed them himself as they watched him through white, pinched faces. He broke down and cried like a child, for it reminded him, of course, of his Rosie and of Claire's lost child, of his mother and father, of all useless suffering. For so this suffering seemed.

They made it in good time back down to the valley, but the nightmare didn't stop here. Homes must be found for the many small children who had been orphaned, and medical help was needed for the grueling task of amputating toes and fingers, sometimes entire feet that had been destroyed by the frost and were useless. Percy stood by and cried when they cut off three of the toes of one of the little girls he had cared for; he couldn't help himself. But it made him feel better to learn that Brigham Young, the prophet, had done the same thing when he looked on the children who sat with frozen feet in the wagon where their dead mother rode.

Ten-year-old Maggie lost only one finger, and she had her mother as well. Melissa, only four, had lost both mother and father. Percy told Claire of her plight, mentioning with as little passion as he could the need to find homes for the children like her. Claire looked thoughtful but said nothing. He had been back for three days. He was getting warm at last, as much from Claire's food, he felt, as from dry clothes and heated rooms.

On the third night she came to him, sat down on his bed where he had stretched out, fully clothed still, but covered with blankets, to read his scriptures out loud.

"Do you always read them out that way?" she asked.

"No, just sometimes when I'm too tired to concentrate and I fear I might fall to sleep."

She nodded. He laid his book aside, wondering what she wanted.

"How can I take her in?"

He blinked his eyes, but he let her continue.

"We still have no room, too little money—" she paused, tried to smile for him, "and too many girls."

He smiled back, but said nothing. He sensed that she wasn't yet finished.

"Besides, what did I do? I made you leave the little sister you loved back in England."

He was surprised at the pain in her voice. He had never imagined that she had suffered about it.

"How could I take in this girl? You might grow to resent her every time you looked at her because she wasn't your Rose."

Because he had really come to know Claire he reached for her hand now. "What a prize you are, Claire! You may mutter and grumble, but your heart is twice as big as most other people's. And in the end you always do the best thing."

She squirmed and protested, but he held onto her fingers.

"I shall love her the more. As you shall. We shall both love her for Rosie's sake."

She nodded, speechless. "All right."

"Poor Claire," he said gently. "It looks like you're stuck with me — one fiery, obnoxious, nearly grown son."

He was only half teasing. He looked into her eyes. "They have boys who need homes, too, you know. You could ask for a little boy — "

Claire was shaking her head. "Why can you always make me blubber like a girl, Percy?" she scolded. "No, it's settled. Melissa will do."

She stood up and he let go of her hand. "Melissa will do," she repeated, "and so will you."

By the end of November all the surviving members of the handcart companies had been brought safely out of the mountains and into the valley. It was a good reason to rejoice, to usher in Christmas and its festivities.

Percy, snug in the warm log house, marveled. *Less than one year ago I was a Birmingham factory lad with a good, solid family and a future carefully mapped for me. Then, in the twinkling of an eye, it all was taken away and I stood in the pool of my own pain with nothing and no one.*

He considered it time after time. Melissa fit so well into their family; Claire handled skillfully the small flares of jealousy between the girls and Percy worked hard to smooth over anything he could, grateful for what Claire had done. Benjamin seemed to thrive on the gentle affection that the child in her need and grief showered on him. *We're a family. Anybody could see that. How does it happen this way? What marvelous powers love has!*

So Percy decided at last. He ceased attempting to examine it, to understand it. With a new, trusting faith he merely accepted it.

The year 1856 was drawing to a close. Percy knew he would never see another quite like it. On Christmas night Brigham Young hosted an entertainment at his new Lion House. A few of the Brethren came, but the party was made up largely of missionaries who had lately returned from their places of labor, many from England and Scotland. Percy happened to walk by the place on his way home from an errand for Claire. He paused; he was drawn to look in.

How brightly lit the windows were; how elegant the large rooms, the new furnishings. That such a home could be established out here! It looked as though it came straight out of a fine English city—from the more prosperous section, to boot. He could hear music, no more than a soft echo, reach out over the snow. He felt the most delicious exhilaration move from his head to his toes, leaving him tingling and happy all over.

"Happy Christmas," he said, to no one in particular, to the clear, silent night, to the mountains he half turned to stare up at, so distant, so cold—so secretive. And yet, hadn't he conquered them? Hadn't he, a young boy, overcome their untamed snares and dangers to come here, to come *home*?

"Happy Christmas, President Young," he said. Brigham Young had known Birmingham, he had worked there, he was of English descent—he loved England. *We are all brothers here. This is home.* Percy thought again of the great ocean that had caught his life up and planted him here. *I will grow*, he vowed, *I will grow well.* He knew he had already sunk his roots into the dry desert soil.

He had better get home. They were waiting for him. They were holding the stories until he got back, and the warm cider and the Christmas pudding. And there would be carols to sing—good English carols, and perhaps a new hymn or two.

He bent his head to the night wind and hurried his steps.

PART II

CHAPTER

1

*I*t was not that Percy forgot or stopped caring, but life didn't slow down for a heartbeat, didn't pause to catch breath. It kept propelling him forward and, as he went, Percy's roots sank deeper and deeper into the desert soil.

Now, returning from his mission to the Lamanites, Percy had occasion to wonder. Claire was having her annual birthday celebration for Melissa. They didn't know when her real birthday was, so Claire had decided to give her a new one, and she chose the day the child had come to be part of their family: November twenty-third. And today Melissa was turning fourteen.

Fourteen—that was nearly a woman! How could she have gotten so old? Fourteen was the age he had been when he entered the valley. Was that really ten years ago? It frightened Percy to think of it.

He sat on the new horsehair sofa and watched the girls gather around Melissa and admire her gifts. Belinda was twenty years old and a wife who would soon be a mother. Ellen, now seventeen, had a special beau she was going to marry next spring. Even Mary at fifteen seemed to be giving serious attention to some of the boys.

Claire sat down beside him.

"Are these beautiful creatures really your daughters?" he teased. "You're as pretty as any, and you look as young as our Mary."

"Don't flatter me," she scolded. "I know it's not true."

"It's nearer truth than you think," he persisted. Then he mused out loud: "Ellen's as good as gone. How long do you give Mary?"

He grinned. "Before you know it, Mother, you'll be stuck with your two odd ducklings, Melissa and me."

"There's nothing odd about Missy," she snapped back. "But you're an old man, Percy. When are you going to bring home a pretty little bride for me to mother?"

He thought of Emmeline and colored a little.

"Well, you'd better make time. You won't get anywhere stuck off in the desert with your precious Indians."

"I know, Claire, I know." He patted her hand in exaggerated comfort. Sometimes he still called her Claire; these days he called her Mother or Claire intermittently. He wasn't sure when it had come. She was his mother in every way possible, and so at some times the word just slipped out. And when it did, it felt right. He liked the freedom he was given to use it at will.

"Look at this place, Claire," he marveled. "You and Benjamin have come a long way in ten years."

"We've been blessed. Has it been ten years, Percy?"

"It has."

"And you've spent over half of it on the back of a horse—no wonder you're still unattached."

He laughed at her concern but, as he thought about it, he was amazed at the truth of her words. The first ten years in the valley he had spent much of the time on the Church Team Train, which meant he went back and forth over the Mormon Trail picking up immigrants at the railway terminal and guiding them back over the mountains and home. It was an actual mission, and he served it well despite the advent of Johnston's Army and the barely averted Utah War. The world was in chaos, or so it seemed as he followed the events of the war that was raging between the Northern and Southern states. In comparison his own life seemed rather calm and well ordered.

Shortly after release from his position as teamster he was called to serve a two-year mission to the Lamanites in the southern part of the state. He was eighteen years old. That did take him out of the marriage market for a spell, he realized. But when he returned the Brethren put him to work on the temple, and that kept him poor. Although he had learned to live frugally while with the Indians, he had but little laid by. So he convinced Brother

Davis to take him on as an apprentice in his blacksmith shop. It was a beginning he felt hopeful about. He had amassed much experience handling oxen and caring for them on the trail, and discovered that he had quick, dexterous hands, and something of a way with animals. He became involved with the Salt Lake Theater group, doing small dramatic parts on the side and enjoying the association, especially of one particular girl. Then came the Indian wars stirred up by Chief Black Hawk, and President Young called many of those who had experience with the Lamanites to go back as mediators, and Percy was one. And that took care of 1865 and most of 1866. Now he was home again, poor as a church mouse, but he didn't mind that. Perhaps he was pampered by knowing he would always have a home with Claire and Benjamin. Perhaps it was shameful to take advantage of that—perhaps he should strike out on his own, make his own way. He was, after all, more man now than boy.

So his thoughts ran all that first week as the days grew colder and another Christmas approached. Percy began to pray about what he should do after he learned that Brother Davis no longer needed a man in his blacksmith shop. Life had gone on without him, but he still liked that line of work. So when Brother Bateman approached him with an offer to come work for him, Percy felt it was right.

Brother Bateman owned a blacksmith shop, a tannery, and a small bootery for ladies—a very progressive kind of establishment. Percy hadn't minded the idea of starting from scratch again. He was home. That was all that mattered. But Emmeline was enthusiastic.

"Brother Bateman is successful already," she reminded him, "and making money seems to come naturally to him. It must mean something that we both work for him, Percy."

Emmeline waited on ladies in Brother Bateman's fancy bootery. She earned pin money that way, money to spend on clothing her parents didn't approve of, money for jewelry and theater tickets. Percy knew that was how it was. Although Bishop Terry didn't approve of all his daughter's doings, he felt she would outgrow some of them with maturity. Percy wasn't so sure. Emmeline had a passion for the theater; that was where they had first met. In fact, it was she who had talked him into trying his hand at acting, who had eased him into that group of gregarious, fun-loving dramatists. He liked it well enough. But it wasn't in his blood the way it was in Emmeline's.

He took the job Brother Bateman offered. When the new year came in, it found him well settled as a blacksmith's apprentice with the promise that in time he would be taught the tanning trade as well. There was much to learn, and Percy applied himself with all his energies. For one thing, the collection of tools in the blacksmith's shop seemed endless, and Percy knew that as a striker or helper he would have to learn how to use them all, and do much more than shoe horses. He knew that the forge and anvil were the heart of the blacksmith shop and he liked to work there, to stand facing the smith ready with a heavy sledge to strike blows as the master directed. He was working to get the rhythm of the thing, which he knew was important. So much was important! But he enjoyed the atmosphere and the smell of the place, and the sounds: the melodious ring of the hammer punctuated with the heavier clanging sound of the sledge. It brought out some sense of rhythm within himself that he couldn't explain. He still helped Benjamin farm the land and care for animals on the place. But he felt he fit here more than he did at the back of a plow. It was hard to say why. Factory born and bred; that must be the answer.

After his long days of strenuous work Percy usually spent his evenings with Emmeline. It was beginning to be a pattern. He knew Claire was pleased. He was pleased himself. He enjoyed Emmeline's company, at least most of the time, despite the fact that she was obviously pampered and a little petulant, and intended to stay that way.

But Emmeline colored his life with bright shades, with new colors it would not otherwise know. He was grateful for that. She made life seem a game, a happy pleasure to be enjoyed, to be savored—never something to be plowed through, to fear, or, heaven forbid, to take too seriously.

So the first weeks of the new year ticked away with the precision of a new clock in crisp, tight working order. Then two things happened.

Percy volunteered a Saturday of work cutting temple block — the fine, more precise cutting that needed some of the craftsmanship he had learned. Just a few hours, but they set him to thinking, and he walked past the site where the tentative walls were struggling up, seeming to reach out for completion, for the beauty of the dream to release them. Percy stood a long time, thinking old, painful thoughts, fingering the button he had had Claire sew inside his pocket, so he would not lose it in all his travelings. He had fairly worn out the coat, crossing rivers, riding through storms, sleeping out on the trail. He wondered how many layers of dust were compressed with the cloth now! The old family greatcoat. The old promise. That seemed not only in the past now, it seemed in another far world, a world he could scarcely bring to life in his memory. *I was only a boy. I meant well . . .*

He walked home in a thoughtful mood. He had no money, no money for passage all the way back to England. And, more important than that, he had just been given his second chance to set his feet into the future; he couldn't throw that away. *What would I find if I went back?* The thought teased at him. *Where would they be? Do they think of me, do they even remember me?* Perhaps he should have tried to write, to contact them. But mail was such chaos, such a hit-and-miss affair here, and he was so young, and always poor, and always on the move. They seemed so far away! Yet he realized that when the temple was completed he could go and do the endowment work for his parents. He couldn't wait till that time. And what about the rest of them, the family he had promised to reunite someday?

Perhaps because he had been thinking about it, he had a dream upon the subject as well; so he rationalized. But the dream seemed so urgent, so real. And it was only the second dream he had ever dreamed with such vivid clarity, only the second one he had remembered upon waking, remembered in careful detail. The first was the dream he had had as a boy in Birmingham of the Salt Lake Valley. This dream was of England. In this dream a young girl was sitting in the shade of a great oak tree, upon a stretch of green lawn. He could hear bird song and there were flowers and the day was most fair. The girl had her head bent; he could not see her face. She appeared to be reading a book that lay open on her lap. She wore a white cotton dress with lace at the throat and sleeves; lovely red hair fell in thick waves over her shoulders. He knew it was Rose. He knew she was happy.

Then suddenly the aspect darkened, as though the sun had been obscured by a cloud. In fact, the scene grew so dark that Percy could scarcely make out the details. Rose stumbled to her feet, dropping the book as she did so, and not pausing to retrieve it. But, lifting her skirts high, she started to run. Percy watched her run, run with frightened panic, first one place, then another, looking over her shoulder toward something that distressed her. He could feel her pain. He seemed to know that she could not escape her pursuer.

The scene shifted and changed. Rose was running down a long, narrow corridor, dirty and unlit. She stumbled, she fell. When she raised her face Percy saw her features for the first time, and the fear and anguish stamped there filled his whole being with pain. It seemed she screamed, or perhaps it was himself who was screaming. With a great start he awoke, and lay trembling. The feeling of the dream was strong upon him, and an urgent unrest stirred like a sickness inside him.

Why this dream? And why now? What does it mean, what am I to take from it?

He didn't know. His mind was as foggy and unclear as the atmosphere of the dream had been. But these feelings of fear, of unhappiness, lingered with him; he could not dispel them. He tried to bring to his mind the picture of his little seven-year-old Rosie, hear her voice, see her smile. It was faded, so faded — nearly lost to him.

He spent several restless days struggling to ignore the dream and the impressions it had given him. He spent several frenzied nights attending any social function he could find with a radiant, pleased Emmeline beside him. Nothing worked in the least. It was with him; it had its effects on him still.

One night he went home feeling so worried he nearly was ill. Claire saw it and fed him an early supper after chores and put him to bed. He had never prayed concerning this dream; something in him refused to. Perhaps he was afraid he would

receive an answer he wasn't eager to hear. If something said *go* —
how could he?

He lay stretched out on his bed in the shadows of the dusky
winter twilight and, closing his eyes, worked with patience to
bring back the images, bring back the reality of the little family
in the old house in Birmingham. Bit by bit they came, hesitant,
perhaps even unwilling, but he summoned them forth and took
a long look at them until he remembered — not so much their
faces, but the feel of them: remembered their love. Each success
brought its portion of pain; Percy was not anxious for that. He
felt the pain had no place to go. He felt the boy and his promise
were a fragment of a world that no longer existed. *Yet that boy
was once me, it was I who made the promise — and boasted of
it — I who was certain I could fulfill it in the face of the worst
odds.*

Yet here he was, trapped in a reality he saw no way out of —
a reality he had sought, a reality he still desired and would have
chosen again.

At last, weary, he crawled from the bed and dropped down
on his knees. He would pray, though he saw little sense in it.
What could be done in this case? What would his Heavenly Father
expect of him? *What would you want of me, Mother?*

The thought came through his prayer; he did not summon
it. It disturbed him yet further. At last he did the only thing he
could think of: he poured out his heart, then he placed it all in
the hands of heaven and went back to bed, wondering what in
the world even heaven could do with this.

The very next day Brother Bateman came into the blacksmith
shop. He seldom worked there; he was the owner and overseer
of too many concerns. David Long, his junior partner, really ran
things with the help of two strikers, and it was Percy's opinion
that he did a good job. He told Henry Bateman as much when
the man took Percy aside and asked how he liked work in the
smithy. Henry tightened his jaw and did not look particularly
pleased when Percy went on in glowing terms about work there.

He chewed on the end of his pen, asking other vague questions that Percy answered with growing confusion.

"What is it you want, sir?" he said.

At that Brother Bateman laughed with outright pleasure. "I'm not much at tact, son, and it appears neither are you. Straightforward, to the point." He put down his pen and leaned over the desk. "I have a special job, an unusual assignment I'd like you to take."

Percy lifted an eyebrow. Something in him urged caution, yet at the same time a small prickling of excitement shot through him.

"What did you have in mind, sir?"

"Well, as I said, it's a bit unusual. But I thought first off of you. You're the most responsible boy I know, Percy, and a kind boy as well, and that's what I'd want in any person I entrust with my family."

Percy leaned forward. "What do you mean?"

"My family's in England, you know. My wife was sick, pregnant with a child when I came across. Her doctor wouldn't let her travel." With a furtive, almost boyish expression he added, "Neither would her mother. She's most unreasonably protective. In her mind there was no way she would allow me to carry her fragile daughter across thousands of miles of ocean, then thousands of miles of desert to a God-forsaken spot—so she looked at it."

He winked a small, deep-set eye. "So I came on ahead. Knew I'd have to. And thank heaven the Lord has prospered me, or I am certain I'd never get my wife and children back again—her mother would see to that."

"But what does all this have to do with me, Brother Bateman?"

"Well, haven't you guessed? I would like you to go back to England and make all the arrangements, put my wife on the ship, take good care of her. There are no men in the family to do it. Her father is long since dead. In return, Percy, I'll pay your passage—all your expenses and such, of course. Haven't you family there? You could stay as long as you'd like and visit— provided my wife's on the first ship possible, with my two little daughters and the son I've not seen."

It was done; it was out. Brother Bateman breathed more deeply, more freely, but Percy sunk back into his chair, trying to take this in.

"When would you want me to leave?"

"Spring. Soon as possible." He scowled slightly. "You might think me calloused to send you in my place. But things here couldn't run well without me and, to tell the truth, lad, I believe the mere sight of me maddens her mother. She'd be more pleased to know that I had remained with my nose to the grindstone making money for her daughter." He chuckled a bit at the thought. "I'll promise you a job still, if you're concerned about that, lad."

"How long could I be gone?"

"Hadn't thought of it." Henry rubbed his broad forehead. "A year, maybe a year and a half. Eight to ten months for travel — give you a few months in England that way."

Percy nodded his head. *What am I hearing?*

"When your wife reaches New York, Brother Bateman, what about that? Won't you want someone with her for the rest of the journey?"

"Good thinking, lad. I've made arrangements for that: mature, responsible brethren coming back with a shipment. And I intend to meet her partway. Perhaps in Wyoming. I can manage that much."

Percy nodded again.

"But there aren't many who would go all the way to England — not many who could. Too tied down. But yourself —" He smiled broadly. "You're just back from your mission. No wife yet, no financial obligations —" He chuckled under his breath. "May be your last chance to go back."

Of course he was trying to be persuasive. Percy had no idea if his powers were good or indifferent. For him the decision was made; for him the answer was all too obvious.

"Will you think on it, Percy?"

"No, Brother Bateman, I'll go."

The older man scratched his thick beard, his face reflecting his pleasure. "Bless you, son, are you sure? This is pretty quick. You may have second thoughts —"

Percy smiled for the first time. "Oh, Brother Bateman, I'm sure. As sure as I've ever been about anything."

They talked on for a while, settling some of the details, posing various questions. All very ordinary and sane. But something inside Percy was making a high, ringing sound. *How has this happened, and why? Is it really important for me to go back?*

He knew what Brother Brigham taught about prayer, but it shocked him to think how directly a prayer could be answered. Was someone up there really aware of him?

Suddenly he thought of his mother. She had come to his mind last night, while he was kneeling. *There is so much,* he thought, *that mortals can't understand.*

He went through the rest of the day in a kind of daze. In some ways he was frightened; he was struggling with some uncertainties already that he hadn't even thought of before.

Emmeline noticed his preoccupied mood and teased him out of it a little. He wished he could tell her, but he didn't feel ready. Besides, he felt pretty sure what her reaction would be, and he didn't look forward to it. *I have no choice. I am duty bound. This is an answer to prayer.*

He told Benjamin, who understood, as Percy knew that he would.

"Isn't it what you vowed to do when you were just a boy, Percy?"

"Yes, it is."

"Well, go on. Don't let your fears prey upon you. The Lord will help you in this." He studied Percy's face for a moment. "I feel certain of that."

Percy wished he shared the confidence. Later, when he had Claire alone, he told her gently. He was worried about how she would take it. Thus he was quite caught by surprise when he saw her reaction.

"I think it's wonderful. Go. Go, by all means."

"But, Claire, what will happen? Will I be acting the fool? Will I waste a year of my life to go poking where nobody wants me?"

Her expression changed. "Answer that question yourself. Really, I'm ashamed of you, Percy."

They sat in silence. *Answer that question yourself.* Suddenly his dream flashed before his eyes, and that sense of urgency. *What a baby I am!*

"You're right, Claire. It is meant that I should go. There is some reason—"

"There may be several reasons. Where's your old faith, Percy?"

"I don't know," he confessed.

"Don't worry about it." She smiled. "I remember those first weeks with you. We were so intent on making a Mormon of you, Benjamin and I. I can laugh at it now." Her eyes softened. "It meant so much to us. When you pulled away after that first taste of conversion, I spent a lot of time on my knees."

"I didn't know that."

"We prayed you into the Church, as they say."

"Do you ever regret it?" His eyes held a twinkle.

"Do you?" She was more serious; she wanted an answer. Percy didn't have to think twice.

"Never. Not once, not for a minute."

Claire slowly nodded her head, and a satisfied expression touched her features with gentleness.

"What would I have done without you?" Percy asked the question in a quiet, toneless voice and he avoided her eyes. She made a small sound. He knew he had embarrassed her a little. "I mean it, Claire. I look back now and I don't know how you did it."

"It wasn't so hard." The affection in her voice made it sweet.

"Well, I won't go so far away, I won't leave without telling you at least once that I think of you—I've thought of you for a long time as my mother. You've been all any mother could be. I—I want you to know that."

He rose to leave quickly, but she wouldn't have it that way. She stood, too, and forced him to look at her.

"As long as we're saying the kind of things that don't often get said, Percy, do you know what? When I think of dying, I think of your mother. Somehow—sometimes, I feel close to her. I'll be anxious to meet her." She smiled through the tears she was fighting. "We have much in common."

"Yes, that you do." He stooped to kiss her. "You both are

angels." She began to protest. "You both have been angels to me."

She could say nothing to that. She gave him a quick hug and left the room, while Percy stood at the window pondering many deep and wonderful things.

He put off talking to Emmeline. Instead he redoubled his efforts, courting her with a charm and intensity born of his fears. She responded with the same intensity, making it all the more difficult for him; she was unaware. Emmeline wasn't the kind of woman who sensed things; he thought that might come someday. Right now she was too interested in herself to ponder the emotions of others.

Therefore, when he spoke to her one March night he took her quite by surprise. She blinked her eyes at him.

"You don't mean it," she said. "It's so—" She caught herself. "Foolish. You have your own life to think about, Percy. Just tell him no."

"I told you, I have reasons of my own for going."

"I know. I heard. But they can't be as important as what you might lose." She threw him a coy look, touching on sour. "You might lose me."

"I've thought of that."

Something in his look shamed her. "Well, what am I to do for a year—a whole year and a half? I'm a bishop's daughter; my folks expect me to marry—"

"And you're a beautiful girl who would find it difficult to turn your nose up to suitors." He was really thinking: *to any form of attention or flattery.* But he held his peace.

"Well, be realistic, Percy!" She stomped her small foot. "How distressing this is!"

Percy worked at gradually reconciling Emmeline to his departure. Meanwhile, he set his plans. Things moved forward. He would leave in April and be in England for the last days of summer, for the fields bright with red poppy and pale heartsease, for the

Travelers' Joy curling over the fences, for the pink dog rose. England!

He made no attempt to write ahead. He was going. He would contact them there—face to face. He harbored an odd fear that if he wrote they would reject him, take some means to avoid him. It would be better this way: *I have come back. I promised you, didn't I? I have come home.*

So he planned and imagined and wondered, and time kept its pace, and before he knew time had the better of him. He took his last wrenching farewells.

"Take care, little mother," he whispered in Claire's ear. Melissa clung just a bit. She was his girl, she had been from the start. The pressure of her arms around his neck reminded him strongly of that other farewell, of the small, loving child who didn't want to let go of her Percy.

"I'll be back, Missy, with presents and stories to tell."

She smiled through her tears. What a lovely face hers was! Some lucky boy . . .

He spent a long, teary session with Emmeline.

"Will you wait?" he asked at last, point-blank.

"I can't promise," she hedged.

"I would not want a false promise, nor a false sweetheart," he countered, his pent-up anger at last breaking through. "Go your way. Do what you must, do what you'd like, Emmeline. I shall do the same." He kissed her a bit roughly, not knowing how his emotions stirred her.

"Percy—"

"No, it's decided. It's the best way. Fare you well. God be with you, Emmy."

He kissed her once more and was gone. So be it. If she was here when he came back for her, well and good. If she was not— But he must not think that far ahead. What was it his mother used to say when he was only a small boy? *Don't sup trouble with a long spoon.* He'd better try to remember that.

His head was filled with a ream of instructions from Brother Bateman, his luggage was bulging as well with little gifts he carried back to his own, and tons of things Henry sent. *For the comfort of my family,* he said, *and the pacification of my mother-in-law.*

He was off. It was a long, wearing journey. He had time to think, time to plan, time to fret and worry. *I am like Mother that way: always courting trouble before it notices me.*

At last he thrust all thought aside and threw himself into the adventure of the journey, drank in the sights, and felt himself relax, then take on an eagerness, a youthful interest in each day as it came to him, no matter what it might bring.

2

*E*ngland. As soon as Percy stepped off the ship onto English soil he felt as though a piece of himself had been fit back in place, a piece he hadn't even known he was missing. It felt like home: it smelled and tasted and sounded familiar in a deep, satisfying way.

He was required by his commission to spend the first few weeks after his arrival in Liverpool, or rather the small village of Warrington that sat just outside it. He found things, a little to his surprise, much as Henry Bateman had predicted: a quiet, slightly nervous wife, sweet and willing to cooperate; a large, overbearing mother who, with only the best interests of her daughter and grandchildren in mind, cowed everyone into doing things precisely her way. She was long accustomed to having what she wanted on a more or less consistent basis. She reminded Percy just a little of Emmeline, and the comparison was distasteful, to say the least.

While he went about his quiet arrangements with Eliza Bateman, he placated her mother. Women liked Percy; he had long known that. It wasn't so much his charm as his openness, something trustworthy about him. He liked women, he enjoyed their company, he felt at ease around them — and this must have shown. Mildred Boswell took to him almost immediately.

This was, of course, a mixed blessing. The more she liked Percy, the more she got in his way. Only Eliza Bateman's eagerness to join her husband saved him; she worked with him side by side packing, preparing the children, filling out forms, talking with authorities, securing reservations, paying each little hidden fee that popped up from some unexpected corner of a tedious, seemingly unimportant form. She was quite a capable woman, actually, and Percy's respect for her grew. And, to his overwhelming surprise, he began to grow fond of Mildred Boswell as well.

It made no sense, this sudden affection he felt for her. She was a fussy, obnoxious old woman; most people saw only that. He saw other things: her odd sense of humor; her weakness for dogs and cats, for any small, helpless thing; her passion for flowers and bright colors; her interesting talk. Once they strayed from subjects of complaint to subjects of interest he discovered that she had a mind as filled with bits and snatches of knowledge and information as an old, stuffed ragbag.

Because they got to that point, the point of real conversation, he was able to tell her stories about Utah and the country he loved. He described the cacti growing side by side with palm trees in Utah's Dixie and the shades of the red rock that even colored the soil. She was fascinated with his tales of the Indians, so he gave her one of the arrowheads he had in his pocket. She slipped it into her fat, clasped pocketbook like a girl and vowed she would carry it always, for luck. Lest she have only the impression of an uncivilized desert he told her of the Great Salt Lake and the city the Saints had built there, of the new theater, of the houses like Brigham's, of the hot springs, and the beautiful fresh mountain streams.

"You could come for a visit. You must," Percy urged. "You would love it, I know. And the people would love you."

She scoffed. "I know what folk think of me." He saw the loneliness behind her mask of indifference and it made him shudder.

"Not so! I think you're truly delightful. We need some color out there, a person who knows how to stir things up some!"

She couldn't help beaming at that.

At last he put Eliza Bateman and her children on the boat with none of the prophesied horrors that Henry had gloomily intoned. Eliza thanked him profusely; she was a sweet, genuine person. She hugged him and kissed both her mother's rouged cheeks.

Percy intended to stand at the dockside and wave them off.

But instead he walked a short distance off, where the crowds wouldn't stare, and held the ample form of Mildred Boswell close while she sobbed in his arms.

Riding in a train through the English countryside was sheer pleasure for Percy. He felt as if he were reliving a dream. Perhaps most people didn't look at their childhoods as something removed from them, but simply an earlier edition of what they now continued to be. But for Percy all had changed: his home, his family, his religion, the place he lived, the things he did with his life — all had changed radically.

He pressed his nose to the glass and watched the green, serene world as it passed him. Cottages seemed to grow out of the heath and the bramble, topped with thick thatch roofs that gave them the look of brooding old men. He had missed that. He knew how they smelled inside. He could close his eyes and see the blackened firebrick, the broad wood floors, the little dark nooks with window seats in them. He saw men in the fields who looked up, wiping their brows, as the trained passed. An occasional dog ran, barking, alongside, or a boy on a horse, or a gaggle of girls, like young geese, walking, skipping, talking, and giggling together, all at the same time.

People have gone on living their lives just the same here as when I left them. Nothing has changed. The age-old routine of things churns its slow way. This is England, as it always has been.

The realization was difficult for him. He *was* coming back to a different world. Most of the people here had never heard of the great American desert, of buffalo, of red Indians. This was their own narrow world, beyond which life may as well cease to exist, for all most of them cared. He felt a little lonely, but that didn't disturb him. He was glad to be here. He wondered for the thousandth time, feeling this world about him, how his parents would have reacted if the gospel had been brought to them. He had come to believe that they had accepted it now in the spirit world, but would they have here? And if so, would they have ever left England? Left this safe, peaceful place as Claire and Benjamin had, as he had?

He was nearing Birmingham, country he knew now and recognized. Something deep inside him had not changed or grown older, and that part of him still belonged, still responded to everything here as though nothing had happened, as though there had been no changes, not even a passage of time.

He had only a loose plan at best. He would look up addresses and start from the top to the bottom; that seemed only fair. That meant Louisa would be first. She was probably married. Ten years, nearly eleven had passed; she was twenty-three, nearly twenty-four now. She could be a mother more than one time over . . . the thought seemed strange.

He walked from the train to a little inn he remembered that stood by the town's edge. The inn was still there. He took a room and unpacked his luggage, fingering the gifts he had brought. They weren't much, though he had tried to make them the best he could. This wasn't how he had pictured it, coming back. He had always seen himself in his imaginings returning a fine gentleman, fashionably dressed, showering exotic gifts on his wide-eyed sisters, perhaps with a girl on his arm whose beauty would make his brothers draw their breaths in envy. He sat in the low, overstuffed chair and thought of Emmeline, something he'd vowed not to do. A year was a long time, a year and a half even longer. He'd been gone nearly six months already; that gave Emmeline time to do heaven knows what — to forget him, perhaps, altogether. He pushed her forcefully out of his consciousness.

There was no pretty girl. There were no fancy clothes, though Brother Bateman had outfitted him well, and insisted he carry enough with him for exigencies that may arise past his modest needs. *I'm not what I thought I would be. How about them? Will they be less than they want to be, too? Less than I want them to be?*

He entertained the unworthy thought for one brief, greedy second, then he thrust it aside. *I have to see her. I'll go find Louisa tomorrow. I have to see Rose.*

He knew the way to the doctor's house, and though the innkeeper offered the use of his carriage, Percy decided to walk. It would be a long walk, but the evening was warm, the sky clear, and he felt that by walking he might ease himself back a little, feel and remember and repossess those places which had been his whole world before he left them behind.

The walk was longer than he had remembered and the city had grown. There were several new factories that rose much higher than the old ones; there were entire new streets, tidy rows of houses built like Prince Albert had wanted them for the sturdy working classes. The buzz of progress was here. He could hear it as he heard the night crickets. He liked the sound. But he didn't know if he could live with it now as he'd once planned to do. Things were very narrow, very crowded and crammed in—there was no City of Joseph plan here. Buildings and streets were placed helter-skelter, in a haphazard manner, and despite the progress, everything here felt *old*. He laughed out loud. *I've become a renegade,* he thought. *A frontiersman.* The idea pleased him. He tipped his hat to the few ladies he passed, and caught himself humming softly under his breath.

As he neared the old street he felt his pulse quicken and his breath become constricted. *What are you nervous about?* he chided himself. *Things will be all right. You'll recognize her. She'll be your old Rosie.*

The lane looked dark as he turned down it, dark and ill cared for. How old the houses all seemed! Was that the one? No, no, two houses further. There were very few lights and it had grown nearly dark while he walked. This was it: the green door, cracked and faded now, but the same. There was the doctor's worn sign, and the tall old barn in the back for his horse and buggy. Percy supposed Turnip was long gone by now—

He walked up the brick path. There were weeds poking through. He would have thought May, even Rose, would take better care of the place. He peered closer. The house looked dark. Dark and shuttered, dark and— He walked up and knocked on the green door. His fist made a small, hollow sound. Dark and—empty! There was no one living there! *How can that be?*

He knocked again, with more resolute briskness. There wasn't a sound. It was so still he could hear the wind soughing through the tall trees. He could hear the silence with its hoard of old memories that the wind stirred and tugged at uneasily.

"There ain't no one there, son."

Percy jumped at the sound of the voice. "Who is it?" he called. He could see no one as he turned to look around him. No shadows moved.

"Up here."

Percy lifted his head. A latticed window in the house next door was pushed open. An old woman leaned out from it. She nodded as he caught sight of her.

"The auld doctor is dead."

Percy put his hand to his throat.

"Dead these six years."

"How did he die?"

The woman shook her head; the breeze lifted the lace on her nightcap. "An ill death it was. One of his patients, delirious, broke in and shot him."

Percy backed against the green door in horror.

"I tell you the truth. Shot him through the heart because Doctor Davies had told him he was going to die. They said the good doctor felt nothing at all."

"What of May?" Percy shouted. "What of May and the little girl?"

"Aw, 'twas awful for them."

"Where are they?"

"Four years past now she married. Took the pretty red-haired child with her. I don't know where they've gone."

Percy wanted to scream, but he barely could speak. "Are they here in the city?"

The old woman pulled her shawl up around her thin shoulders. "I don't rightly know. She couldn't live here after what happened, and she can't sell the place—no one wants a thing to do with a house where a good man was murdered."

A chill ran through Percy's body. "Do you know the man's name? The name of the man May married?"

"Sorry, young man, I can't tell you."

"I thank you, grandma," he cried.

She nodded her gray head to him. "Be on your way, son. Don't tarry around here. Naught but ill spirits in this place."

She reached out a thin arm and pulled the window in, pulling the small square of light back in with her. There was nothing but darkness. He could feel the wind rising. But it was a warm summer wind. There could be no menace in such a wind. Yet the chill came again and he wished he had a jacket to put round his shoulders.

This happy place. This happy old house of laughter and healing.

Percy shuddered again. He had left his Rosie in this place to be happy. Where was she now? *Perhaps this is what my dream tried to tell me. Perhaps this was the pain, the danger my Rosie was in.*

With a last look at the sad house he turned and retraced his steps. *Louisa will know, Louisa will be able to tell me.* Perhaps it had been foolish to run breathlessly so soon after his arrival. He had come so far and waited so long, it was nearly impossible to slow, to postpone his quest now. But who would ever have dreamed?

He walked the long way back to the inn. It would take him some time to locate Louisa. First he must talk to the Bascoms and, if Louisa had married, find out her new name, and hope against hope that she lived close, that she lived right here in Birmingham. And of course, she would know about Rosie. Of course.

He felt deflated. This wasn't how he had imagined it. He went up to his room and fell, dressed, on the narrow bed and stared up at the ceiling. *Perhaps this won't be as easy and as pleasant as I've imagined.* He pushed back thoughts of his dream. It would do no good to frighten himself over something he wasn't sure of, something he knew he did not understand.

With a tired reluctance he got ready for bed. He was eager for the morning to come, but his uneasy feeling, the spell of the doctor's house and the old woman's words, wove a new sense of uncertainty that was the last thing he felt before falling asleep.

CHAPTER

3

The bakery was there, with the same name on the signpost that swung over the door. Percy remembered the sour-sweet smell of the place that made his nose twitch. He walked briskly inside. There was a young girl behind the counter, a stranger to him. She looked thin-faced and tired.

"Mrs. Bascom?"

"In there." The girl nodded in the direction of the kitchen.

"Will you please fetch her for me? Tell her Percy Graham is here to see her. From America. It's very important."

"Yes, sir." The girl perked up, and began to eye him, he thought, as an oddity. She was back in no time with Mrs. Bascom standing there broad behind her. The woman was far more stout than before. Her face was all jowls, the color and consistency of her bread dough. Percy held out his hand.

"Percy Graham at your service, ma'am."

She wiped her hand along her apron, but didn't extend it to shake his. "And what might you want?"

"Word of Louisa, ma'am. I'm recently back from the States. I'd like to see her again."

"She found herself a man, though it took her a long while—"

"And who might that be?"

"Oh, she found her a good one. She held out for a good one." Edith Bascom showed her yellow teeth when she smiled. Percy ground his own silently.

"Victor Maughan is his name. Fancy name, isn't it?"

"Does he live hereabouts?" Percy could hear his own heart.

"Heavens, yes. They live right over there." She nodded her

head in a general direction. "Up on the hill a bit. That kind of folk."

"Do you know the address?"

"That I do." She took one of the slips she used for billing and wrote it out for him. Percy snatched it right up, anxious to be out of there. The smell in his nostrils would be with him all day.

"Aren't you gonna buy nothing? Favor for favor? I've got some lovely things here."

Percy swallowed and ordered six raisin buns, which he paid the young girl for; then he turned and pulled on the door, eager for fresh air. He found a small, scraggly boy on the street and handed him the sack of warm buns.

"Thank you, mister," the boy called, with one already stuffed in his mouth. Percy mounted his horse. He had hired a horse from the inn, a nice, spirited beast, though not like the animals he had been used to in the mountains.

He steered through the choked confusion of the main streets. His whole insides were on fire with an anticipation that felt like pain. As he drew near to the place he could see that the houses here were large, fine ones, many of them new. They boasted wide porches and small, manicured yards with brick coach houses set discreetly behind them and out of the way. His curiosity mounted. What would Louisa be like? What would she say? How would she react to him?

He tied his horse and walked up to the door. He wondered if this house looked like Louisa, if it reflected her spirit at all, the way the cabin in Salt Lake spoke of Claire and her tastes, the way he remembered the dark, quiet house of his mother reflecting her sweetness and her own quiet ways.

He knocked on the door. His breathing was fast now. When it opened he saw immediately that the woman who stood there was a servant of sorts, and could not have been his sister.

"Is Mrs. Maughan at home?"

"Yes sir, she is. May I tell her who's calling?"

Percy nearly laughed out loud. *Yes, she is at home, sir. Who's calling? Who's calling? What madness!*

"Tell her Percy is here. Percy Graham, her brother from America."

"Very good, sir. You may step inside the hall to wait." *The woman is well trained,* Percy thought. *Louisa's doing, no doubt.* Nothing but a quick arch of an eyebrow betrayed her interest.

She turned and left him alone. He listened hard, but he heard very little. At last her footsteps returned, from some pattern of inner rooms she walked toward him. There were two sets of feet; he could hear two people walking toward him. The older woman, the housekeeper, the maidservant, stepped aside. Percy closed his eyes for an instant, then looked on her face.

Louisa stood and stared back at him, aware of his scrutiny. She had wide, honest eyes, broad cheekbones, good skin. Hers was a pleasant face, nearly pretty, framed by masses of rich chestnut hair that increased its softness. The wide eyes were filling with tears.

"Percy! Yes, it is you!"

She held out her hands. He moved, started to take them, then embraced her instead. She leaned against him; she did not resist. He heard her whisper his name.

"I told you I would come."

She laughed and pulled away from him. "Yes, yes you did." She was shaking her head and her eyes brimmed with pleasure. "You're quite the handsome young man. More slender than Stanley."

"It's frontier living."

"I don't know about that. It's the Miller in your blood, I'd warrant. There's more red in your hair than I remembered, and it curls in the back."

She reached out to run her fingers through it. "I'm embarrassing you!"

"Yes, you are, and it obviously pleases you."

"Percy, it's you! I didn't really believe I'd ever see you again." She stood back, she couldn't take her eyes from him. "How did you find me?" she asked.

"Mrs. Bascom. She said you married well."

"So I did." There was a hint of defiance in her tone, or of pride.

"I can see," Percy said. "Is he a good husband?"

"Victor?" It seemed she wanted to laugh. "He's a good husband, yes. And I have that nephew I promised to show you." A slight glow touched her features. "But he's sleeping upstairs. And I have a meeting I must leave for shortly. It's lucky you caught me at all." The expression that lit her features was something he remembered. "I was never one to be on time for things, was I? Remember how that frustrated Mother? I wish I didn't have to leave right now."

"We'll have time."

"Yes. Yes, I hope so." She blinked her eyes at him. "Come inside for a few minutes. Where do we start?"

"Start with Rosie. Where is she?" Percy could hear the urgency in his own voice.

"That's a long story, Percy."

"I know. I was there at the doctor's house. I walked over from the inn last evening. Some kind old lady stuck her head out of the next door window and told me."

"It was dreadful for all of us," Louisa murmured.

"I'm sure it was. But what about Rose?"

Louisa looked thoughtful. "I went to the doctor's funeral—"

"I'll hear of the funeral later. I want to hear about Rose."

She cocked her head at him. "You've grown up, brother, and so has your temper. You talk differently, too."

"That can't be."

"Yes, it is. An interesting mixture of accents which, I suppose, is your own." She sighed. "I'm anxious to ask about your life, Percy, so let's get through this first. Four years ago May married, a nice fellow, young like herself. He and Rose took at once to each other. He moved his new family to Warwick. I know that's close—"

"Quite close, Louisa."

She stared back at him boldly. "I've seen her once or twice, but not for a while."

"For how long?"

Louisa shrugged her shoulders: nice, rounded shoulders, not thin like before. "A year, maybe two. She's eighteen, Percy, a girl nearly grown. I was pregnant with Ian and sick. You must know how such things are."

"And now? Has she seen your baby?"

"Of course she's seen him. She came to the christening."

"A year ago?"

"No, it's been longer than that. More like eighteen—I guess Ian's twenty months old now—"

"Louisa!"

"I'd forgotten how you say that! No one else says my name that way!" she flared back at him. "And what's more, you've no right. You come back, out of nowhere—"

"All right, all right," he soothed, "I'm just worried, I'm just—" He couldn't go on. She took the moment and used it.

"She'll be well, Percy. You can ride over and see for yourself in the morning. But you must have dinner with me."

"What about Stanley?"

"Stanley goes his own way. He does well enough!" There was a tone to her voice that warned Percy. "Do you know what he's done? Gone and talked the old Squire into leaving him everything. Squire died last year. Stanley is now Master Beal." She was watching him. "Don't look so surprised. You shouldn't be."

"What's he like?"

"Mean, nearly as mean as old Geoffrey himself." Her face softened a little. "Did you expect different, Percy? Come, sit over here. Sit and tell me about yourself."

"All right, I'll sit for a spell, but don't make me stay. I want to find Stanley."

"Yes, yes."

"What of the other two?"

"I nearly forgot." Louisa rose with a grace that surprised Percy and rushed to a desk that stood before a long window. "I have Laura's letter right here. She's to be married—" She paused and read for a moment. "Why, in only five days!"

Percy's face lit with sudden interest. "Will you go up with me?"

"No, I don't think so." She replaced the letter and ignored Percy's look. "I wasn't planning to go before, so why should I now? I'll send an expensive gift, that's all she'll be wanting."

"Louisa—"

"Really, Percy, are you such a babe still? I haven't seen her in years. You go on up there, I know that you must. But you should go alone."

"I don't understand. It seems it would have been simple to keep in touch with them, Louisa—"

"It seems, does it?" She turned on him. "Well, think harder, dear. Remember back to how it was when you left us. Remember life for me then. I didn't have two minutes in a day to call my own, Percy. I worked twelve hours at a spell. I fell into bed dirty and crying with my hands sore and bleeding."

He began to remember. He sat silent, and listening.

"How I hated her then! That fat sow, that mean, fat little woman!" Louisa stopped herself. "I'm sorry, but that's how it was. I bided my time, but it wasn't easy. I had offers, you know." Her smile grew a bit crooked. "I wanted nothing more than to just get away. But I bided my time until the right one came along."

With a sweep of her hand she indicated the large, sunlit room with its costly appointments. "I waited for this. I waited and I got what I wanted."

"Did you, Louisa?"

She glared at him suddenly. "I got more than most people get."

She didn't answer him *yes*. He took note of that. She didn't say: *Yes, I'm happy, I really got what I wanted.*

Percy was deeply disturbed. He felt drained by all he had learned, and all he had not learned.

"I'll come back later," he said. "I'll come back and hold little Ian and tell you about the mountain men, the cougars, and the Indians."

"Are there really such things?" Her voice sounded suddenly girlish.

"There are. I lived with the Indians one winter myself, with a tribe of Utes down by the Sanpete." He suddenly grinned. She wouldn't have the slightest idea what he was talking about. He changed the subject abruptly. "What is his name? The man May married?"

"His name is John Thomas."

"John Thomas," Percy repeated. "What made you choose Ian for your first son?" He wanted to say: *you should have named him after Father.* But he didn't.

Louisa made a small, nervous movement with her hands. "Ian is Victor's younger brother's name." Seeing Percy's reaction she hastily added, "And his father's as well."

Percy nodded. "I may be back tonight, but in case I'm not, in case I find Stanley and then just go on to Scotland—"

"Yes, you'd better hurry if you're going there."

"In case it's a few days before I next see you, will you take this for me, please?" He pulled out a book from the small bag he was carrying. She leaned forward to look at it. "It's the Book of Mormon. Will you take it and read it for my sake?"

She was already shaking her head at him. "No, Percy, no."

"It can't hurt anything, Louisa, just to read, just to find out what—"

"I already said no." Her voice had grown emphatic and hard, as if she'd pulled herself into a shell and was speaking to him now from a distance. "You don't know what you say. I have a reputation, my husband's reputation to uphold now, and my own social position—"

"And reading this book would interfere with that?"

"Mormonism would interfere with that." She drew herself up almost haughtily; for the first time Percy caught a glimpse of this new Louisa, this Louisa who was the wife of the man Victor Maughan. "The Mormons around here have a reputation quite different from the one I must cultivate."

"It is life and breath to me," he said, making her look at him. "Would you not read it just to find out what I believe, Louisa, and why?"

She met his gaze and her own didn't waver. "I've paid a price for my life. More of a price than you know—" Again that fluttering, nervous gesture. "It would cause trouble with Victor if he even discovered a copy of that book in his house."

"All right. I don't wish to come between a man and his wife." Percy slipped the offending volume back into his satchel. "I've other presents as well. But I'll bring them next time, when Ian's awake."

"I'll look forward to it, Percy." She walked him out to the door. "Be careful. I hope things go well in Scotland."

When he extended his hand she took it in both of her own. They were soft, gentle hands now, unroughened by work. "You made your choice, Percy, long ago," she said, "and no one stood in your way. None of us blamed you for it. Why can't you let us live our own lives with the same freedom?"

"Because Mormonism has made me so happy—and I want that same happiness, Louisa, for you!"

She pulled her hands away. He had distressed her. "Leave things be!" She nearly hissed the words at him. "Leave things be, Percy, please." She sighed and shook her head at him. "It was you, Percy. We were all young and frightened and unhappy over what was happening, how our very lives were snatched from us—" Her eyes grew dark with remembrance. Percy stepped unconsciously closer. "But you were the only one who believed we could stay a family." She met his eyes squarely. "We *were* a family then." She seemed to shudder. "It's been a long time since I've thought about it, at least thought deep enough to remember the feelings."

"We're still a family."

"No, no we're not, Percy. You must be able to see that."

His own eyes grew dark. "I've seen precious little so far, Louisa." He reached out his fingers, wanting to touch her again. "But I have seen you. You are as lovely as I remembered. And as brave and sure."

Her eyes softened at his words, at the love she felt in them. "I'm glad you're back. I am truly. But just be careful, Percy. Please do that."

It was a strange parting admonition. It cast a shade in his mind; it lit a slow, burning anger inside him.

Well, I've botched things up royally, he chided himself. *I'm sure I can't expect any better with Stanley. What about Rose? This isn't going to be easy.* The need to see her, the sense of urgency was building. But Warwick was in the other direction from Scotland; Rose would have to wait. He needed to get to the borders for Laura's wedding, he knew he did. It would mean so much to him to share this time with her. It almost seemed an act of fate that the chance had been given him.

I'll try to find Stanley right now. If he's home I'll spend the evening with him, then get an early start before sunup for Scotland.

It seemed a good plan. He rode out to the Squire's estate. It looked as big as before, perhaps even bigger and more impressive than he had remembered it. He rode straight to the foot of the door, the wide front door that rose three feet above him at the end of a long flight of stairs. He tied his horse to the heavy gold ring that topped a polished granite post. He thought briefly of all the gold and brass fittings Stanley had polished.

He knocked at the door, letting the heavy lion knocker bang three times, then another three. No one came, not even a servant to ask him his business. He went back to his horse, feeling deflated and drained of all purpose. What to do now?

He rode to the inn and ate a hot meal. He could go back to Louisa's, but he didn't want to. There was one thing he hadn't done yet: he hadn't looked up the Church, made himself known to them.

The closest chapel to the inn was the one on Thorpe Street. He rode to the place, but the building was empty, though there was a sign on the door with the schedule of meetings posted and two or three names. Any of these men might be able to help him.

Percy tried the first one. No one answered his knock at the door. He tried the next name, then the next. Where could everyone be on a late Thursday afternoon? At the third house he tried, someone answered his knock. At last! It was only a young boy, but he smiled kindly at Percy. "There's a baptism, sir."

"So that's where everyone is!"

"Are you from America—from Zion?"

Percy grinned back. "Yes, boy, I am. How in the world can you tell?"

"I don't know." The lad looked down at his feet and shuffled a bit. "How you dress, how you speak—just something about you."

Something about me! Percy wasn't sure how he felt about being recognized by everyone for such an obvious stranger, especially when he wanted to feel at home, when he wanted to seem to fit back in here.

He found his way to the spot on a broad, sloping bank of the river where large trees offered shade—and seclusion. He might as well join the others; there was nothing else he could do. He heard the music before he came in sight of the party—the sweet, well-known strains that brought a flood of memories and feelings tumbling over him:

> Now let us rejoice in the day of salvation,
> No longer as strangers on earth need we roam—

He urged his horse faster. He felt no longer a stranger; his loneliness fell from him. Here was home. Here were people like himself who would welcome him.

> Good tidings are sounding to us and each nation,
> And shortly the hour of redemption will come—

He came in sight of the group. It looked like a heavenly scene: men and women dressed in white coming out of the river, being beckoned ashore, people embracing one another with tears of joy running down their cheeks.

> When all that was promised the Saints will be given,
> And none will molest them from morn until ev'n,
> And earth will appear as the Garden of Eden,
> And Jesus will say to all Israel, Come home.

Percy dismounted, he mingled among them, he shook their hands and answered their questions. He basked in their love. Many here were new converts, one or two he thought he might recognize: there were twenty-five or thirty in all. One of the young boys just baptized asked that Percy join in his confirmation. He placed his hands on the boy's head, on the tousled hair that was wet still, and with a strong voice pronounced the ordinance that was so sacred to him. He called forth blessings as well, blessings and admonitions that came to his mind unbidden. He knew the Spirit was there.

He had nearly finished when he felt the earth tremble; it would have been no surprise to Percy if the trembling came from the rushing of angels. He opened his eyes. A group of horsemen surrounded the party. Their animals churned up the dirt as they rode in short, angry circles around the small group of people, who drew in closer together, their eyes on the men.

"We'll have none of this here!" one of the young ruffians shouted. "We've told you before. We'll have none of your calling of angels and spirits." He moved his horse close to one of the brethren and spit at his feet. "You don't belong here!"

The contempt in his voice cut through Percy like fire. There was such hate in his face, in all the faces that leered above him. He felt a hand on his collar that jerked him back. He struggled to keep his footing.

"This is English soil; we'll have none of your heresies practiced here."

Percy didn't know what to do. He looked from one face to the other. They all were shuttered and still; shuttered and still and accepting.

"We've as much right as they," he snapped to the man beside him.

"We want no trouble," the man soothed. He looked about him. "These are powerful men." As he spoke he moved toward a small group of women huddled under a tree.

"Could you take Sister Anderson on your horse, brother?" he asked Percy.

"Of course."

"Thank you. Just follow me."

The man moved with quick precision and purpose. Percy thought: *He's done this before. This isn't the first time this kind of thing has happened.*

He followed the other's lead. He felt sick inside. The mounted men taunted them, calling out oaths, filthy words that made Percy's cheeks burn. The young women dropped their eyes. He helped Sister Anderson climb up behind him. He felt a sudden sharp pain in his arm, and another that snaked up his leg like a fire. It came from the kick of a boot, a hard-tipped boot that had been aimed precisely. *They're pelting us with dirt and stones. This is madness!* Percy looked across at a young, bearded face, directly into eyes snapping with hatred. This was the man who had kicked him!

"We've seen your evil work," he was shouting. "You are devils who pose as men, who prey upon innocent women—"

The man's shout was a roar in Percy's ears. He was trembling all over with enraged indignation. He bent his powers on guiding his horse through the churning of horses and bodies to follow the brother who had first asked him to take Sister Anderson out of here. He drew up the incline, away from the press of chaos behind him. He still heard the wild oaths in his ears. He bent low over the horse's thick neck; he could feel the woman's arms at his waist. He kept his eyes on the man before him who cleared the crowd and headed west down a road Percy knew. Percy followed him with speed and skill. When they had gone a few miles, when there was nothing but dust and silence behind them, the man drew aside, off the road, into a small stand of chestnuts. Percy pulled up gratefully.

"Brother—Clark, is it?" Percy asked a bit breathlessly.

"Yes, lad, bless your heart for your timely help." He smiled past Percy to Sister Anderson, who relaxed her tight hold and leaned out to smile at the woman riding behind Brother Clark, who Percy assumed was his wife.

"What's happening? What was that back there?" Percy was trembling still. "I don't understand why you didn't resist them. We had more men than they."

All three smiled at him with a sad condescension that only banked Percy's rage.

"You haven't been here, you don't know." Brother Clark spoke with patience. "We've had much opposition of late—"

"They attack the missionaries when they preach on the streets, they come right into our meetings—" Sister Clark couldn't keep an edge of bitterness from her voice.

"Well, why doesn't somebody stop them? What about the authorities?"

"That's it. These men are powerful, some highly placed. Right now we haven't got much on our side."

"Why? I don't understand. When I joined the Church here in '56 I don't remember such scenes, such bitterness."

"You were only a boy then," Sister Anderson pointed out softly. "You probably weren't aware."

She is right, Percy realized. *And I had other things on my mind.*

"It comes and goes. Sometimes something will fire it, sometimes one man gets some sort of a personal vendetta against us—"

Like the man on the black horse, the man who kicked me so viciously.

"What can you do?"

"Ride it out, try not to occasion their anger, pray for patience and faith."

Percy made a short noise that had no patience in it. "That doesn't sound right to me. You'd think there'd be something—"

The faces that watched him smiled gently. *You'll learn in time,* they seemed to say.

"We must get out of here." Brother Clark looked behind him. "Can you follow me still? See Sister Anderson safely home?"

"Of course." The tight hands closed at his waist again. They moved cautiously back to the road.

"Where are the others?" Percy asked.

"They all went by different routes, several different routes," Brother Clark called back to him.

"So you had a plan. You knew this might happen."

"That's right," Sister Anderson answered. They headed out, gathered speed. He lost track of just where they were going after several turns. He had a feeling they might be doubling back, doing some kind of zigzagging into town, anyway.

What a strange welcome home. What a strange, unexpected homecoming.

Well, at least he had lost his drugged feeling of lethargy. He was wide awake now, alive with all sorts of tingling, sensational feelings, all sorts of stirrings inside. He rode through the streets of Birmingham. The unpleasant thought came to him: *I'm a marked man. I'm a Mormon, which makes me some kind of vermin, something less than human.* He wanted to laugh, yet he knew he must not take this lightly; he knew there were those who thought it a most serious matter. He would be foolish to underestimate them.

He rode again in the twilight of early evening to the Squire's great house, marveling, as he considered its magnificence, that it belonged now to Stanley. Was Stanley a happy man? Percy thought that he ought to be. Would he marry and raise up a good, solid family? Louisa's words raced through his mind: *He's mean, nearly as mean as old Geoffrey himself.*

He knocked at the door with as much emphasis as he could. He was more than curious now; he was anxious to see this younger brother, to talk to him. At last he heard movement, a rattling of locks and chains. The man who stood before him was young and, though liveried as a servant, he had an obviously insolent air.

"Is Master Stanley at home?" Percy asked, with what he hoped was a voice of authority.

The young servant regarded him stiffly for a moment or two. "Master Beal is out for the evening, sir."

Percy checked his disappointment so the man would not see.

"I do not expect him until late—" a wry expression touched the impudent features— "very late. Would you leave your name, sir?"

No, not yet. I want to surprise him.

"No, thank you, but I shall be back in a few days' time and hope the young Squire is not too drunk to receive me."

The servant's expression confirmed that Percy's comment had been highly accurate. What else should he expect?

Once more he mounted his horse and rode, empty and dissatisfied, down the long lane. It almost seemed he could see the two boys in the shadows, scurrying from tree to tree, hoping to avoid detection, hoping Master Beal's coach would not bear down upon them unexpectedly from around some dark bend. Two brothers stealing an hour together in a world that no longer existed.

He rode back to the inn. This meant he would have no trouble getting an early start in the morning. Perhaps it was for the best.

Stanley would hold. He hoped that Rosie would, too. If it weren't for Rose he would welcome the journey that lay ahead. His dream had meant nothing more than a message that he should come here, nothing more than the death, the horrid death of the beloved old doctor, and Rosie's grief.

So he told himself. But something inside him proved stubborn, and refused to believe.

CHAPTER
4

*I*t was a picturesque route Percy traveled and, though restless at first, he soon succumbed to the green, peaceful charms of the rich countryside. He had chosen horseback as the most affordable mode of travel. Although it took longer, it was a pleasant way to see things, and it gave him the freedom he felt he wanted, especially once he reached the borders.

He passed up through Liverpool and Preston and out of the industrial district, fighting rain all the way; this was certainly not the desert. No wonder things here were so green. He spent the first night in Sheffield. England was falling behind him. Before the second long day of riding had ended, he was nearing the Lake Country: Windermere, Keswick, and Cockermouth. This was nature at her most sumptuous, most flagrant, most fair. Percy felt the tensions of the past days fall from him. Here was meadow made gold in the sunlight, here were stretches of blue — deep, languid blue lakes framed in flowers and shades of green that no bright blossom could fairly compete with. Here was ageless peace, untouched, unmarred by man's passing.

Near the close of the third day he approached the border, through Carlisle and on to Selkirk, "the proudest of all the border burghs." *Of course Aunt Judith would live here, where else?*

It was night in the town; the wide town square was swathed in shadow. He found a good pub, The Queen's Head, and ate a hot meal there. Just off the square was the old street of Kirk Wynd, where Judith lived. The men in the pub had described her house for him, and he rode up, but there were no lights in the windows, and he hesitated waking the place.

There was an old, half-ruined church on the corner. He pulled up there to think, to walk around a bit in the fresh moonlight. He read the gray plaque inscribed to the greatest of Scottish heroes: William Wallace, the guardian of Scotland, who raised archers here to fight alongside Robert the Bruce for the freedom of their country. The night was so still that he could hear his own breathing and the occasional snorts from his tired horse. He kicked at the short, wet grass that hugged the leaning gravestones.

When Wallace came here he had a mission to perform. Was he tired, even a little frightened, as I am? Percy wondered. *Have I come all the way here in vain? Have I set myself on a fool's errand?*

He felt a long way from home. Despite the beauty and peace of the night, this was foreign soil. Perhaps he was an adopted son of the desert, but the desert was home. He knew that now as he never had known it. In his uncertainty, he longed for what was loved, familiar—and so far away.

This was Scotland, it was not England. Although just a few miles stood between them, the speech here was different, the customs, the ways. Percy stood before the stout door on Kirk Wynd and knocked with his might, as much to bolster his own courage as anything.

She answered the door: not a servant, not the imposing Aunt Judith, but Laura herself, looking as lithe as one of the young, graceful larches he had passed through last night riding into town. She stood perplexed, not recognizing him, but recognizing something. She tilted her head. "Sir?" Her voice was still sweet. Percy suddenly longed for its laughter, for the petulant poetry of it.

"Laura, lass—don't you know? Don't you know who I am?"

Her eyes widened. "Do not toy with me, sir. You look like someone—someone . . . but that was so long ago."

He feared he might make her cry. She was always close to tears, and with her wedding tomorrow—

"Percy, could it be you?" She whispered the words with her head down; if she was in error she could cover the mistake and go on.

"Yes, Laura, God bless you!"

She smiled into his eyes; she flung herself into his arms. She wept in the same passionate, almost abandoned manner he remembered. He let her cry herself out, smoothing her hair, saying soothing words to her. When she lifted her head her eyes were shining with tears and gladness.

"Heaven brought you to me. Heaven brought you to be here for my wedding. Isn't that so?"

He wanted to laugh: at her lovely earnestness, at his own happiness. "Yes, it is so, I believe it is so, Laura."

"Come. Oh, come quickly inside. Aunt Judith will have one of her fainting spells!" She tugged him along. "Sit right here. I'll have old Jacob get Randall. No, no I won't—" She pulled herself up and with a small, gloved hand smoothed out her skirt front. "No, Randall can wait. I shall have you all to myself for a while."

She was pleased with that plan. Percy laughed. "You haven't changed, little Laura."

"Oh, surely I have. I've grown up to be a beauty, Percy—everyone says so."

"Well, in Scotland, I'm sure. But I'm used to rosy-cheeked American women who—"

"Percy, don't tease!"

"All right, since it is your wedding tomorrow I'll please you."

"Just tell me the truth."

"The truth is that you are the proudest and prettiest little chit I've yet known."

She fluttered over and kissed him in exuberant gratitude. She smelled like roses in spring. She smelled like fresh spring rain on a hillside.

"Is Aunt Judith well? Are you well, Laura? The man you will marry—" He thought of Louisa. "Do you love him truly?"

"Oh, Percy, he's the most marvelous person! Have no doubts of that. He is gentle with me, and I adore him!" She unconsciously lifted her head. "He is an Armstrong." Percy's blank look annoyed her. "That's a name to be reckoned with here on the borders. Don't forget that."

He nodded his head and brought her smile back again. She *was* a pretty girl, with darker hair than the rest of them and a fine oval face, a gentle chin, high cheekbones, and large, deep-set eyes. *Can this Armstrong boy handle her?* Percy wondered.

"Aunt Judith is ailing, you'll see. At times she looks like a walking skeleton, but yet she holds on."

"She is a stubborn woman, Laura, you know that. Has she been kind? Has your life here—"

She waved a hand at him. "We've gotten by. She's tolerable most of the time, and she's fond of me—"

So Laura had kept her hold upon her.

"And Randall?"

"Well, there—there have been some problems between the two of them. At last she apprenticed him out, to one of the best shoemakers in Selkirk."

"Is that what Randall wanted? Does he live here with the two of you still?"

"Well, he takes his meals here and sleeps in the small room at the back." Laura played with a lock of her hair. "It hasn't been easy for Randall, Percy. He's a sensitive boy. I think he's lonely; he always seems lonely. That bothers her—they rub each other the wrong way; you know how it is."

"Does he like being a shoemaker?"

"I don't really think so. But it's a noble trade here. Selkirk is known for the fine shoes we make. In the Forty-five it was our lads who made shoes for Prince Charlie and his men."

"*Our lads?*" He couldn't help teasing her just a little. "Are you a Scots lassie now? No more to do with the Sassenach devils across the border?"

"I guess that's right. I guess I have become Scots in my heart now. It's easy to do."

Percy thought of the desert and the mountains and nodded.

"You're different yourself," she went on.

"So they tell me."

"You even sound different. But I like how you talk. And you've grown quite handsome, Percy, though I always believed you'd be handsome. You look more like Mother than the rest of us; I always thought that unfair."

"You haven't come out badly yourself."

"Is my frankness embarrassing you?" She smiled at him impishly. "You do have a shy manner about you, but it takes people in. Have you a way with the girls, Percy? I imagine you have."

This was too much. He stood and strode to the window. "Where will you live, Laura, after you're wed?"

"In Jack's family home above Ettrick Bridge. It's one of the old Armstrong strongholds."

"So you'll be happy here?"

"Yes," she laughed, "I'll be happy here."

He thought of the book in his pouch.

"And I'll be the happier to have you here for my wedding day."

He returned her smile. "Laura, do you and Jock attend church here—"

She scowled at him. "*Jack*, Percy! Heavens, his name isn't Jock! We'll be married in the Kirk of Scotland. Is that what you mean?"

"Not exactly. Do you attend church meetings often?"

"Living under Aunt Judith's vulture eye? Of course we do; even Randall never misses his meetings. Jack's father is one of the Elders of the session."

"Oh, I see."

"Why, Percy?" She had grown suddenly wary. "Are you one of those strange Mormons still? I suppose you are, if you still live in America. I yet remember how shocked I felt when your letter came, all those years ago. Aunt Judith went into a fit and had us all three in tears. I was afraid you'd go straight to the devil, Percy. I could just see the flames licking at you—" She shuddered. "It was awful. I never did understand."

"That's just it, Laura. I know Mormonism is different, but it's really quite easy to understand. I would like you to understand it, for my sake."

The guarded look had returned to her face. "There's no reason to, Percy. If it's what you want, I can accept that. There's no other reason—"

"There may be, Laura. There may possibly be something in Mormonism that you need, something that would make you happy, make you—"

"Percy, Percy! I'm happy now! I couldn't be happier." She

shook her head at him and her long ringlets quivered. "I believe Aunt Judith's awake. I've developed an ear to hear when she's moving about. I hope the shock of seeing you won't be too great for her."

She glided to the foot of the staircase and cocked her small head. "Stay put, Percy. You won't disappear on me? I'll just run up and check."

With graceful energy she raced up the stairs. Percy took a deep breath. He wished he didn't have to face the old lady. But the sooner the better, he supposed. He stood with his hands clasped behind him to receive her.

She swept down upon him with an air almost regal; he could hear the stairs creak, and wondered that her thin, brittle bones did not creak with them. She was more bone than flesh. Her face was gaunt and pulled tight, but she had all her hair still, stark white and piled up on her head, and she had all her teeth, or enough to season the smile she gave him with a stamp of authority.

"This is a day I never thought to see in my life," she snapped briskly. "Death may take me now, for I swear there could be no more surprises in store for me to compare fair with this."

Percy took both her hands and leaned forward to kiss her cool cheek. She pulled back, flustered and pleased.

"You're the image of your mother, lad, at least about the eyes you are. The eyes and the mouth." She shook her head at him as she settled herself, rustling, into a black horsehair chair as straight and austere as herself.

"Have ye come back from the dead? We've never heard a word from you all these years, you must know, and your sister's no better. And her close enough to come visiting if she'd a mind to. Especially now with that fancy husband she's got—"

Over Aunt Judith's head Laura rolled her bright eyes.

"But he's here, Auntie," she gushed, rushing forward. "That's all that counts now. He's here, my own brother, to see me married." She turned with sudden inspiration to Percy, her small hand to her throat.

"Will you give me away, Percy? Randall hated the notion; he's so backward with people. But you're the oldest, 'tis only proper."

"Of course, whatever you'd like." He wondered just what it

meant to "give away" a bride. He had never attended a wedding. Benjamin and Claire had been sealed in the Endowment House in Salt Lake and she had told him something about it. But he was sure this would prove quite different from what Claire had described for him.

"So you come from the West, from the great, wild, American wilderness?" Aunt Judith peered at him more closely. "Are there really grizzly bears there? Buffalo and bloodthirsty Indians?"

He nodded solemnly. "Yes. I've killed a grizzly myself, and many buffalo, and I've lived with the Indians in their own tents and more than once known of one who wanted my blood."

She snorted back at him, almost in fear. "I'm not sure I believe you. Are you still one of them heathens, lad?"

"A Mormon? I am, Aunt."

"Well, that explains all." She settled herself back against the unyielding chair. "Will you be with us for long?"

"Just a few days—"

"Well, good. We can visit then, after the wedding. Today this missy and I have our hands full—"

"What can I do to help?"

"I'll make out a list. Several things, to be certain. Have you breakfasted yet?"

She read Percy's blank, wide-eyed stare to mean *no*.

"Laura, go call old Mary to heat up the porridge and cook a few eggs for this starving lad. I've never yet met a man who could work well on an empty stomach."

Laura jumped to obey, catching Percy's eye long enough to give him a saucy wink as she sailed from the room.

Percy wondered several times during the day how they would have made it without him. He did the work of three men and ran more errands, he was sure, than a henpecked husband who had been married all his life.

He didn't see Randall until they sat down to supper, and even their supper was late. Every item on Aunt Judith's list needed to be scratched off before anyone ate.

He watched his brother come into the room, unprepared for

the shock of how large he was: he stood inches taller than Percy himself, and in width he was twice Percy's equal. But you could not call him stout. He was solidly built and well muscled, with a great shock of hair and large, quiet eyes that sat deep in an expressionless face: a broad, innocent, well-guarded, poorly shaved face. The color seeped into it when he recognized Percy and he cast his eyes to the floor, as though embarrassed or ashamed for some reason. Percy held out his arm and made Randall shake hands with him. Something warned him not to do more. They sat to the table with this awkwardness between them. Talk of the wedding concealed it, but that wasn't what Percy wanted. He would have to get Randall alone. But before they were fairly through with the meal the boy slipped away and Laura cajoled Percy to come meet her new in-laws, and he could not refuse.

"Jack and I will take off for a wee tour tomorrow after the wedding. Will you be here when I come back?"

"I don't think so, I haven't that much time to stay."

"Then this is our last night together," she pouted. Percy gave in with grace. She had a right to him now; he would do her bidding, and then confront Randall when the wedding was over.

She *was* a delight to be with. The glow of beauty and youth was upon her, almost an aura of joy. "Do I leave you in good hands tomorrow?" he asked her. "Will you be truly happy, my dear?"

There was no room in her young, bursting heart for doubt. "Jack is a darling, he'll take good care of me, Percy. He's a kind, honest man."

"Will you be a good wife to him, Laura?"

She blushed a little. "I'll try. I mean to make him the happiest man in all of Scotland."

She was ever one for superlatives. How could he say: *When you get down to the level of everyday living, Laura, will you serve him without complaint? And be happy whatever life brings you?*

"Do you have your button?" he asked.

"The old button from Father's greatcoat?" Her eyes grew warm. "Of course I have it. Come see."

She drew him up to the room, which was all frills and flounces, as feminine a concoction as she, and opened a small velvet, heart-shaped jewelry box. There in its folds, nestled down among earrings and necklaces, the brass button shone. He picked it up between thumb and forefinger.

"Do you have yours, Percy?"

He thought of the night of the terrible rainstorm when he had laid the coat over Claire; he thought of the time when he had covered the small, half-frozen girls with it. "I have it," he said. "It's sewn inside the pocket of the greatcoat itself, so I couldn't lose it."

He had drawn her interest. "Do you wear Papa's coat, then?"

"I've worn it many a time. I even traded it once to an Indian chief for food." He smiled at the memory.

"So have you lost it?"

"Oh no, I got it back. The old fox knew I wanted it, and I earned it, you might say, by saving his grandson."

Laura settled back, ready to listen. "How did you do that?"

"He had been shot, the wound had festered, and he had a terrible fever. I nursed him with white man's medicine for days and he rallied some." Percy paused. He decided he may as well tell her the truth. "At last I gave him a blessing, laid my hands on his head the way Mormon elders do, and blessed him to recover."

"How in the world would he recover just because you did that?"

"It wasn't through me, it was through the power of the priesthood which, as an elder, I hold. Through God's power."

If you say so, her eyes said. "So the chief was so grateful he gave you your coat back?"

Percy nodded.

"I like that story," she surmised. She reached out for the button. "Do you ever think about us, about England — about any of that anymore?" she asked.

He had to be honest. "I used to a lot. I shut it out after a while; I felt I had to get on with my life."

"I know. I've done the same thing in some ways. When I was younger I used to try to get Louisa to write, to come, to pay some attention to me. When Aunt Judith was nasty I would lie on my bed and sob and make up daydreams where Louisa would march in indignantly and take me away." She lowered her long lashes. "Of course, she never did. Nothing ever did happen. It got easier after a while."

She rose and put the button back into its place. With her back toward him she said, "Do you ever think about—them? About Mother and Father?"

"Yes. All the time. That's somehow different. It's been a great help to me sometimes."

Laura sighed. "I don't know. I was younger than you were when they died. Sometimes I've forgotten what they look like even." Her voice trembled. "When I think of her, I think of times when I was very little. And I think of the time—the time I saw her standing in the air by the mantel—"

"I remember," he said. "It *was* her you saw, Laura. Do you ever doubt it?"

"Oh no, Percy, no."

"I'll be gone when you get back," he said, "and you have a new life to live now." He placed his hands on her slight shoulders and turned her to face him. "Will you promise me this? Keep the button still, keep it for bad days and difficult times. Let it help you to be brave and wise and good, as Mother was."

She was crying by now. Of course, he knew she would cry. Being Laura, what else could she do? He drew her close, felt her head on his shoulder. "I won't really leave you this time. I'll keep in touch, I'll write letters, I'll try to be a help to you, as a big brother should be—"

"You'll be so far away."

"Fifty miles can be as far as five thousand, and you know it. There are things I can do, ways I can help by just loving you, Laura."

She cried all the harder. He found her handkerchief for her. This wasn't easy for him; it was much harder than he had expected.

When at last her tears had all dried they walked out into the moonlight together. He closed his eyes and tried to capture the feel of the evening, the scent of the night and the young girl beside him, her voice, her softness.

"How proud I shall be to walk down the aisle on your arm, Percy," she murmured. "It makes everything right. It sets a benediction on my marriage." She leaned over and kissed his cheek.

"I'm glad, dear," he whispered. But his own heart was aching. *There could be so much more to your marriage, to your happiness, Laura. If you only could know!*

It was a lovely wedding; it was one of the gayest the borders had seen in many a year, men told him. It seemed madness to him. There was the stately march in the early morning down a flower-strewn path, the entire wedding party moving to the strains of a single piper. In the fresh morning air it seemed other-worldly in a sweet, haunting way.

Once inside the church Percy didn't remember much. He must have made it somehow down the aisle with Laura's light hand on his arm. He did remember the look in young Jack Armstrong's eyes, and that warmed him considerably.

In the chaos afterward of pipe and fiddle, dancing and drinking, eating and toast-calling, he did make the chance to draw Jack aside and exact the old promise from him: "You take care of my girl"—half entreaty, half threat. Jack grinned at him.

"Don't fret yourself, sir. I shall be ever gentle and loving with Laura."

She crept up from behind. "And if you are not, Percy will send one of his Indians out here to get you, to cut off your head with a tomahawk." She made a gruesome face.

They both laughed at her and Jack answered back, in true border fashion, "He'll have an Armstrong to reckon with, lass. Ask the Sassenachs what it is like to come up against hot Scots blood."

It was a good marriage. Percy could feel that. These were good people here. The happy hours slipped away and, all of a sudden, the bride and bridegroom were leaving. Percy watched them trip off together, looking into each other's eyes, lost in each other. He felt a sudden sharp stab of envy. The crowd parted for them, cheering them, reaching out to them with their hands and their hearts.

Then the moment was gone; the bright young couple was

gone and the crowd turned, as if with a single breath, to the continuing pursuit of their own pleasure. For most who were there the merrymaking would continue until morning. For Percy the pleasure was gone; the reason for the celebrating, the flame that had lit it, had burned out, and had left him feeling a little bit lonely, a little bit chilled.

Percy excused himself from the revels early and went in search of his brother. The house was empty, even the room that was Randall's. But the old manservant, Jacob, watching Percy's perplexed searching, volunteered a suggestion.

"Try 'is favorite pub. The Hawk's Head, just over on Back Row."

Percy thanked him. He found the place easily. Once inside he had to adjust his eyes to the dim light and the hanging curtain of smoke. He didn't mind the smell of the strong pipe tobacco; the liquor smell bothered him more. He squinted his eyes and searched for the big shape that was still unfamiliar to him. It was hard to tell. There were many large men bent over their mugs, dressed in rough working clothes.

A hand on his shoulder made him jump uneasily. He looked into the face of the bartender. "Over there. Your brither's at the table in the corner."

Randall had seen him, then. *I must stand out in such a crowd*, Percy realized. He walked to the corner table and sat down at the chair Randall had pulled out for him.

"I've been looking for you," Percy said, putting as much warmth into his voice as he could.

"Who steered you here?"

"Old Jacob."

Randall nodded. He sat very still, with his hand on his cup. His eyes, like two dull but steady beams of light, burned into Percy's face. "Do ye go back tomorrow?"

"I go back to Birmingham. I'll stay there for a spell. I haven't seen Stanley—I haven't even seen Rose yet." His mouth felt dry and he swallowed.

"I haven't seen Rosie in years. Bet she's a pretty little thing now." Randall's voice had a slow, musing quality.

"I'm a little concerned about her." Percy hadn't meant to say that.

"Why so? May's of as fine stock as the old doctor, and the man she's wed would be a good sort. Rosie's sure to be well off."

"And what of yourself?"

Randall's gaze never wavered. His eyes said: *What's it to you?*

"I get along."

"Are you happy here?"

"What's happy, Percy? Happy has little to do with life."

"Laura said she didn't think you particularly wanted to be a shoemaker. She said Aunt Judith and—"

"What does that chit of a girl know? She does go on!" There was bitterness in his voice, but the fire burned low; it was a slow, smoldering ember he had tended a long time.

"Most of these lads in here are doing something they'd rather not be doing."

"I don't believe that."

"What of yourself?" Randall's voice was still quiet. "Are you *happy* with your life?"

Percy thought for a moment. "On the whole, yes, I am. I like the desert and the mountains, I like what I see around me, and I like what I do."

"Have ye a woman?"

"She's the thorn in my side right now." Percy grinned. "But Claire and Benjamin, they've been very good to me."

"Some is lucky, some ain't."

"You're only nineteen, Randall, you can do anything. You don't have to stay here."

For just a moment the calm eyes wavered and dropped their gaze.

"Come with me, Randall. The West is a man's world, it's wide-open country full of—"

"Come be a Mormon!" He spat out the word with more venom than Percy would have thought possible. His mind stumbled, wondering how to proceed.

"There's California: gold and land to be bought, and shipping. There's more than Mormons in the West."

Randall nodded. "Why'd you come back, Percy?"

"I made a promise."

"I know that. But I asked you why you came back."

The anger that had been building in Percy, born of frustration, began to flow like a heat through his system; he could feel it pounding in his head. He put his elbows on the table and leaned closer to Randall.

"If you really want to know, Randall, I had a dream. A dream that reminded me of my old promise. Then the man I work for asked me to come back and help his wife and family prepare to go over; he paid my way here. I thought it was fate; that's how I looked at it."

Randall nodded again. "Are you glad that you came?"

Percy nearly chuckled. How dogged this brother was! "It's been harder than I thought it would be—"

"Most things are."

"Most things are," Percy agreed. "But sometimes there are unexpected surprises. I thought—I hoped my homecoming might be one of them."

"For Laura it was."

Percy smiled gently. "Yes, yes, I suppose so."

Randall took a long drink from his mug and held it out to Percy, but Percy shook his head and tried to hold Randall's eye again. "You know, I meant what I said. I didn't say it out of a sense of duty or politeness."

"What do you mean?"

"I mean, I think you'd be happy in Utah. There's room for you there, room for a man like you."

Randall's eyes seemed to darken. "And what kind of man might that be?" he asked gruffly, as much as to say: *What makes you think you know what kind of a person I am?*

"You can't have changed all that much," Percy pressed. "There are certain things I remember. Do you still like to draw?" It was a shot in the dark. "There's room in the kingdom for artists as well as artisans. There's room for a man who may think and feel more deeply than his neighbor does—"

"Wait, Percy, hold on. What do you want? You want to convert me, you want to take me back as another Mormon?" He laughed, though not unkindly. "What a romantic you are! Would you want me if I came with you the way I am, unconverted?"

"Of course I would. I would want you any way I could get you!"

"Why?"

"Because you're my brother! Because I believe in the family."

"Blood's thicker than water and all that? Nonsense! Why should I believe you care when nobody else does? Aunt Judith is family, and so is Louisa, and that spoiled, haughty Laura, and what help is that? Are you some kind of do-gooder? Is that what Mormonism's made you?"

Percy shook his head. "You wear me out, Randall. What is it *you* want?"

"I want nothing from you."

"Don't you? Why not? You have claim on me—"

"I don't see it that way."

"See it or not, Randall, you do. Do you still have your button?"

Randall looked at him darkly. "What difference can that make?"

"No difference, I guess." Percy felt drained. His anger, with no outlet to extinguish its energies, was wearing him out. He stood. He was tired from the day and its demands.

"I'm worn out," he said bluntly. "Will you walk home with me now?"

The calm eyes bored holes through him. "I'd be poor company, brother, and I've scarcely got started here." He held up his thick glass. "A refill here, Maisie."

Percy ducked past the barmaid as she made for his table and walked out the door without once looking behind him. He didn't see that Randall sat, staring holes through the thick wood of the old door, his drink untouched, his hands clenched on the top of the table, his eyes wide and wet.

The wedding was over. There was no reason to linger; Percy saw that at once. Aunt Judith, despite her words to the contrary, was in no mood to visit, to chitchat. She made that quite clear. She was one of the few women Percy could make no headway with, much less charm; that in itself annoyed him.

"Do you intend to go back to that heathen land, Percy?"

How haughty her manner was! Where did she acquire that? Percy thought of his mother's meek, gentle ways and wondered.

"Yes, I'm going back, Aunt."

"You mean you have been here, seen your homeland again, your own people, and yet you *choose* to go back?"

Percy was weary of this. "There is much to go back to, Aunt Judith. It is wicked of you to judge what you do not know. Unchristian, at best."

"Well!" She drew herself in, nursing her ruffled feathers like a tall, affronted bird. "I see maturity and experience have not mellowed you much, young man." She clucked at him a moment. "At least I know I have done my duty, done it to the best of my ability. That's Christian, young man!"

Duty! What of love, Aunt Judith? How different they are!

"Yes, you have done your duty," he admitted, more gently, "and you shall be rewarded for what you have done." *And no more.* He kissed her thin, sunken cheek. "Hug Laura for me when she returns," he said. Her eyes grew wide, but she nodded. "I'll get my things and be going. Perhaps I'll swing past and say goodbye to Randall."

"That would be kind of you."

"Take care of him, Aunt Judith," he said as he started up the stairs. He couldn't see her face, so he mustered the courage it took to go on. "He needs more care, more love."

He heard her snort, but he didn't turn around. He took the small satchel that held his belongings from the room where he'd stayed and brought it downstairs with him. On a last, crazy impulse he ducked back into the room that was Randall's, opened his bag, and snatched a copy of the Book of Mormon out of it. *What harm can it do?*

He set the book on the bedside table. He could hear Aunt Judith's clipped step. He met her in the hall.

"Are you ready, lad? Here are some scones and a slab of bread and cheese the cook wrapped for you."

"That was thoughtful. Thank you."

The farewell was easy for both of them, though Percy rode off in pain, pain and a burning anger after he stopped at the shop and the foreman told him Randall could not leave his bench now. He wanted to know if what the man said was true, or if his brother avoided him on purpose, avoided even this last moment together, this last chance for farewell.

He rode into the stillness of the new morning longing for answers, yet knowing in his heart that there were none to be had.

CHAPTER

5

The White Horse Inn, after the long, lonely journey, looked a little like home. Percy was glad for the comfort it offered, though vague and anonymous.

He ought to report the results of his trip to Louisa, but that could wait. Although it was late in the day, he wanted first, first of all to see Rosie!

His route out of town would pass by Squire Beal's; he ought to stop there once more. It was broad daylight, perhaps Stanley would be in. He turned off on the long, private path up to the door and knocked, but the same servant answered.

"What a gadabout your master is," Percy complained. "Tell him Percy was here, his brother—his long-lost brother from America."

That drew a response. "I'll be back," Percy promised. *Now to Rose.*

He bent his energies to traveling quickly the few miles that separated him from the village of Warwick. Long before his approach he saw the old castle rise up, a gray standard above the line of the horizon, riding tall in the warm air, against the blue sky. *How old England is,* he mused. *How long she has nurtured our race. How long she has sent out her children to people the ends of the earth with her sturdy blood.* He thought of the Saints back in Zion; so many of them came from this island, or boasted mixed English blood. It was a joy that moment to him to be English.

He rode down the main village street. The home of John Thomas should not be difficult to locate here. At the open market he stopped and asked a vendor or two if they knew of the young man and his family. One of the old ladies buying bread said, "They lived over my way, young stranger, before they was gone."

"Gone?"

She scratched at a large wart that stood out on her forehead. "You do mean young John who married that pretty widow, the doctor's daughter?"

"Yes, yes, I mean him."

"Well, he's gone. Packed up and went off to Australia."

Percy felt faint. "Are you sure?"

She nodded and turned with a shrug of her shoulders. "I'll take this loaf," she said.

Percy leaned against a pile of stacked bushel baskets. "Are you all right, sir?" one of the vendor girls asked. He stared back at her blankly. Then a thought pierced his fogginess.

"Did all of the family go? Ma'am, did the whole family go?" He tugged at the arm of the large woman who turned, with her bread loaves, annoyed.

"How should I know? I suppose they did."

"How can I find out for certain?"

He had hold of her sleeve still and she shook him away from her. "See that lane veering off to the left here? Take that to the top, then turn left again and stop at the fourth house you come to. They ought to know there. 'Tis the neighbors who lived next door to them."

"Thank you, ma'am!" Percy was gone as he said it. His mind was reeling. This couldn't be true! *Father, don't let Rosie be lost to me!* he prayed.

He knocked on the door of the fourth house with a trembling hand. The old lady who answered invited him in. She was pleasant and concerned.

"I remember Rose well," she said sweetly.

"Could you tell me something about her?" he urged. "Anything. I'm her brother, I haven't seen her since she was a little girl."

The woman closed her eyes as though trying to remember. "She was distressed and unhappy after they first brought her here, after the old doctor's murder."

A shudder seemed to disturb the air between them. Percy nodded. "I know about that."

"But she was a great strength to May," the woman continued, "a great strength to May. She was a sweet, gentle thing, but amazingly strong-minded, a trait one wouldn't expect upon first knowing her." She seemed to smile at her own memories. "And she was a fine-looking girl. Bright eyes and clear skin, and that beautiful mass of red hair, perhaps more gold than red." The woman sighed. "Yes, she was a lovely young thing."

The use of the past tense was bothering Percy. "Then you believe she went along? You believe she went with May's family to—" He couldn't finish saying it.

The old woman squinted her eyes and considered a moment. "I believe she must have, my dear. That was three, four—perhaps even six months ago. I've not seen her since." She nodded her head, as if recalling something of importance. "I know the poor thing seemed sad, sad and disturbed the last time I saw her. And I remember John said, 'Rose doesn't want to go away to Australia, but I don't know what May would do without her, nor the little ones either. They're so fond of her.' I remember he said that. You know they had two little boys, John and May did?"

Percy felt tears forming behind his eyes. "Do you have an address? Do you know where they are in Australia?"

"No." She seemed downcast to have to answer him so, then she perked up a bit. "The parish priest might have an address, though he's gone for a fortnight. But you can check back with him. Thomas Brewster's his name, and the church is right up there at the end of the street."

"He'll be gone for a fortnight?"

"I fear so. Gone to Liverpool to visit his wife's folks. But you must come back and ask him. He'll be able to help you, I know."

Percy thanked her kindly. He wanted to lay his head against her motherly shoulder and cry like a boy. He felt more desolate, he was sure, than he had ever felt in his life, even when his mother died, even when he left England. *Even when I lost Rose.* He felt himself trembling. *Have I come this great distance and lost her again?*

He stumbled out to his horse and rode back to Birmingham,

not seeing the road, not seeing anything, but riding blindly like a man in a trance. When he came upon the small knot of men at the center of town, he instinctively gave them wide berth. Somewhere in the back of his consciousness a sensation gnawed at him: he had seen them before, these rough, coarse men on black horses. He drew in his rein. There were six riders, and caught in the midst of them were two men on foot.

Percy turned and rode just a bit closer. *I should have known!* The deep anger within him at last had a direction, a target! He spurred his horse and made a break in the cluster as he forced his way through.

"What's going on here?" he demanded, in the roughest voice he could muster.

"Mister, it's nothing to you," one of the dark riders scowled.

"We're just takin' care of some scum," another called out.

The dark-bearded leader bore down. "Leave it be, it's none of your business!" he growled, his voice thick with threat.

Percy knew by now that the two men being harassed, being beaten with canes, pelted with mud clots and tomatoes, were missionaries. He had seen one of them before; he recognized him from the river baptism.

"Don't you think the odds a bit unfair?" Percy kept his voice pleasant. He didn't wish to arouse the leader's rancor.

"The odds are nothing to you. These men are wicked in ways you can't imagine. We want no part of them here."

"Well, it's still not a fair fight," Percy persisted, for want of a better tack. "I think they've got the point of your message by now, don't you?"

There was some hesitation in the ranks; the men turned to the scowling, dark-haired one for their lead. During that moment the two men on foot melted into the shadows, sidling close to Percy's horse, then splitting ways and heading off behind the houses. Percy stepped his horse carefully in to close the opening and obscure their passing.

"The scoundrels have gotten away!"

Upon that discovery there was much cursing and moaning. Percy edged his horse back, quite aware that he was the only outsider left in the group now.

"Let the wretches go! We've scared them enough for now; there'll be other nights."

It was quite dark. Percy wished he could see the men's features. All he really got was an impression, and the impression was frightening.

The horses stomped around in an uneven circle to accentuate their riders' emotions. Then they formed into a line, the dark young man at their head. He called back over his shoulder to Percy, "You, stranger. From now on stay out of the way. Next time I catch you poking your nose into other folks' business, I'll assume you want the same thing they're getting!"

His comrades laughed at his words. Percy felt himself go hot all over, then cold. *The vain little bully! If I could get him alone, off that black beast of his, I'd show him a thing or two.*

All he needed was another frustration! He rode on toward the inn, his mind struggling to comprehend this senseless opposition, this persecution of Mormons. He never would understand. What had they done to harm anybody? What was it men feared? What was it they hated about Mormonism?

Percy was exhausted when he reached his own quarters, but his mind would not rest. He went down and ate a cold supper, but back in his room he found himself pacing the floorboards back and forth, back and forth, until someone in the room below pounded on the ceiling and shouted a mild threat up to him.

He stretched out on the bed. How far away Utah seemed—how removed from this life! It was a Wednesday night in July; there would be a dance in the Valley tonight. In his wretchedness he brooded upon what Emmeline might be doing. He knew her flirtatious ways, her fondness for masculine attention. He also knew she was easy prey and would be simple to catch if someone took half a mind to do so.

Do you want such a girl, if she can't be faithful to you for even this short time? The old question again, the one he had battered down into silence time after time. Emmy was so lovely, so overpowering to be with. Percy smiled at himself. Overpowering. A good choice of words, there was no doubt of that. She would be a handful to whoever married her, that was for sure.

He missed Melissa. He wished he could show her all the things he'd been seeing, share this world with her. Strange. He should be thinking such thoughts about Emmy. What would Claire say? How would she advise him? She had that rare gift of putting things into perspective so as not to overwhelm one. How he missed her right now!

It was late; he wished sleep would come. In the morning he would go to Louisa and find out what she knew. She must know something! He closed his eyes. The long journey had taken its toll. He slept, and for a while all his dark troubles ceased to exist.

He wasted no time the next morning in getting to Louisa's. Even her housekeeper's face registered surprise at the early hour. She came back with word that her mistress was not yet ready to receive guests.

"I'm not a guest," he retorted. "I'm her brother, and I'll see her right now."

She left the room with his message, and when Louisa came down to greet him, she was alone. She wore a long morning dress and her hair was combed hastily.

"What is it that could be so important?" she demanded. "Have you come to report on your trip?"

She's a calloused little thing, Percy thought. "No, it's more than that. I want to know what you know about Rosie."

"I already told you—"

"Louisa, she's gone! May's whole family has picked up and moved to Australia. Don't tell me you didn't—"

"I did not! I remember—I remember one time when she said something to me about it."

"Well, what did she say?"

Louisa ran a hand through the long hair piled loosely on her head. "It was some time ago." She thought for a moment. "She sat over there in that little green chair. She said John was all fired with enthusiasm about Australia and the opportunities he'd heard were opening up there." Louisa closed her eyes. "I think she frowned and said May would go with him, but she never would. I told her it might be fun and she said it was important for her to stay here."

Percy was hanging on her every word, striving to hold down the hope that began beating against his reason.

"That doesn't sound like she would have gone."

"Percy, her words meant nothing. She was just a young girl expressing her feelings. Young girls do as they're told."

"But she wouldn't have gone without telling you, Louisa, without saying good-bye!"

"I don't think she would have," Louisa said slowly. "That part of it seems strange."

"I must find out for myself," Percy said. "I can't wait for this priest to return in a fortnight's time."

"It will do you no good to go out on a wild-goose chase after him, Percy. You can wait two more weeks. Weren't you going to stay on for a while here?" She gave him a tentative smile. "Sometimes I think Rose is the only one you ever really cared for."

Her words struck a tender nerve. *How true they must seem to her!* "Louisa, please don't, don't think that. Remember how we were, you and I? It's just that Rose was so young, and Mama's favorite and the last one to leave me—"

"I know, Percy." She placed a gentle hand on his arm. "I didn't mean to distress you."

How narrow and bullheaded he felt! "Where's that baby?" he asked. "I haven't even seen my one and only nephew yet. Bring him out here."

"He's not had his bath yet."

"I'll give him his bath. I'm a good hand with children. Then when he's all nice and clean I'll give him the presents I brought from America."

Louisa's face became sweet when she smiled. "Are you sure?"

"Yes, I'm sure. Wait till you see me in action."

Something about her grateful pleasure almost made Percy cry. *What a blind, self-centered fool I've been,* he berated himself angrily. *Even in this thinking only of my own needs and desires.*

He followed her out of the room, checking an impulse to

hug her, satisfying himself with this second chance she had given him.

When Percy headed back to the White Horse Inn it was late afternoon. He was caught up with a sense of peace and well-being, and he rode slowly, enjoying the scenery, watching the people. He had needed this day. What a balm to the spirits a child could be!

He pulled into the inn yard. There were extra horses tied up; he knew the first dinner crowd must be gathering. He gave his horse to a stable boy and was nearly inside before he noticed it. He stopped and turned back to be sure: the large black horse, glistening under the late sun, taller than any horse here. He had seen that horse twice already. Was the young mobber inside?

He went in cautiously, adjusting his eyes to the dim interior. There were fewer men scattered throughout the large public room than he had expected; the bearded young man was not there.

He went up the stairs to his room in a thoughtful mood. He would wash up before dinner. He had a good appetite tonight. He pushed the door open, walked into the room, and had his coat half off before he looked up and noticed the man, sitting like a still, dark statue in the shadowed corner. The high leather boots, well polished, but with a layer of dust now, the well-cut coat, the black, wiry beard, the dark, insolent eyes.

"What are you doing in my room?" Percy snapped. "Who allowed you to enter when I was gone?"

"I have my ways; I am known here." The man did not move; his voice held no expression.

"What do you want of me?"

"No, what do *you* want of *me*?" The young man leaned slightly forward. "It was you who left word for me—Percy." The dark eyes were fixed on him keenly. Percy felt his head reel. Suddenly the sullen face broke into a smile. "Welcome home, brother!"

Percy stood frozen. He knew he revealed no expression; his mind and feelings were blank, wiped clean by this preposterous shock. He stood staring at Stanley until slowly, slowly he *saw*

Stanley there, beyond the insolent bully he had felt almost a hatred for. Stanley watched too, and waited with the poised patience of an experienced alley cat. It was he who broke the thick silence.

"Yes, we are one and the same. I am the rude ruffian who ruffled your feathers."

"Did you know it was me?"

"Know you were the stranger who made a fool of me? In the devil's name, no. I'd not have put up with it if I'd have known then. You have some nerve."

"*I* have nerve! You're an insolent braggart, a petty bully, a—"

"Whoa! Hang on, brother. I'd forgotten that temper of yours." Stanley leaned back and folded his hands over his crossed knee. "You don't look like a hotheaded man." He was enjoying this. "But then, looks can deceive."

"Yours don't. You—"

"Yes, I look mean and little." There was a snarl in his eyes, though he kept his voice even. "Tell me, Percy, do I look rich? Rich and powerful?" He smirked openly. "You see, I am right."

"Why the Mormons? Why them?" Percy demanded.

"I have my reasons!" The snarl was strong in his voice now. "I have my own reasons, you can be sure."

"Beyond what you said when I left, that you decided you would hate the Mormons?"

"Indeed! Beyond that!"

Percy backed off. Something warned him about exploring those reasons right now.

"So, I come back to find you a rich, spoiled Squire." Percy tried a slightly new tack. "How did that happen?" he asked.

Like the cat who had just cleaned the canary's bones, Stanley grinned. "By my own wits I gained the title, Percy. By my own wits! He was a mean man through and through, meaner than you knew, old Geoffrey Beal was." He raised a dark eyebrow. "There is much you don't know."

"Tell me." Percy sat on the edge of the bed. "How did it happen?"

"Well, let's start it right. He was cruel to me, Percy. I didn't even sleep in the house, did you know that? His big house had no corner in it lowly enough for the likes of me — it was that way from the start. But after Geoffrey lost the election, after he realized he was stuck with me, an insolent orphan boy he never wanted in the first place, then the real cruelty in him came out."

Stanley leaned forward, watching Percy's reactions. "He worked me like a common servant, almost like a slave. I ate the leftover slops, I never took meals with him. When he was drunk he'd come home, wake me up, and beat me — usually with the whip that he used on his horses. Do you want to hear more?"

Percy ignored the cold leer on Stanley's features and the sick feeling in his stomach. "Yes, I want to know more." He could hear the voice of the hurt, frightened boy he had known, and it pierced through his head.

"Well, the fact is, I took it. What choice did I have? But I studied him: I learned his habits, his ways. And I knew his weaknesses. When I saw what drink did to him, I took to sneaking into the house at times when he was gone and planting a bottle or two where he'd find them. When the doctor first came I waylaid him and mimicked concern for my poor benefactor, and he told me that the Squire had a serious disease of the liver and drink would kill him if he didn't stay away from it."

Stanley's dark eyes were glowing. "I knew then that I had him in my hands. I laid my plan. I bribed one of the serving girls who was sweet on me to give me the key to his liquor and made sure there was always a bottle at hand. When he was drunk he would talk. I found out where he kept his money and all his deeds —" Stanley grinned at Percy's expression. "Have you had enough?"

"No, go on."

"During the day, during his sober hours, I kept out of his way. When he drank himself into a stupor one cold winter night I found him passed out in the snow and mud. I dragged him into his bed and stayed all night with him. When morning came, I took over. I told the few servants he had that the master was ill, very ill, and had instructed me to take over his house. They were poor, worthless old bags, most of them; they had no heart to challenge me. I had the old doctor sent for. As far as he knew I was the orphan boy the Squire had adopted; it made sense that

I would care for him now. He examined the half-conscious Squire. It seemed his condition was bad, very bad. The doctor left one costly medicine. 'Without it,' he said bluntly, 'the Squire won't live. Give him the medicine, feed him on broths and liquids, and don't let him get chilled. And if we are fortunate—'"

Stanley leaned back, uncrossing his legs and stretching his long boots out into the room. His eyes had a glazed, faraway look. "If we are fortunate! Ah, I would make certain of that! For the first day I did as the doctor instructed and the Squire rallied. I shall never forget the look on his face when he saw *me* bent above him! I made it plain that if he wanted to live, he must give me my dues, he must comply with my terms. Of course, he told me to go to the devil; I knew he would. So I opened all the windows and I kept back his medicine and gave him no food. After a day and a night he was shivering and shaking, burning with fever, and begging for help. I brought in his strongbox with the deeds. 'Sign them over,' I said. 'Make me your heir, and I'll help you to live.'

"Even then he refused. It took a few more days for him to know I meant business."

Dear heaven, Stanley, what is in that head of yours that you could do such a thing and stick to it? Percy marveled. But he kept quiet. Stanley went doggedly on, seeming scarcely aware of his quiet listener now.

"I brought a notary in. I had the deeds witnessed and all made legal. When I knew I had won, when I knew all was legally secured and safe, then I played my hand. I poured out the medicine and filled the bottle with whiskey. I cared for the good Squire myself. Throughout the day I was the picture of decorum. Even the old servants said they couldn't believe how good I was to him who'd been so cruel to me." Stanley's whole face was dark. It made Percy shudder to look upon him.

"What happened then? Did he rally and live?"

"Haven't you been listening, Percy? I poured out the medicine! I didn't feed him—during the cold nights I opened his windows. It didn't take long. Within two weeks he had wasted to a mere pain-racked shadow of himself; in another week he was dead."

Percy stood. He couldn't hold still and listen. He walked to the window and looked out at the approaching night. "For the love of heaven, Stanley, don't you know, don't you know what you did, what you—"

"Come, tell me, brother. He was a cruel, wretched beast; you could not call him a man. *Self-preservation.* That's all there was to it, Percy. He would have died anyway. Maybe that time, maybe the next time. So what harm was done?"

What harm was done!

"You stood by and watched a man die, you—well, you tortured him, Stanley."

"You are melodramatic, Percy. I merely let him stew in his own juices. It was he who tortured me and many others besides— tortured and cheated and turned out homeless." He threw back his shoulders. "It no longer matters! It's over and done! I'm the Squire now. I've got what I want."

"Do you?"

"Oh yes, I do!"

Then why are you so unhappy? Don't you know I can see how unhappy you are?

Percy gathered his wits. He had to go on from here somehow. "What gives you pleasure, Stanley? What's in your life? Do you have a girl you are sweet on?"

Stanley cursed and his voice shook. "I've sworn off women for good! Talk about cruel! Women are weak, heartless creatures!"

"I see. Women and Mormons."

Stanley laughed. "That's right, Percy."

"So, what do you value in life?"

"Power and pleasure." He seemed to caress the words as he spoke them. "Nothing else can be trusted; nothing else lasts."

Percy didn't reply. He could think of nothing to say; he could think of nothing at all.

"I shock you, brother." Stanley's voice was stone cold. "I've been forced to see a darker side of life than you have. You'll get over it, though. Once you go back to Utah where you Mormons belong."

Percy roused himself; the effort was tremendous. "I didn't come back to quarrel, to discuss morals or religion, I came back—" *Why did I come back?*

"You came back to prove a point, and you've done it. You've impressed me, brother."

"To keep a promise," Percy protested.

"Same thing." Stanley shrugged, but his eyes were bright pinpricks. "I mean it when I say you've impressed me. It took some courage to come back. Not to speak of money. Are you in need of money, Percy?"

"Shut up, Stanley. Does all this mean nothing to you? Do you think me a fool?"

"Well put, Percy. You said it yourself. Be honest for once, if you've the stomach to. Why did you make that crazy promise in the first place? You made it for *you*. You needed it more than any of us did, Percy. And why have you come back? Because you *needed* to come back! Not for our sakes. What's in it for us?"

He hasn't really changed. He was like this when I left him: unsure of himself, unable to love, to give in, to reveal anything that might come back and hurt him. Percy had no reply. Behind the twisted cruelty of Stanley's words there was a strong strain of truth. He felt his brother had stripped him and he stood naked, without purpose, excuse, or defense.

"Don't take it so hard, Percy. You're human like the rest of us." Stanley stood with a long stretch. "Though I suspect you don't often like to admit that, nor to think of yourself in those lowly terms." He laughed at his own cleverness. "Mormons are such arrogant fools! How did they dupe you, my lad? You don't look like the type who'd—"

"Leave it alone, Stanley. Stop it!"

"All right, brother, all right." He paused for a moment, as though to catch his own breath. "Will you come down to supper with me? Compliments of the Squire."

"You could really eat, Stanley? You have an appetite?"

"You're a strange one, Percy. I thought life on the frontier would have hardened you."

"It's taught me a few lessons."

"It has? Well, they don't show." Stanley reached for his black hat. "Some other time."

"I'll hold you to that. But there's one more thing."

"What's that, brother?"

"Where's Rose?"

For just an instant a look crossed the dark face, but it passed too quickly for Percy to read or to name it.

"You mean you haven't seen Rosie yet? I would have guessed she'd be the first one you'd go to."

"I've tried. Don't tell me you know nothing of her, that you've kept no better track of her than Louisa has."

"The black sheep who has been busy securing his fortune? Why would I have time for Rose?" He flicked a piece of dirt from the rim of his hat and twirled it around in his hands. "Rose has been the best cared for of any of us. Why should we be concerned about her?"

"Do you see her often? Did you know May and her new husband have emigrated to Australia?"

"I knew that they might."

"And what of Rose? Have they taken her with them?"

"It looks that way, doesn't it?" Stanley stood back and grinned. "Poor Percy. Things aren't working out how you wanted them to, I can tell. I believe you shall have to go home without seeing Rose, Percy. Are you going back soon?"

"Not too soon," Percy growled. He had the distinct impression that Stanley not only didn't care about him being here — he wanted him gone! "I've come a long way to do certain things, Stanley, and I'm going to do them."

"Well, enjoy your stay, but don't get into any trouble."

"What does that mean?"

"Take it how you like. But you can read one meaning into it for certain: don't get mixed up with the Mormons while you're here."

"That's absurd. I am a Mormon, I'm mixed up with them already."

"Why does that have to be? Why do you have to associate with them during this brief time?"

"That's just how it is. Mormonism's a way of life. Wherever you are, you indulge in it." Percy stressed the last words slightly; the effect was not lost on his listener.

"Well, you'll be taking your chances, then."

"That's fine with me."

Stanley nodded his head in slightly exaggerated acknowledgment. "I'll be off for now. Will you come to the mansion some evening for dinner if I invite you?"

"Of course I will."

"Good." Stanley had his hand on the door.

"You're not going to tell me any more about Rose?"

"I have nothing to tell."

The devil you haven't!

"All right, Stanley. Thanks for the visit. If you don't come around soon, I'll be in touch."

"Good night, brother."

"Good night."

Stanley walked out and the small room went still. Percy could hear the creaks in the stairs as Stanley walked down them; he could hear the low, indistinct murmur of voices from the public room, like the backdrop of insects on a still summer day. He could hear his own breathing. He stared into the stillness and asked the question out loud: *What in the name of kind heaven do I do now?*

6

*B*y the time he was through shaving and dressing in the morning Percy had made up his mind. He would leave for Liverpool this very morning. He could stay with Mildred Boswell in Warrington and with her help find this priest. He ought to check with May's neighbor first to see if she might know the name of the relative the priest was staying with. He had to know now, know for certain if Rosie had gone to Australia with May and John Thomas. If she was gone he would somehow face the pain of it. But if not, then where was she? Where was his Rose?

He would speak with the landlord and make some travel arrangements, then come back upstairs and pack.

As he started down the stairs he ran straight into a young boy who was fairly flying up past him.

"Easy, lad," he said, steadying the boy. "Is there something the matter?"

"Might you be Brother Graham, Percy Graham?" the boy asked.

"Yes, I am."

The boy leaned against the railing to catch his breath. There was an open relief on his features. "Would you come with me, sir? My father said you would."

"Who is your father?"

"Phillip Clark. He's the president of the conference here. You met him at the baptism."

"Oh yes, of course. What is the trouble?" Percy thought at once of the black horse and its rider.

"My sister. She's ill, very ill. My mother called Father from work, and there are no other elders available to administer to her. You will come?"

"Yes, I'll come." The journey could wait; it would have to wait for this, no matter how his impatience plagued him. "Let me lock my room. I'll meet you in the front of the inn, lad."

It was only a short distance to President Clark's home. When they got there his boy took the horses and Percy went right into the house.

"Thank heaven my son found you!" Brother Clark pumped Percy's hand. "It's my Allison. She's been sick for a week now, but last night she grew worse. Her fever's been rising all day, she's near delirious, the doctor despairs. I know of nothing else that will help her but this, Brother Graham."

"Do you have oil?"

"Yes, I have oil."

"Where is she?"

"In here, in the small room behind the stairs where her mother can care for her."

They walked back and entered the hush of the little sickroom. How unexpectedly cheerful it was! Chintz curtains hung at the small, high window, a patterned quilt lay over the bed, there were pictures on the walls and a flowering plant by the bedside.

"What a lovely room," Percy cried. "One could get better in such a room."

Brother Clark smiled. "This is my Dorothy's doing; she has a homey touch. If Allison would just open her eyes—"

"She'll open her eyes, President Clark." Percy said the words calmly, but once they were out he thought: *Why? Why in the world did I say such a thing to a worried father, when I know nothing at all?*

"Would you pronounce the blessing? Would you be voice?" Brother Clark asked him. The request took him a bit by surprise. "I feel it should be you."

Percy drew a deep breath. He had done this before. He had a reputation, in fact, with the Lamanites; some of the tribes called him "the healer." But this was different. He felt out of tune here in England, as though a film lay upon his awareness, his faculties.

"I'd like to have a prayer first. Alone, for just a moment?"

"Of course." His host tiptoed out of the room and shut the door behind him. Percy knelt by the bed. As soon as his eyes were closed he felt a sweet spirit enfold him; he felt all his own cares relax, fall away from him, leaving him open and willing, cleansed. He rose and looked down at the bed.

The sick girl was very lovely. Long, dark ringlets curled around her pale face; she had an aquiline nose and a small mouth quite perfectly formed.

Percy went to the door and admitted her father. He smiled at the worn, anxious man. They placed their hands on the dark head and proceeded with the ordinance that never failed to thrill Percy. Perhaps he was a little unusual that way. All the ordinances of the gospel had this influence upon him, this solemn effect on his heart and senses.

As soon as he started to speak, the words he should say came to him. He promised recovery, total recovery, and the prospect of health and a long, useful life, and a blessing of being a mother in Zion. He wondered where that last had come from. When he pronounced the amen he felt drained and yet peaceful, and in some way, renewed.

He looked over at President Clark; there were tears in his eyes. The girl, Allison, stirred; her father moved to bend over her. Very slowly she opened her eyes: small, deep eyes, summer blue, touched now with the faintest of smiles, a very faint, glowing light.

"Father . . ."

"Yes, my love, I'm here, I'll get Mother." He turned and slipped out of the room. Allison sighed and moved her head slightly, and her blue eyes met Percy's. Without the expression on her face seeming to change, her eyes smiled at him, smiled with a warmth that seemed to penetrate all the way through him.

"I know you," she said. "You blessed me just now, didn't you?"

"Yes," he answered.

"I heard your voice—I recognized it." Her voice was weak, but her words perplexed him. *The confusions of a sick mind.*

Her mother glided into the room, took up the slender, limp hand and kissed it.

"Oh, my Allison, thank heaven you are back."

Allison smiled at her mother, but then her eyes searched for Percy. As she lifted her head something slid from the folds of her nightgown: a small golden locket. She reached up to her neck and felt for it with her free hand. Percy watched, thinking nothing, except perhaps of the pretty scene before him of mother and daughter. Then something reached out to him, drew his attention.

The locket Allison's long fingers played with — he had seen it before. *No, surely not.* Her fingers slipped from it; Percy leaned carefully closer. He knew that thin oval shape, the faint *M* in a fine scroll etched on it. *It couldn't be.* Some kind of coincidence, some trick of the mind. The old gold blinked back at him.

"Allison," he whispered, "what is that locket — " The blue eyes were closed; long lashes brushed her white skin.

"She's gone to sleep. It's a good, peaceful sleep," her mother murmured. "She will wake up refreshed."

The locket trembled with her breathing, disappeared under the lace of her gown. Her parents were leaving the room. Reluctantly, his thoughts churning into confusion, Percy followed them.

"May I come back?" He hoped he didn't appear to them as strange as he felt. "I must speak to Allison soon — as soon as she's able."

"Of course. Why don't you come back tonight?" Her father was smiling at him.

"Come here for dinner," Sister Clark urged.

"No, I couldn't do that."

"We would love your company," she persisted. "And you need a good, home-cooked meal. Don't try to tell me you don't." She squeezed his thin arm with her own plump, white hand.

"All right, I'll come."

"Good. Be here by five o'clock, my lad, and no later."

"I will, ma'am, and thank you."

"Heavens, Brother Graham, no, we thank *you*. You have a gift for healing, haven't you?" Her eyes were misted and her voice very soft.

"Some say I do, Sister Clark, and if it's in any way true, I'm very glad to have been able to use it for you and your child."

There was too much emotion in the atmosphere for Percy to handle; he was relieved when he reached the front door, when he found himself out in the warm summer morning. There was a climbing rosebush by the door; he hadn't noticed it when he went in. Several small, perfect buds were breaking out. They looked white, but they were really pale pink. He bent to smell one. *Liverpool!* He had completely forgotten. Well, he wouldn't be going there now. Obviously the trip was no longer his primary lead. The most important thing now was the locket. *It couldn't be!* And yet he had seen it with his own eyes.

He walked out to his horse. He didn't see the three riders approaching. Not until he had mounted and turned did he look, did the sight of them register. He moved his small, ordinary brown horse until it was blocking their way. They pulled rein angrily, with an abundance of colorful oaths.

"What are you doing here?" he demanded. "What is it now?"

"This is the Mormon leader's house," one of them growled back at him. "We've got our own business here."

"You have no business here, not on this day." Percy moved close to the man, so that their horses' noses were nearly touching. He spoke over his shoulder. "Stanley, what's this about?"

He wasn't sure his brother would give him an answer. "If you must know, Harry here works at the mill where Mr. Clark works — we keep our eye on him that way." His tone was lazy, almost disinterested. "He left work early this morning, in some haste. We wondered what business he might be about."

Percy turned to face Stanley. "Don't you get sick of this nonsense?" he demanded. "Stanley, don't you get sick of it?"

"What is this, Stanley?" one of his companions growled.

"Shut up, Harry!" Stanley lowered his head, as though wanting to rush Percy. "No, I don't."

"You enjoy persecuting innocent people?"

Stanley swore fiercely. "I enjoy persecuting Mormons. There's no such thing as an *innocent* Mormon, Percy."

He believes it, Percy thought.

"Now, get out of my way!"

Percy moved closer. He leaned across to his brother. "I've just been in there," he said. "His daughter is very ill. That's why he came home. There's nothing mysterious going on today, just a sick daughter. So leave him alone."

"Who is he to tell us our business?" Harry growled, inching closer.

"Shut up, Harry, I said!" Stanley's eyes were dark pools of hatred. They drew a feeling from Percy that was part anguish, part rage. "Do you remember what I told you last night, Percy?"

"I remember." He forced his own gaze to remain steady. "Do you want to fight it out now? I have no intentions of backing down on this."

To his surprise Stanley laughed. "Do you recall how I told you I gained the inheritance, brother? *By my wits.* I gain what I want by my wits. If I want something from you I will find a better way than a street fight to get it."

The disdain in his voice was unmistakable. Percy felt the force of it like a blow.

"You're trying my patience, Percy. This is the last time. Don't get in my way again." Stanley turned his horse sharply. "We're going back, boys," he announced. Though the others looked dark, they hazarded no reply.

"Go home, Percy, you don't belong here." There was a melancholy in his words Percy didn't expect. "I repeat: don't get in my way again, or next time you'll be sorry."

I'm already sorry. Percy held Stanley's eyes though his own burned. For a moment the cold gaze seemed to waver, grow soft. Then Stanley threw back his bearded head and rode off. Percy watched him. The peace of the sickroom was shattered. The fragments, like small shards of glass, cut him.

Stanley was no longer in sight. Percy rode slowly back through the city, and as slowly gathered his wits. Now and again he would pass some place that was known to him: the school he had attended as a boy, a millinery shop his mother had frequented, the house of a friend. Each one seemed to jar him in a way that was painful. When he came to the church, the tall, dark church with the old manse behind it, he slowed his horse to a walk. Here rested memories in plenty! He drew up by the fence, past the main gate that led to the buildings. This fence stood on the side that sloped down to the river and shaded the graves of generations of parishioners, three hundred years' worth and more.

He tied his horse to one of the fence posts and went in. Here was peace again—peace too deep for any human emotion to hinder. He stretched out on the grass, closed his eyes, and let the feeling seep into him. *Why didn't I think to come here? Is my brain so addled that I'd have gone back without paying respect to the graves of my parents?*

He lifted his head, aware of the bee that buzzed by his left ear; he had always been wary of bees. Otherwise there was no sound. There seemed to be no living creature in this place besides himself and the lone working bee.

He rose to his feet. He knew where the grave was. He worked his way through the unpatterned forest of gray stones that leaned at haphazard angles to the ground and each other. He liked the feel of this place. He had often wandered here as a boy; he knew many of the names and inscriptions, although some of the oldest ones were faded past reading. He knew most of the families that held distinguished places from generation to generation; he even knew some of their histories. His father's people were buried here, but few of his mother's. He was reaching the row of Joneses, the line of his father's mother, now the small cluster of Grahams.

The last time he was here the grave had been new, lately dug, scantily covered with the grass that needed time to force its tough roots deep again. Now he walked past the place the first time because it looked so much like the others.

Over ten years they have lain here. He bent down and pulled a small cluster of weeds from one end of the headstone. *They have lain sleeping while I have pushed and struggled my way into manhood, while I've traveled half the globe and made a life that is foreign to all they ever knew.*

He realized they had not really slept as their bodies did. But, nevertheless, they were gone: as silent, as lost to him as if enclosed in that grave. They were buried on top of each other and shared one common stone: *Oscar Graham*, it read, and *Beloved Wife— Suzanne Miller Graham.* Names. Just names, like the hundreds of others here.

Percy dropped to his knees. *Mother, Mother, what shall I do with Stanley? How can I help him?* He had never longed for her more. *I'll find Rosie and take care of her, Mother. I promise I will.*

He lowered his head, humbled by his own feelings. *Here I am, at it again, making new promises when I've not even kept the old ones yet.* These brothers and sisters were grown people now who in some ways were strangers to him. Strangers formed by the good and bad of the lives they had lived, the strengths and weaknesses inside them.

He didn't see her approach; he didn't notice a shadow, a movement, a feeling. When she spoke his name it brought him back from the world of his memory with a terrible jolt.

"Percy Graham! Are my eyes deceiving me? Is it you?"

He looked up. The direct sun in his eyes mottled his sight, but he knew her instantly.

"Jane Evans, my old guardian angel." He rose and held out his hand to her. "Yes, I'm back for a spell, for a visit." She clung to his fingers a minute. Her hand felt pleasant and cool. "How is the vicar?"

"He is well, we are both well."

"You look well—you look good. I recognized you instantly because you haven't seemed to age any."

What he told her was true, but he wished to please her, nonetheless. A slight blush touched her cheeks. She was not an unattractive woman at all; he could see that now. When he was a boy, when she had borne down upon them with her self-righteous zeal and that touch of cold thoroughness, he had seen only that: a thin, dry, small-hearted woman. He saw more than that now.

"You look marvelous yourself, young man," she returned with an effusiveness rare to her. "You still favor your mother. Goodness, I never thought to set eyes upon you again."

"Well, life is strange."

"Yes, it is." She looked down at the grave. "Have things gone well for you, Percy?"

"I believe they have. I've been kindly cared for and loved by good people, and I've had experiences I would never have dreamed of."

"So I have heard." The pursed mouth, the slight chill to her speech—he could smile at it now. He thought he would try his hand at wooing her out of it. "I must ask—and don't take offense, Percy—but is it true that those people who took you in were really Mormons—were of that *persuasion?*" She spoke the word as though it might be a disease.

"Yes," he answered mildly.

"Did you know that at first?"

"Heavens no, I didn't find out until much later—when they took me to church."

Jane Evans stifled her horrified reaction into a handkerchief. "How dreadful for you! They made you—attend with them?" She could not quite speak the word *worship* in such a context.

"No, I really must be fair. They never forced me, they just requested that I give their religion a chance. Since I would be living with them they wanted me to at least have some under-standing of their way of life."

"I see." She had to give justice where justice was due, yet she drew herself up, in that straight pose which lent her authority.

"So I studied their books, all I could find printed about them." He fixed his eyes on her eyes. "And I came to know for myself that Mormonism is true, that it contains the fullness of the gospel the Savior taught, as well as the authority to administer it."

He paused. He gave her his most beneficent smile. With a sentence he had slain her. She stood defenseless, dumbfounded. He took pity and broke into her suffering.

"By some chance have you any of those tea cakes with the raspberry jam in the middle that you used to make?"

She blinked a time or two. "You remember those, Percy?"

"I do."

"Well, as a matter of fact, I have a fresh batch in the cupboard from yesterday's baking."

"Fine! If you'll invite me inside I'll tell you all about my adventures with runaway buffalo herds and wild Indians."

The hanky went up to her mouth again. "Are such things true?

I have often wondered if they were not simply tall tales invented in some overrich mind."

What a gem she is! "I'm afraid they are all true, Mrs. Evans—too true." They began walking up the slope to the manse, which stood stern in the shadow of tall, age-old trees. "Most of the Indians wear little more than breechcloths, you know, and they eat red, uncooked meat and at certain seasons insects—"

She shuddered. "Percy, my dear! And you have seen this?"

"With my own eyes, and much more."

They entered the tall, solemn house, already lost in the world of Percy's lurid descriptions and preposterous tales.

Percy dressed carefully for the evening, though he couldn't have answered precisely why. He would certainly be under only a friendly, casual scrutiny from the kind Brother Clark and his agreeable wife. And the sick girl, Allison—what a lovely name that was—at best he could hope to find her awake and coherent enough to understand and respond to him.

He arrived precisely at five, thoroughly wet from a downpour that darkened the hours before their time. He had never seen a place where it rained so much! He didn't remember this much rain from his childhood. Dorothy Clark met him at the door. The aroma of rich, well-cooked food reached his nostrils before he had entered the house.

"If your food tastes half as good as it smells, Sister Clark," he told her, "I'll wager that I'm about to eat the best meal I've tasted in over six months."

She smiled, pleased, and her husband said, "Get ready, then."

The air was a festive one. Allison must be improving. "Is your daughter better?" he asked.

"Better?" The president roared out the word. "She's a new girl. As fit and sassy as she was a fortnight ago, before the fever struck."

"It is your doing," Sister Clark said, as though pronouncing a verdict.

"I had a little help," Percy laughed.

"Well, we are being careful with her to make sure," her

mother admitted. "Only soup and teas taken in bed, for a few days at least. Though she wanted dearly to sit at table with you, Brother Graham."

"Call me Percy, please."

"All right, I shall."

"May I talk with her after the meal?" Had she forgotten his morning's request?

"She's looking forward to it—by all means," Brother Clark assured him. "Shall we eat, my dear?"

"Yes, all is ready. Sit here, Percy, where I can see you and make sure you're well fed."

He passed the bounds of good manners, he knew; he filled his plate up three times. But the homemade biscuits, the lamb, the thick gravy, the fresh garden peas, and the rich trifle she served for dessert—there was no way to resist it. His friendly prediction had been right on the mark: Sister Clark was an excellent cook. The two sons—the one who had come for him and a younger boy—kept the table in enough commotion that Percy hoped no one took too much note of his excesses. For a time he even forgot the sick girl and the actual purpose of his coming. When he recalled it to mind, his full stomach churned and he begged for a stroll in the shadowed garden to walk off the effects of his meal. As it was, he played ball with the two boys and filled half an hour that way, and felt much more prone to face the languid recoverer than he had when sitting to table.

When he walked into her room he was not prepared for the change he saw in her. She was sitting in bed. Her hair was combed and her face, though pale, seemed to shine with an interest he would not have expected from a girl who had been at the point of death.

There was a chair by the bed; he sat down in it. Allison smiled, a bit shyly. "I want to thank you," she said. "Mother and Father are convinced you saved my life."

"It wasn't me. They know that."

"Yes, they do, but they're so grateful." She smiled. She had a low, lovely voice and her blue eyes were as deep as he re-membered them. "Father says you're just visiting here."

"Yes, that's right. I lived here as a boy; this is where I accepted the gospel."

"But you live in Zion now?"

"Yes, I went to America when I was only fourteen."

"What an adventure that must have been!"

"It was an adventure. In fact, it still is. I suppose my life has held an unusual amount of adventure."

"Father seems to think so. He said you drove wagon teams for the Church and you've lived with the Indians and smoked peace pipes and been on buffalo hunts. Is that true?"

"All true. But it's not as fantastic as it sounds, really."

She lifted a hand from the coverlet in a small, resigned move-ment. "To one who has been nowhere and done nothing out of the ordinary it seems fantastic enough." She closed her eyes for a moment and sighed. "I have dreams about Zion. I long to go there. But I don't think we ever will. Father hasn't much wish to leave England, and he knows the Church needs leadership here. So he seems content to work and organize and send everyone else off—as long as it isn't himself."

I'll take you to Zion, he wanted to say, but how could he? "I hope you will be able to go. If you want to that badly."

Her smile turned a bit sad. "Don't you wish life worked that way? If you want something badly enough, it will be given to you?"

Her fingers played at the lace of her collar, played with the thin gold locket that nestled there. Percy leaned forward. "Alli-son?"

"Yes?"

"I have something I must ask you. Please don't think me rude, but it's important to me. Very important."

Her blue eyes were wide with innocent interest. "What is it?"

"That locket you wear—can you tell me anything about it? Can you tell me where you got it?"

She glanced down. Her eyes clouded. "Why do you want to know?"

"For very personal reasons. Please tell me anything that you can."

"It has a quite singular story," she said, "and I've never told anyone before." She looked at him closely. "But I suppose I can tell you."

She leaned back against the pillows with a sigh. "I don't know where to begin. Last year, a year ago last spring, I noticed a new girl who had begun to attend some of our meetings. She always came alone, and seemed not to know anyone, so I made her my friend. I lent her the materials she wanted to read, I answered her questions. For her birthday I gave her a Book of Mormon." Allison smiled sweetly, remembering. "We talked easily, she and I, and got along as well as sisters would. When summer came I remember how distressed she was. She said she might have to leave, go far away from here, and she didn't want that. For a time she seemed fearful, preoccupied."

Allison paused for a moment. Her blue eyes were disturbed with her contemplations; her small mouth was pursed thoughtfully. "It's strange, I never really thought about it, but I realize now that, although we could talk upon a variety of subjects — music, nature, poetry, pastimes, and friends — she never spoke about herself or her own life. I knew very little of that." She shook her head as though the idea distressed her.

"No matter. Whatever it was that disturbed her must have resolved itself, for she told me one day, *I have made new arrangements, I shall not have to leave.* I was happy for her and along with her; I had not wanted to lose my dear friend. For a time all seemed smooth, she seemed happy, happier than ever before. Then a slow change came about: she grew quiet, at times almost timid, almost fearful, it seemed. If I asked her about it she would say, *Never mind. There is nothing you can do except pray for me.*"

Allison looked up at Percy, her eyes were misted. "I did pray, you know."

"When was this? Over what length of time?"

"I believe the change came after Christmas and progressed slowly until some time in April when she came to me."

She. Percy could bear the suspense no longer. "Who is she? What is her name?"

Concern flicked in the blue eyes. "Suzanne."

"*Suzanne!* That can't be!" He rose with a vehement move that nearly upset the chair. She leaned out from her pillows as if to assist him somehow, but she had no strength. Percy saw what he was doing.

"I'm sorry," he soothed. "You're not strong enough for this. Try to calm yourself, please. I must hear to the end. I must!"

"I am fine," she assured him.

"All right," Percy pressed. "This Suzanne came to you and gave you the locket."

"She did."

"She wanted you to keep it for her. But why?" Percy was almost thinking out loud.

"She seemed beside herself, almost incoherent. She came to the house and we walked outside in that very garden. I asked her if she were ill. She smiled back wistfully, but she gave me no answer."

"What else did she say? Try to remember every word she spoke."

Allison closed her clear eyes. Percy could see the strain of her concentration. He held his breath.

"She said: *I have tried so hard, Allison, but there is no help for me.* I didn't know what she meant. It was then that she gave me the locket. *You must take this for me,* she said, *please.*

" 'Suzanne, why?' I asked. 'It is your treasure, you wear it constantly. It looks old, it looks dear.'

"*It was my mother's,* she said, *but it is not for that reason alone that I value it. Someday my brother will come looking for me, he will look for this locket.*

"Her beautiful eyes filled with tears; I remember that well. *He will come looking for the most lovely of all the young girls he finds to see if she is wearing this locket. And then he will know he has found me again.*"

Percy had put his head down between his knees. He had grown very quiet. Allison studied him a moment and then continued more softly.

" 'Then you should be wearing this,' I argued, 'not I.'

"*Something might happen to me*, she said, *but if he comes he will find you.*

" 'How do you know that?' I demanded, confused, but she would not say. *If he comes, if he comes looking for me, tell him not to give up. Tell him I am near and I need him, and I love him.* That's what she said. I wrote it in my diary, and I've read it back to myself often."

"Did you ever see her again?" Percy's voice was muffled; he did not raise his head.

"Yes, I did, once or twice. Then suddenly nothing, just as she said—no word, no appearance. I have not seen her since."

He could not move; he was aware of nothing but this terrible pain and the need to control it before the young girl who was watching him. He felt her hand come to rest on his shoulder. Its tenderness drew what was left of his resistance. The tears ran down his cheeks.

"You are crying," she said softly. "Who are you? Please tell me what you know. You know something that I don't."

"She said her name was Suzanne. Suzanne what?"

"Suzanne Miller."

"Of course. That was my mother's name." He raised his head slowly. "She did that for some reason of her own. Suzanne isn't her name. Her name is Rose, Rosie Graham. She is my little sister. I am the brother she waited for, the brother she believed would come for her."

"Can this be true? Are you sure?"

Percy feared Allison would faint before his eyes, she appeared so pale. He took her thin hand and laid it gently back under the coverlet.

"When our parents died ten years ago we were all parceled out; the vicar's wife found places with whoever would take us. It was dreadful," he said. "Rose was only seven years old and Dr. Davies and his daughter, May, who had just lost her young husband, took Rosie in. The day she left—" He paused, finding it hard to go on. "The day she left I gave her Mother's old locket to keep. She was afraid I wouldn't recognize her when she came back, so—"

"I see," Allison whispered. She lifted the locket on the palm of her hand. "And this is that locket?"

Percy bent over it. "Yes, it is."

She sunk back again. He had worn her out. He took her hand and said gently, "I am sorry to have put you through this. Rest now."

"Will you come back tomorrow?"

"To torment you more?"

"Please."

"If you want me."

"Yes, we've only begun . . ." she closed her eyes. "Good-bye, Percy Graham, till tomorrow."

"Good-bye, Allison," he replied. There was a strange feeling upon him. "Rest well."

It was difficult to walk out of that room into the real world. Allison's parents noticed a change in him, or seemed to sense something.

"Is she resting now?" her father asked.

"Yes."

"Then we'll let her alone."

Percy made pleasant conversation with them for a few minutes, then slipped away. He picked one of the rosebuds that had begun to blossom and tucked it in his lapel. *Love is like a lovely rose, the world's delight* . . . he still had so many unanswered questions! Yet this much he knew: Rose was not lost to him! She had not gone with John and May to Australia. *But where was she?*

This is what my dream meant! It seemed preposterous, yet he knew that she was not safe, that at this moment she was suffering. The thought drove him wild. It would be a long, painful time until tomorrow when he could see Allison and talk with her again.

7

*H*e found Allison in the garden next morning. It was a picture he saw. She was stretched out on a long reclining chair that was covered with cushions and pillows of various shapes and sizes. Her thick, dark hair was pulled back into loose curls at her neck. She wore a bright red skirt and a blouse of some filmy material with long, flowing sleeves that tightened to show her thin wrists. She held out her hand.

"Percy! I've been hoping you would come while I was still up and feeling strong." She sighed happily as he sat down beside her. "The garden is yet lovely," she murmured, glancing around, "though the heat has wilted some of the more frail of the blossoms."

Her voice is music, Percy thought, *low and sweet, like the sound of the spring wind in the mountain pines.*

"I've been thinking," she said. "I've tried very hard to remember more of what Suzanne, I mean Rose, more of what Rose said that day. I have a few little bits that might help you."

Percy felt his pulse quicken. "Yes?"

"Well . . ." she was hesitant, "they might mean nothing at all. But there are two things. I remember once, close to the beginning of our friendship, asking her why she always came alone. She replied, *No one else wants me here. I have agreed to certain conditions in order that I might come* — or something like that."

Percy was perplexed. "Would May have been so hard on Rose in a matter of religion?" he wondered out loud. "Perhaps. Although she was a sweet, gentle person, I did not know her well.

Even the old doctor — people do strange things when it come to religion — "

"To Mormonism in particular."

"I've noticed."

"But it might not have been that. It might have been something to do with family," Allison suggested.

"I doubt that," Percy responded reluctantly. "Although all three were right here in Birmingham, my brother and sisters have not stayed in close touch."

"You have another brother?" Allison demanded excitedly.

"Yes."

"That might explain it, then." Her eyes widened to reveal her excitement. "When she gave me the locket, when Rose spoke of her brother, she may not have always meant you. Once she said, *He doesn't mean to be violent, but there are times when I fear.*"

Percy leaned forward. "What else? Anything else?"

"I don't remember. I believe there was more, but I don't remember." She was distressed; he took her hand — so soft, so cool it felt.

"Allison, please. Please don't upset yourself. You've been a great help. And more than that; it is a pleasure to be in your company. Tell me something of yourself, of your own life — "

"You're just being polite." Again he sensed the girlish embarrassment behind her shy smile.

"I am seething with questions and fears and half-impressions, I'll admit. But putting all that aside, I meant what I said," he urged.

There is something about her. I can see why Rose was drawn to her.

"Well, then, tell me: what is Rose like?"

Allison smiled, glad to turn the subject away from herself. "Very sweet. A little quiet in her ways, but given to enthusiasm when she feels strongly about something."

Percy laughed. "That's a family trait."

"She's very pretty," Allison continued, "with masses of golden-red hair and a nose that is more adorable than pretty; it nearly turns up on the end. Kind eyes, but sad in a way." She paused. "I wish I had a picture to show you."

"I wish I had a picture of the two of you," he mused, "the two prettiest girls in England."

She laughed out loud, but she colored a little. "What are you going to do?"

Percy tilted his head and gave her a long, thoughtful gaze. "I'm not sure. Lots of possibilities I could try. I know only one thing for certain: I'm going back to question my brother. I believe that's the best place to start."

She was watching him carefully. Her eyes made him uncomfortable. "But, meantime, go on. Tell me something about yourself, Allison. I'll not leave till you do."

She hesitated a little, but once he got her talking the minutes fled past, the slight awkwardness between them dissipated into the rich summer air, and they were both startled to see her mother approaching to shoo Percy off. Allison would not let him leave until he had promised to return.

"I must know what your brother has to say," she reminded him.

He nodded grimly. "It may not be fit for your ears." He lifted her hand and kissed the delicate fingers.

"Take care, Percy."

Why did she say that?

He left her feeling strong inside, resolved, and — happy. There was no better way to describe her effect on him, to put words to the way he felt.

Percy tried Stanley's house several times during the course of the day; the master was never at home. At last he camped out, as it were, on the doorstep until Stanley's man admitted him.

"I'll wait here in the library," Percy informed him, after looking around. The rooms were grand indeed, richly furnished. Percy guessed most of the things had sat in their places for three or four generations. He believed some of them could use a good dusting and polishing, but he didn't say that. The whole place could use the touch of a woman.

"It may be some time yet, sir," the servant reminded him.

Percy nodded agreeably. "I feel at home with these books, I'll be fine."

The man scowled, but had to leave him. Despite the books, the hours did grow long. Percy feared he must have drowsed off once or twice; it was the sound of voices that woke him. He straightened his clothes, ran his fingers through his hair, and went out to face his brother.

The five young people he saw, stumbling and leaning against one another as they made their way across the front hall, were quite thoroughly drunk. An impatient anger flared at his temples. This was not what he wanted—but never mind, it would just have to do. He walked with long, purposeful strides out to meet them. Stanley saw him and scowled, hunching his shoulders the way Percy had seen angry bears do.

"What's your pleasure, brother?" he grinned. "Come to join the party? You're in luck, we've got an extra girl."

"I'm here to talk to you, Stanley."

Stanley ignored him and slipped his arm around the waist of one of the girls, then bent to kiss her neck. "I'm busy," he slurred.

The sullen servant had appeared. Percy addressed him with an assumptive air that he hoped carried more confidence than he felt. "Escort these people to wherever they're going. I'm sure they can occupy themselves. The Squire and I will be in the library for the next little while."

He stepped up and took Stanley's arm firmly. The limp girl slid away and followed, giggling, after the others. With an oath Stanley shook Percy off, but he went along with him.

"What in the deuce do you want? Haven't you had enough yet?"

"Not by a long shot."

With exaggerated nonchalance Stanley sprawled on the leather sofa. Percy, infuriated by his insolence, pulled him up by the collar. Stanley reached out to hit him, but Percy grabbed his flailing arm and held it.

"Where is Rose, Stanley? Where is she?"

"Is that why you came?" Stanley leered at him.

"Stop the pretense, brother. I know she's had contact with you. I know she's *here*. She did not go to Australia with May—"

"Who says?"

"I believe she's here, and in trouble. You know something, tell me! You know where she is."

Percy had twisted Stanley's collar until he was choking him. With an ugly threat Stanley pulled back. His eyes had narrowed to two mean, glowing lights.

"You don't know what you're talking about!"

"Oh yes, I do. I'll thrash you to within an inch of your life if—"

Stanley laughed and thrust Percy's hands away from him. "Don't threaten me." His voice had turned suddenly mean. "Don't threaten me here. You'll get more than you bargained for, brother."

He straightened himself surreptitiously. "For the last time, Percy, I have no intention of helping you. I'll tell you this much: Rose is beyond your power. You'll never find her!"

Percy went cold at his words. "She's your sister, for the love of heaven, Stanley! What have you done?"

"Don't start your family bit again, Percy. You sicken me," Stanley growled.

"Do you have the button I gave you?" Percy asked. "Did you keep it?"

"Your precious button?" Stanley leered at him. "Oh, I kept it, like the pathetic fool that I was, out in the carriage house in a box I had hidden beneath the gear. I kept it until the day old Geoffrey gasped his last. Do you know what I did then?" He stumbled to his feet and stood tottering unsteadily. He moved in a crooked line to the window and clutched the thick folds of the drape as he yanked it open.

"Do you see the large pond out there? When the old man was good and dead I walked out to that pond, I gave one long shout of triumph, and I took your button—" He reached into his vest pocket as if to reenact it. "I took that miserable thing and flung it as far as I could into the water."

Percy dropped his gaze before the anger and hatred reaching out to him.

"Do you know what that means?" Stanley was shouting now; Percy's own anger was trembling.

"That means I am no longer an unfortunate, unwanted orphan. I am Master Beal!"

"Amen to the old life and all that it meant?"

"That's right!" Stanley leaned against the drapery, breathing heavily, his eyes hot and glazed.

"Then why did you help Rose at all in the first place?"

Percy saw the hesitation, the pain Stanley was working so hard to mask. "She came to me, she's a pretty young girl. Could I turn her away?"

Percy moved a step closer, but Stanley had caught his mistake. He lunged forward and locked both his hands around Percy's neck. With a series of ugly names he accused him. "Don't trick me like that again!" he threatened. Then with a savage move of contempt he shoved Percy away from him.

"Get out of my house!" He hissed the words; his voice bordered on madness.

The door opened. Had he pushed some concealed button? Percy was struggling for breath, gulping air into his burning lungs. Stanley was a big, brutal man. If he hadn't been drunk—

"Get him out of here!"

Percy felt hands pass under his armpits and close tight on his chest. The weasely little servant was as tough as new wire. It took all Percy's effort to shake him off.

"I will leave, but I leave of my own accord," Percy stuttered. He was almost breathless now.

"Don't come back, don't come here again, Percy. I warn you!"

Percy stumbled out of the room, through the swimming hall toward the fresh outside air. He could hear Stanley's terrible curses thudding after him like fists. They rang in his ears long after he had climbed onto his horse and ridden off into the full stillness of the warm, cloud-shadowed night.

The following day was the Sabbath. Percy went to meeting with the Clark family and spent the day at their home. He was well cared for, fussed over, really. He was amply fed. But he was too occupied to sort out his feelings. He had made no progress the night before. The turmoil and exhaustion, the late hour, had blunted his reasoning. He had let his anger get the better of him. And now, even with reason to aid him, there were too many unanswered questions, too much that made no sense.

"Her relationship with Stanley has something to do with her parting from May and John Thomas," he told Allison.

"I agree," she encouraged him. "Maybe Rose went to Stanley for help."

"And he must have helped her, at least at first, perhaps allowed her to stay with him. But then something happened. *What* happened? And why?"

They went over it again and again. *Does Stanley's hatred of Mormonism come into it?* Percy wondered. *It must. Did he find out she was involved with the Mormons? Is that what angered him? If so, what did he do in his anger?* He had no clue as to what had happened to Rose. Had Stanley sent her away? Married her off to some brute like himself? Percy didn't dare think upon that. Nor could he understand the extremity of Stanley's abhorrence of Mormons. It had to be more than Percy's joining the Church and going away from him; it had to be more. But here again, he had no clue to guide him.

Percy and Allison exhausted themselves going round and round the thing, attacking it from all sides, as if it were an impregnable fortress they must somehow penetrate. When evening came on and the heat of the day became muted and blown away by the cool night breeze, they went for a walk—a short walk, for she was not strong yet. He carried a cane, the lion-headed cane that had been his father's. In place of a shawl, she wore the new fashion: a soft braided Zouave jacket. He told her stories of home, of the mountains and deserts. He thought he might tire her, but she only wanted to hear more. He told her of Claire and the love between them, of Benjamin and his gentle, stolid example, of the handcart tragedy and Melissa. In the telling of tales he revealed much of himself; it surprised him how safe he felt, how at ease in her company. There was no sharpness here, no sarcasm, no self-interest. He craved the nearness of her, the sound of her voice, the scent of her skin and hair, the solemn way she studied his face, as though striving to look beyond what little was written there. He liked the touch of her hand, the cool, soft skin against his. Their slow feet ate up the distance too soon.

"I don't like going away from you," he said to her honestly. "How can that be? I've only known you for a matter of days."

"But you know me in some ways better than people who have lived with me all my life."

She explained it in part. Yet, how did it happen?

"I feel the same way with you." Her voice was a low caress. "From the very first I sensed a familiar spirit in your spirit, something that drew me to you." She leaned against him. She had used her small store of energy. He lifted her up, above her protests, and carried her the short distance back to the house.

"I'll see you tomorrow," he promised. "But I told Louisa I'd come over for tea. After that I think I'll poke around Stanley's a bit."

"Do you think you should? Oh, be careful."

"He won't be about. If the black horse is gone he's out stirring up trouble; if not, he's in bed sleeping off the night's drinking."

She let him go. He walked home; he preferred walking to riding, despite the light rain that settled over him like a mist. He refused to entertain any longer the dark thoughts that had marred the day. Instead he tapped his fine cane on the pavement, stopped to smell flowers, smiled at the ladies he passed, and gave in to the weakness of daydream. He thought only of her: what it would be like to take her back with him, to introduce her to Claire, to share the things he loved with her, to—

He refused to allow his mind to go beyond certain safe points. It would be foolhardy to do so. But it took the greatest effort to deny his desires, to make the pleasant dream stop.

CHAPTER

8

*L*ouisa was happy to see him. He enjoyed being with her, but she was no help at all. Her concern for Rose didn't penetrate as deeply as his did. She scoffed at some of the things he was wont to surmise.

"This isn't the Wild West," she reminded him. "People are civilized here. Even Stanley wouldn't be capable of some of the things you're suggesting."

"Then, tell me, where's Rose? Where is Rosie?"

She didn't answer him at once. She played with the child. He was a bright, fine-looking boy who responded with unspoiled charm to the attentions of his mother and the tall, smiling stranger. Percy couldn't help noticing that in her son's presence Louisa relaxed—pleasure softened her features and shone in her eyes. He recognized more of the girl in her, revealed unknowingly through the simple joy her child brought her.

At last, with some reluctance, she gave Ian to the nursemaid and turned her attentions upon Percy. He could see that she was trying to be gentle. "There's some simple explanation, I'm sure. She's moved away for some reason of her own—she wanted to remain incognito for a spell."

"You'll have to try harder than that, Louisa. You're the one who makes no sense. There's some trouble at foot here; I can feel it, I know it. What did Rose herself say: *Tell him I am near, and I need him.*"

"Yes, according to your girl, that's what Rose said." She tried to soothe him; she had good intentions.

She had become a person of expediencies; he was beginning

179

to see that. Suffering and unkindness had made her cautious. Her naturally efficient manner had narrowed into a protective self-interest that ill became her and distressed him. For he could see in her eyes none of the relaxed happiness a life such as hers should hold. Did the key lie in this wealthy husband? This man he had not even met yet? Why couldn't men contrive to be successful and kind at the same time? So few seemed to be. Sensitivity seemed the first encumbrance men shed on the long climb to power.

"You worry too much, Percy." Louisa's voice was sweet and soothing. But it drew him back with a start. He felt guilty; he wondered if his morose thoughts were visible to her. She pushed an unruly lock of hair from his forehead and smoothed it back into place. She had done the same thing with the same deft motion often when they were children.

"You're too serious. You always were," she accused. "You take responsibility for everyone onto your shoulders, Percy. No one can do that."

"I only want you to be happy."

The lines of her face rearranged themselves slightly. "I thought you were brooding on Rose."

"Rose isn't the only one I care for, Louisa. I've told you that."

"Well, my happiness or lack of it isn't your responsibility." She attempted a smile. It didn't come out well.

"You aren't very happy, then? Life is still hard?"

She fidgeted in place. "I wouldn't say that, Percy. How many people really know when they're happy, anyway? Things could be worse with me."

He nodded. "I'm sure that's true."

"Are you happy, Percy?" She was purposely turning his attention away from her. But he answered her thoughtfully, almost apologetically.

"Yes, I am. I've been well treated. I love Claire and Benjamin the same as my own."

"Do you enjoy life in such an uncivilized atmosphere?"

It was his turn to smile, and he did so with boyish pleasure, which roused her curiosity more. "It's hard for some folk, that's true." His smile became a wide grin. "But it's been a heyday for me. I've taken to it naturally for some reason, Louie." He shrugged his shoulders. "The freedom, the sense of newness, the space—until you've felt it, it's something that can't be described." He cocked his head to regard her more closely. "Would you ever come out and let me take you on a grand tour?"

She shook her head. "I don't think so. It's too far—too expensive—"

"Too irrational."

She nodded.

"Then I'll settle for Ian. Send him out to me when he's twelve or fourteen and I'll make a regular mountain man of him."

"I might do that." She laughed. "By the time he's fourteen that might sound very good."

"Would you like more children, Louisa?"

"You *do* ask the questions!" She drew back a moment, then relaxed. "I'd like a little girl. Maybe two little girls. Do you have a sweetheart? Someone you might grow serious about?"

He frowned slightly. "I suppose in a way I have. She's a peppery little thing, a real handful—"

"You would fall for that kind." Louisa sighed. "Love's a strange thing. I used to think one could control it at will, make it come, make it go . . ." She sighed again wistfully. "I've learned my lesson."

"I'm sorry," he murmured.

She lifted her head. "It's all right, I'm all right, can't you see that?" She kissed his cheek. She smelled good and her touch was gentle. "Some people expect more out of life than others."

"Meaning anyone in particular?" He knew she spoke truly.

"Meaning just what you think."

She walked with him to the door. "It's right that you've come, Percy," she encouraged. "You've done us all good in some way already. Don't expect a lot more than that. Don't expect to remake us in the image you hold of us."

Her words rang so true that Percy felt glad to escape, to give the horse his head and taste the exhilaration of speed as they took to the country roads. There was certainly not the feeling of wide open space here that he was used to back home. *Back home.* That's how he thought of it. England had been home once; it would remain that way, but only in the past, only tucked in his heart like a treasure.

There was no sign of movement or activity as he approached the Squire's estate. He skirted the house and saw nothing. In the barns there were stable boys moving about at their work, so he avoided those, too, and drew up by the sheltered south side, which was shielded from view. Here were the pleasure gardens, the summerhouse, the slope of the pond where ducklings and lily pads floated and Stanley's button lay sunk in the mud of the bottom.

He didn't know what he was hoping to find, but he dismounted and set about the pleasant task of exploring, walking long strides, drawing in the fresh air — wasted in this place — that ought to reflect beauty and laughter and happy times.

It was obvious that the summerhouse had not been used this season, nor for several before it. The paint around the doorways and ledges was peeling; one of the doors hung awkwardly on a broken hinge. Leaves hugged the foundation, and cobwebs and dust smeared the windows. There was nothing for Percy here.

He trudged out to the small toolshed behind the pond, again finding nothing. It was locked up tight. Through the dirt-streaked window he could see it was empty except for a few rakes and other small implements. Percy didn't know what he had hoped for. But certainly there was no life out here, and no sign that there ever had been. He shaded his eyes. Beyond the toolshed the grass turned to meadow, and where the two met, merged together, rose a huge, gnarled oak whose spreading arms, laden now with green leaves, took up a large space of sky. Although the old trunk was stout enough, wide in girth, Percy wondered how it supported the forest of long-reaching branches that tangled together and pushed off past each other in a wide, glorious crown. They seemed to dwarf the sturdy trunk that supported and balanced them.

He stared at the tree. A strange feeling began to creep over him. He had seen it before. Had he been back here at one time with Stanley? No, he knew he had not. *What was it, then?* He walked closer. The ground was smooth here and even, scattered with a soft yellow carpet of meadowsweet. He drew in the fresh smell. Out past the tree the jaunty buttercups raised their gold heads and danced to the slightest breath the summer air would lend them.

It was a sight so enchanting that it drew tenderness from him as a bee draws nectar from flowers. He moved on until he felt the thick branches draw their shade over the heat of the sun above him. The coolness tempted him further. Down beneath the branches the air, unstirred, was damp still with the dews of morning. He spread his coat over the thick surface of dead leaves and old grass and crushed stems. He stretched out with the rough trunk supporting him. He could see a great distance, though his long sight was narrowed by the shelf of green leaves: out past the fenced fields to a stretch of wood, a hill on the horizon, low and gray against the blue of the sky.

I have never been here before. He closed his eyes and tried to cup the elusive feeling in his mind to examine it. It was too indistinct. He brushed a clump of wet moss from the sleeve of his coat and his hand touched something hard, something solid, yet warmer, more yielding than wood.

With both hands he dug through the debris, brushing it back carefully, blowing the last trailings away. He drew out a book, a book shrunken and soggy with the damp of the earth and who knew how many rains. As Percy held it he felt his grip tighten. All of a sudden he knew. How could he not have known? How could his confused mind have obscured it?

This is the tree in my dream. This is the tree where Rose sat. He could see it again: she was turning the leaves of a book. *Was it this book?* Then something frightened her, she scrambled to her feet, the book dropped from her hand. She began to run, the book forgotten behind her, lying still on the ground beneath the sun-dappled shade of the great oak that had sheltered her . . .

With a trembling hand Percy turned the stiff, wet, misshapen cover. On the flyleaf he read: *The Book of Mormon — an account written by the hand of Mormon upon plates . . .*

A small sound escaped him. He turned one more page. Smeared across the surface were handwritten words. He could make out only one or two. *To S—nn—.* It *was* Rose's book, the book Allison had given her! *To Suzanne*, it must read. He could nearly make out the word *friend* and several letters of Allison's name. He hugged the ruined book to him. The feeling of urgency assailed him with a power that was frightening.

Rosie, where are you? He uttered the plea out loud. *How long has this book lain here, waiting for me to discover it, waiting to lead me to you?*

Yet Percy felt helpless. He only knew surely now what he'd known by instinct before: Rose had been here, under Stanley's protection. And then something had happened, something had turned him against her. He had grown mean and angry. He had *what?* Hidden her off somewhere in punishment, done away with her? Pain was obscuring his thoughts again. What of Rosie's own cry for help? He would go to Allison; she would see it more clearly. Perhaps she would be able to help.

He ran back, crushing the pungent meadowsweet under his feet. He stumbled breathless onto his horse's back; he was certain he hadn't been seen. That didn't matter now; nothing mattered but to go one step further, to figure out what his discovery might mean.

Although it was a release to talk things through with Allison, she could provide no more answers than he. He gave the scarred book into her safekeeping; she would treasure it well. She was as elated as he had been at the discovery of it. It made Rose seem more real to them both.

"You should get a warrant to search Stanley's house, any of Stanley's holdings," she suggested.

"I could never get that." There was a tinge of bitterness to Percy's voice that she had not heard before. "He has too much power where power counts. What I ought to do is get him good and drunk and see if I could draw him out that way." He gave a short laugh. "But that has its drawbacks as well."

Sister Clark interrupted and made them eat the good dinner she had prepared. There was still concern over Allison's health, and Percy meant to leave early. But some of the members he had met at the baptism came to call. One or two of them remembered him; quite a few had known Claire and Benjamin. They drew him out, talked him into telling stories of Zion. One thing led to the next, and Dorothy Clark's homemade peach compote didn't help. When the party broke up it was very late. Percy lent his horse to Brother Bellows, whose only mount had gone lame. He needed to ride over Warwick way the next morning. At first he hesitated.

"What will you do?" he asked Percy.

"I'll walk home as I love to, and you can return the horse to the inn when you're through with her in the morning. I won't need her before that."

Though it was late Percy lingered a few moments after the others to take his own private farewell, to kiss the fingers Allison put to his cheek.

"I'll be back in the morning," he promised, "before I try anything else."

She watched him walk off until his form was lost in the darkness; she kissed her hand to him, she whispered his name. He walked slowly, tapping his cane in the stillness. Perhaps a night's sleep would help. Perhaps he would wake up to some new plan he'd not thought of. A little time on his knees wouldn't hurt.

In his preoccupation he stumbled against a passing stranger and nearly upset him. The man smelled strongly of drink and muttered some foul oath at him. Percy apologized and thought again of what he might do to dupe Stanley. If he could get past Stanley's man he might be able to go over the place when Stanley was absent and not have to worry about the hazards of getting him drunk. Perhaps Louisa might be able to help. If they confronted him together . . .

He saw the lights of the inn before he knew it; he was tired, perhaps he would sleep. Perhaps he would talk the innkeeper's wife out of a tall glass of her thick buttermilk before going up to his solitary room.

The two riders bore down on him from out of the shadows. He stepped back as they blocked his path and stopped in a swirl of dust and spewn stones. He thought of Stanley and his boys and his pulse quickened.

"What's going on?" he complained. "You nearly ran me down."

The men were off their horses. "Are you Percy Graham?" one of them asked.

"I am," he replied. As they approached he could see that they wore uniforms of some kind; yes, they were policemen.

"Will you come with us, sir?"

"Whatever for?" The pounding pulse hurt his temples.

"Were you walking down Reed Street during the last half hour?"

"Yes, I was. I was walking home from a friend's house. What is it?"

"A man's been beaten and robbed along that stretch. The description the victim gave fits you, sir."

Percy shook off the hand that had been placed lightly on his arm. "That is ridiculous," he said.

"Be that as it may," replied the older of the officers, "you must first come with us before anything else can be determined." The hand came down again, firmer this time.

"There is no need of force, I'll go with you, gentlemen."

"That's a good sort," the officer replied. "You can climb up behind me. We'll be at the station in no time at all."

Percy rode with his face against the broad, rough coat of the officer. *Of course this is a mistake. But how could it happen? What an unfortunate mess! I have no time for this.*

That was the extent of his thoughts as he rode along. He entertained no real fears until they showed him the man who had been beaten. The attacked man was the one he had stumbled into; he realized that right away. That was why the fool had identified him. Someone must have come from behind, after Percy passed, someone the man hadn't seen, and done the work displayed here.

He explained as much to the policemen. The older one, Officer Graff, who seemed to be in charge, simply nodded his head. "Could be," he acknowledged. Then he lifted up the man's coat.

"Looks to me like it was a thick stick or cane that struck the blows, lad. Something like that one that you're carrying?"

Percy glanced down at the lion's head, frozen in a grimace.

"You tell me this man was robbed. Of what sum?"

"Thirty pounds."

Percy couldn't help scoffing. "You mean to say a man like this would be in possession of thirty pounds?"

"Seems unlikely, but that's right. Regular as the Sabbath his mum sends him forty pounds a month from London. He usually drinks it all up. He hadn't gotten very far when you found him."

"This is preposterous," Percy raged. "Look, go ahead, check my pants, my coat. I've no money on me but a pound note or two and some change."

"We intend to do just that." The younger policeman moved forward. Percy clenched his teeth at the prospect before him. The man's hands moved with slow deliberation. Percy shuddered at the touch of them. They felt inside his front pants pockets, shirt pocket, vest pocket, the inner lining of his coat. Just as Percy began to breathe freely again Officer Graff, reaching inside the deep pocket at the side of his tweed jacket, made a small, satisfied sound and drew out a wad of creased, dirty money. "It was here all the time."

For the first time Percy felt the cold touch of real fear. "There is something dreadfully wrong. I did not put that money there, I did not rob this man. The money was obviously planted, I have no knowledge—"

They weren't listening to him. "We'll have to imprison you, sir. The evidence looks awfully convincing."

"May I send a message to—"

"No, sir, it's late, it can wait until morning. You've got plenty of time."

Percy was stunned. He couldn't believe what was happening. He walked woodenly back to the cell. This small, enclosed place was where they wanted to put him! Everything in him cried out to rebel, to fight back. The officer grabbed hold of him firmly.

"Now, don't give us trouble, sir, we're just doing our duty."

He was inside, they were leaving him, they were locking the door, the criss-crossed lines that marked the door of a cage! Through the roaring in his head Percy heard other voices, new voices that seemed to grow closer.

"He's in here, sir," the turnkey said.

A man stepped forward. Percy knew the man, knew the dark,

insolent eyes, the unruly beard, the full mouth that could grow mean and little.

"How did you find me?" he cried. "Thank heaven you've come. I don't think I—"

Stanley looked right past him. "Bobby came to tell me, I rode immediately over. Is this the man that you found?"

"It is, sir. The man Frankie identified."

Stanley glanced coldly at Percy. "I should have known."

Percy grabbed the steel bars and shook them violently. "What's going on here, Stanley? What are you up to?"

The policemen exchanged glances. The young one hit sharply at Percy's knuckles with his stick and Percy dropped his bruised hands.

"This man is my brother, or he was my brother," Stanley explained in a cool voice. "I haven't seen him in years. He came back from America with some harebrained notion of going into business together—"

The listeners nodded with interest. Percy put his hand to his head.

"I didn't think it was a good idea and I told him so, but he wouldn't give up. Got a little nasty after I kept saying no to him. He's had a violent temper ever since we were boys."

"Then you think he's capable of this little business?"

Stanley frowned. "I'm afraid so. And in a way it would be my fault. Last week he asked for a loan, said his funds had run low. But I wanted him out of here. I thought maybe he'd just go home, back to the States, if I refused him. I didn't think he'd try—"

He left the sentence unfinished. The policemen nodded again.

"It seems a fairly clear case, sir," Graff said apologetically. "Do you happen to know if the cane we found with him was his?"

Stanley lifted his head. "The one out front that I saw, with the lion's head? It belonged to our father. I would know it anywhere."

The men were growing sorry now. Too sorry. Percy saw it, and hope flared, but Stanley saw, too.

"Well, it's a sorry affair, but you'd best keep your eye on him. Once he gets this way, once he lets go—"

"We understand." The three men turned to leave together.

"Stanley!" Percy cried. "Answer me, you coward!"

Stanley turned slowly back around. A look of satisfaction curled his lips for a moment, burned behind his black eyes. Then it was gone. There was no other emotion Percy could feel or identify.

"Do you remember what I told you, Percy?" he said, his voice expressionless. "It's as simple as that. You should have listened."

He shrugged his shoulders. He turned and walked from the cell to the large outer room of the jail. Percy heard quiet voices, then the sound of the big front door closing. Stanley had walked out into the night, into freedom. With sick dread Percy recalled the words of his brother: *I get what I want by my wits. If I want something from you I'll find a better way than a street fight to get it.*

Percy shuddered. *I've played right into his hands. I was a fool to underestimate him. He warned me again and again.*

There was no window in his cell and very little light from the half-open door. Percy sat down on the hard, narrow bed and put his head into his hands. He'd been frightened before. He'd been in some pretty tough spots in his time, with runaway teams, wild animals, Indians on the warpath. But never before had he been in this kind of predicament. He had never known this feeling of helplessness, this bitter taste of despair.

*T*he night was long. Percy slept only fitfully, and he was bothered by dreams: vague, meaningless, troublesome fragments, the kind he usually had. When he awoke at last he was aware of a dull pain in the small of his back and a throbbing ache at his temples.

They brought him cold oatmeal and coffee for breakfast; he tasted neither. He wrote as brief a note as he could to President Clark, with an even shorter p.s. to Allison, and had to pay to get them delivered. This feeling of being a condemned man had an element of shame to it, and shame was an emotion Percy knew little about. It ate at his insides; it disoriented his thinking. He wondered weakly what Allison would feel when she discovered his condition. Would she believe him wholeheartedly, or might she entertain even the slightest doubt, the least lack of faith in his integrity? He sensed, without really understanding, how important it was that she believe in him with all her heart.

And he knew at the same time that he had never felt these kinds of feelings for Emmeline. Nothing about her had touched him this deeply. Her good opinion of him, her faith in him had not held the weight, the vital importance that Allison's did. Nor had he really cared about Emmeline's happiness. Nothing had stirred that concern. And yet he felt more interest in Allison's welfare than he did in his own. He longed to please her, to protect her, to labor for her happiness, to comfort, to spoil her. Yet look at him now! Helpless, and for all practical purposes useless, dishonored. How could he face her like this?

The morning wore away with a slowness that dragged at him.

In desperation he begged for something to read, anything at all that would take him outside himself and this staggering reality. They brought him a couple of maps and an outdated magazine from a corner of the office. "Very accommodating," he mumbled to himself.

He would flip through the crumpled pages for a few minutes, then pull out his pocket watch to check on the time. This material could not hold his interest, not when its competition was the morbid contemplation of his impending fate. In one of his moments of forced concentration someone came through the door. The person must have come quietly, for Percy heard nothing until a voice said, "I never expected to find you here! Stanley maybe, but not you. Do I have brothers changing places on me, the world turning upside down?"

"Randall!" Percy looked up, dumbfounded. Randall's face was all grin. "I never expected to see you again in this lifetime," Percy stuttered at him. "You look amazingly like Stanley now that you've grown your beard out. You gave me a start."

"Well, it is myself. And I've brought you something you'll be even happier to see: your breakfast."

At his nod the turnkey stepped forward with a large, napkin-covered tray. One smell told Percy. "Dorothy Clark!"

"That's right."

"I don't understand. Have you been there, met them?"

While Percy was eating the warming, delectable food, Randall told his story.

"Let's start at the beginning," he said. "You left that miserable book in my room. When I came in and saw it I threw it against the far wall and it lay sprawled on the floor a few days for me to trip over. But I got a sour feeling every time I looked at it, so in a fit of depression I took it back to the garbage and tossed it in."

Percy was watching wide-eyed; Randall was enjoying the telling. "Would you know it, the very next day I got ill, deathly ill with a cold. I couldn't eat, couldn't talk, couldn't breathe. Aunt put me directly to bed. And soon as she'd done so, old Mary comes in toting your grease-stained book. She asked if I knew anything of it. Had your name in it; she was afraid you had left it here. 'Give it to me,' I growled, and she handed it over."

Percy had stopped eating. Their eyes met, unblinking.

"Well, I'm sure you know the rest."

"Tell me," Percy breathed. *Let me hear it, let me make certain it's true.*

"I read it through, hardly stopping, then I read some parts again. As long as it was daylight I couldn't stop reading, and when I was alone in the night I couldn't stop thinking about what I had read. It didn't take me long, really, to know it. Even before I had prayed, I could see the reasonableness of it." He glanced down. "I haven't prayed much before in my life. Maybe around the time Mother and Father died; I don't remember, but I think I must have. But never since then. It was a hard thing to do, Percy."

"Yes, I know."

"Don't get me wrong. I still have unanswered questions—"

"That's why you're here."

"I suppose so. I didn't hate Mormonism as you must have thought. Nor yourself. Rather something in my own life, in me." He lowered his head a little sheepishly. "Recognizing that is a beginning, anyway."

"So it is! A good beginning." Percy wrapped his arms around the big man beside him. Randall shrank back from the show of feeling, but Percy didn't mind.

"I don't know for sure where I'll go from here, and I make no promises."

"I wouldn't want you to, Randall. It's enough right now that you're here, that we're together."

"I'm no longer the child you left. And you must know, growing up the rough way I did isn't exactly a pretty affair." Randall paused, perplexed at his own words. "Can you accept that? Accept me as I am?"

"Does it seem that I can't?"

"Well, you're awfully demanding, and your head's in the clouds. You always were that way." The soft, lowland Scots accent gentled his words. But they stung nevertheless.

"I'm learning," Percy replied through a tight throat.

Randall's slow smile began. "Good. Because I intend to give you a run for your money."

Percy relaxed a little. "That's fair. I still intend to do all I can to entice you to come home with me, back to Zion."

"I suppose that I might. If you'll still have me by then."

Percy hugged him again. "What a time we shall have!"

"Don't you start crying, Percy. You did that the last time you acted this way. I can't take it; I'm a man grown now."

Percy blinked back his tears. This unexpected joy had caught him at a weak, very vulnerable time. He forced his mind to ask questions, take over, think him out of this spot.

"How long have you been here?" he asked.

"Just got in last night. I went to the old inn, thought you might stay there, but they didn't know where you were. The keeper's wife remembered you mentioning to her once where you were going, she remembered the name. So I looked up Phillip Clark and I found him, and he put me up for the night."

"Were they worried when you said I was missing?"

"I wouldn't say worried. They thought you might have gone somewhere else; to Louisa's house, maybe. But this morning, when your note came—"

Percy shrank back. "What did they do?"

"Well, Mr. Clark got very quiet, serious-like. But his wife set in fussing and fuming at what they were doing to you."

"And Allison? Did you meet Allison?"

Randall grinned in a slow way, as though it were uncomfortable for him. "I met your sweetheart, all right. You know how to pick them, brother."

"Randall—"

"She cried some. I thought she got pretty pale, but her Mum said she'd been sick, that was part of it."

Percy slumped back against the cold wall. He had no more appetite, even for Dorothy Clark's food.

"Can I eat that piece of sugar toast if you don't want it?" Randall asked.

Percy nodded. "Go ahead."

"That woman sure can cook, can't she?"

Randall chewed on the toast and this time Percy heard. Through the stupor of gloom he swam in he heard her voice, the music that lifted him out of himself. *Not here,* he thought.

Not under their begrudging gaze, not like this! He lowered his head at her step, reluctant for the first time to meet her eyes, to read what might be there.

"Percy, Percy," she was calling, "where are you?"

He could no longer resist. When she came to him his head was lifted and ready. She went into his arms, as if it were the most natural thing in the world for her to be there. She rested her head on his chest, those dark, fragrant curls swept his neck, touched his cheek. He wanted to cry from sheer joy.

"Percy, have faith," she said into his ear. "You will not be alone in this trial. Papa will see to that."

"It isn't your father I need."

"I won't leave you!" She seemed to draw closer. "I know you are innocent. This is Stanley's doing, isn't it?" She didn't wait for his answer. "I've been praying all morning. We'll find a way, Percy. I know we will."

The turnkey had drawn back, but Randall was watching them; he was too near. After the first impetuous greeting she pulled reluctantly away. "Father will be here any moment," she assured him. "Did you enjoy Mother's breakfast?"

Percy's smile answered her. "So you've been getting to know my little brother?"

She knit her dark brow. "He's a hard one, like you. Quiet, a little withdrawn."

Percy started. "Did I appear that way?"

She laughed a little. "Yes, you did, but it's all right. It drew me to you, it gave you a certain air of—"

"That can't be muckle true, it never did so for me!" Randall's interruption was sincere, though unwanted. "Just made people call me slow. It wasn't his shy way that drew you, Miss Allison, it was his charm. Those big, innocent eyes and his curly gold hair and the way he moves."

Allison blushed a becoming pink color and lowered her eyes.

"I appreciate you taking him in," Percy continued, making discreet signals for silence at Randall above her head.

"It was our pleasure." Her eyes said: *for your sake.* Her eyes said much more. He didn't want to face the struggle before him; he wanted to stay lost in her eyes.

But her father came, and with his coming Percy's last scrap of hope fled. He knew the news was bad when he looked on Phillip Clark's face, though the man shook hands heartily and tried to act cheerful enough.

"I can't get them to set bail. They give me one story, then another. I believe they have orders to talk to your brother first."

"That's encouraging."

"I'll get Stanley's attention," Randall blustered. "There are ways much more effective than talking—"

"No," Percy warned him. "I want no more of that. If he discovers you're on my side he'll use any excuse you give him to slap you right in here with me—or perhaps to do worse."

"He's right," Brother Clark agreed.

"I must get out if I even hope to fight for my innocence. What can I do from in here?" Percy fought the panic that crept into his voice.

"We can do much for you that you'd rather do yourself," Phillip Clark replied gently. "Though I don't know where to start to find the real culprit."

"Start with Stanley; it all goes back to Stanley," Allison said. Percy was surprised at the vehemence in her voice.

"Perhaps we should start with the matter of bail. They will eventually have to set one. It goes without saying that they will set it as high as they dare, given the offense and its circumstances."

"Yes, and how to get that?"

"We will find some way." The president did not sound encouraging. "Have you any friends with money, Percy? Friends who are not Latter day Saints?"

Friends? Here? "I have none," he said softly.

"Never mind, we'll find some way," Phillip Clark said again.

Meanwhile? Meanwhile?

The talk grew dismal, desultory. They got ready to take their leave. The panic of being alone in this place settled over Percy. He fought it, forcing a bright, cheerful manner. He kissed Allison's cheek. They had walked off, they were out of his sight when her name came to mind, popped into his head out of nowhere. He shouted for them to come back.

"What is it?" Allison asked, her voice fearful.

"It is the first light in the tunnel, our first hope for help."

She looked at him, puzzled.

"Mildred Boswell of Warrington," he said. "She likes me, she trusts me, I know she would help."

"I'll go to her, whoever she is," Randall offered. "It won't take me long."

"You'd best take the train rather than go by horseback."

"All right." Randall grinned, in his slow, uneasy manner. "Mayhap I'm not the best man to go. I won't be able to charm her the way you did, Percy."

"Off with you!"

It was a starting point. They talked over arrangements. President Clark was the first to leave. He had responsibilities, a job to go to. Percy couldn't reconcile himself to the fact that he was not free to walk out of here, free to go with the others. He kept up a brave front for their sakes, but when they were gone he sat on the edge of the bed with his face in his hands and prayed while the tears ran down his cheeks.

Randall was on his way; Allison had seen him off safely herself. Her mother would not expect her home for a while yet. She took the address from her purse and gave it to the coachman. During the ride she leaned back against the cushioned seat, forcing herself to rest. She felt amazingly strong, every day she felt stronger. After the first shock of Percy's imprisonment, which threatened to dissolve her altogether, a new, tough strength seemed to be building inside her. It was a strength born of need. She did not recognize it as such, but she was grateful for it.

It was a lovely house, this house where Percy's sister lived. Allison knocked on the door, smoothed her skirt, straightened her bonnet, and took a deep breath. The woman who admitted her was courteous. Allison stood just inside the front hall waiting for a moment, then the woman returned and escorted her to a small inner parlor. Louisa was there. Her smile was perfunctory, her gaze harsh and examining. It made Allison want to shrink back.

She told her story as briefly as possible. Louisa did not interrupt her, though Allison thought she looked pale and the hands in her lap clenched until her knuckles were whitened.

"Percy doesn't know I have come," Allison concluded. "But I know your husband is a man of some means. I was sure you would want to help him."

"Poor Percy. He had the best of intentions. He tries so hard. I do want to help him." Louisa lifted her head. "But my husband's means, as you put it, are not at my disposal. There is no way I can help."

Allison stared; she could not think how to respond.

"Don't gawk at me." Louisa's voice was not unkind, but it was brusque and Allison felt the brusqueness in it covered softer emotions. "How is it you know my brother?" she asked. "I've forgotten."

"I was very ill; nothing was helping me and my father despaired of my life. He asked Percy to come and administer to me—"

Louisa leaned forward. "What does that mean?"

"The elders place their hands on the heads of the sick and anoint them with oil, and pray for the healing power of heaven."

"And Percy did that?"

"Yes."

"And you recovered?"

"Almost immediately." Louisa leaned back again. "I can see that you're having trouble believing me," Allison went on, "but it's true. Some men seem to have a spirit for healing, a faith or whatever. I believe Percy has that. Whether or not that made a difference, I believe I was meant to recover, and so I did."

"Well." Louisa had not sorted out her own reaction. She sat awkwardly.

"Then you're not going to help?"

"What would getting Percy out on bail do, anyway?"

"Could you talk to Stanley?"

"I could. That would do less good, and you know it. The fact that he's done this thing, that he has gone to such pains to entrap his own brother—well, he wouldn't listen to me. I'm not even sure he'd receive me."

Allison fought a small sense of panic. "Will you at least go visit Percy? He's having a difficult time."

"I'll try to do that, but I don't want Victor to discover me—"

"Would he disapprove of you visiting your own brother? Percy has visited here."

Louisa rose and walked to the desk by the window. "My dear, this isn't a jail." She paused. Her back was to Allison. "Besides," she continued, "he doesn't know Percy has come."

"Doesn't know? Why? I don't understand—"

"Of course you don't. It isn't your business. I doubt you'd understand if it was explained to you." Louisa put her hand to her throat. "Here comes Victor now! I wasn't expecting him." She spun around quickly. "You must leave, my dear."

Allison rose. Louisa took her elbow and steered her. "Tell him we met in town—no, tell him we serve on a committee together and you just dropped in for a moment—tell him that, if he asks."

"All right."

When they opened the door Victor was framed in the doorway. He peered down his long, narrow nose at the pair of them. "And who might this be?" He had a nasal voice, which one would expect, looking at him, and small, close-set eyes very indistinct in color so that they looked almost faded.

"My name is Allison, sir. I work on one of the ladies' committees with Louisa."

"I see." There was no smile. He leaned across his guest to give Louisa a chaste, tight-lipped kiss on the forehead. "Are you coming or going?" he asked.

"I'm just leaving," Allison assured him. Although his features were lean and concealed his years well, she could tell he was older than Louisa. He seemed more of an age with her own father. She curtsied and walked down the path, feeling that his gaze followed her, but she had no chance to look back and see. She climbed into the carriage and the door closed behind her and they rattled away.

"I will not grow depressed," she told herself fiercely. "So my first efforts have failed. I shall only try all the harder." She directed the driver to take her home. Her next move would be more difficult than this had been, and require a little more thought. And a great deal more courage, she knew; but she wouldn't think about that.

Allison saw Percy in the afternoon. She told him nothing: she didn't want to know what he would say, and she didn't want to give him the chance to forbid her. This had to work! There was no other thing in the world she could think of.

She rode out alone, on the gray pony she had ridden since her childhood. The pony's footing was sure and reliable and he had a good sense of home. If anything were to happen he would come back here, even without her. But she refused to think about that. Nothing would happen. Things would work out as she wanted them to, as they had to!

She knocked on the door. A servant answered. He raised his eyebrow and stood staring a moment, but he said his master was home. That was the answer she needed to hear, though it made her tremble inside, made her legs go weak. She put her hand against the cool wainscoting to steady herself.

Stanley came into the room. He stopped when he saw her. She smiled across at him weakly.

"What do you want of me?" he asked. He spoke the words coldly; he made no move toward hospitality, he did not even offer her a chair. She feared by his expression that he might turn and leave her.

"I wish to talk with you," she said.

"I am not in the habit of talking with strange young women," he answered, "even when they happen to be pretty things, like yourself."

"I need your help," she said. She feared that she looked it. She took her hand away from the support of the wall and felt herself sway. He must have seen, too. He moved a step closer. "Who are you?"

"My name is Allison Clark, sir."

"And why are you here, Allison?"

"Might I sit down?"

"We shall see. Answer my question."

She leaned against the firm wall. She was angry at the weakness that gnawed at her. She mustered her faltering forces. "I have come to seek your advice, sir, and perhaps your protection—"

"What nonsense is this?"

He was becoming impatient, yet his curiosity was growing. She took a deep breath.

"I have been acquainted of late with your brother, Percy. He has made advances toward me. I have just learned of his—crime, and I'm frightened."

She had Stanley's attention. It was focused upon her so intently that she fancied she could feel it, feel the force of his gaze.

"If you are acquainted with Percy then you are no friend of mine—" his lip curled ever so slightly— "and I am no friend of yours."

She was desperate now; he could see that, even if he misread the cause of it.

"But you must be my friend. I have no other." She seemed to slump, to sway again. With a catlike quickness he moved close to her, put his hand to her waist.

"Here," he said awkwardly. She allowed him to take her to a chair, help her sit. "Are you better?"

"Forgive me sir, please." She blushed and the slight color became her. Stanley wanted to touch her. She looked like a piece of fine china.

"Can you speak now? Would you like me to get you a drink?" He had been too long away from women. He was awkward and he knew it. Allison could sense his frustration. She held out her hand.

"I feel foolish. I'm much better, really."

"Well, what is this nonsense, then?"

"The jailer said that you knew the details of this incident, that you might advise me." She hurried ahead. "I fear that your brother has been courting me under false pretense."

"And what of it? Many a man has done that."

"Yes, but I am young, and I don't wish to marry, I don't wish to leave home. My father wants this marriage, he wants to send me to Zion—" She was near to tears now.

"Your father's a Mormon zealot?" Stanley's dark eyes were glowing.

"Oh yes, sir, he is."

"And yourself?"

"I am a young girl, I am not ready for marriage, to leave my home and my country."

Stanley pulled a stool up beside her. He had to make sure. The nearness of her excited his senses. "I find it hard to believe you, girl. Percy is a fine-looking man, young and appealing. Has he been unkind to you?"

"He is most charming on the whole, sir. Just now and again, when I show reluctance to go with him to Zion, to wed him." Allison placed a trembling hand on Stanley's arm.

"Women wed men, they bear children; that is the way. Why do you wish me to interfere in your fate, girl?"

She looked into his eyes. Her own were swimming in tears now. "There is more to it—there is a woman in Utah—"

"I don't understand." Stanley could not concentrate well, due to her nearness, due to the fragrance he breathed in from her. But Allison didn't know that. She lowered her voice. She hoped she could trust it to serve her.

"I have heard, sir, that there are some Mormon men who indulge in the practice of plural marraige—"

She could feel Stanley go stiff; beneath her fingers she felt his arm tighten.

"Ah, Percy, the devil! The greedy bigot!" She could hear his teeth grind. "He'd be attracted to that. He'd doubtless fancy himself well suited—"

Allison pressed her advantage. "So you see, sir, if it is true that your brother beat and robbed another man, that he is unstable, that he is not worthy—"

"I can serve your purposes in that," Stanley assured her.

"If my father can be convinced—"

"If I can snatch away the girl he desires as well as his freedom—"

"Will you be my protector?"

"I will, child. We shall keep that demon behind bars, you'll see." She trembled at the confidence that backed his hatred. "That's where his kind belongs, not out breeding more Mormon vermin."

He took the delicate hand from where it rested against his arm and caressed the cold fingers.

"You were born for better than that," he crooned with surprising tenderness. "So was she, my little Annie, my beautiful Annie." He murmured the words. Allison couldn't quite hear what he said, but she shrank at the touch of him. There was a sinewy strength to the fingers that brushed her skin. She was aware of the size of the man, and how alone the two of them were in the big, silent house. She had never lied in her life, beyond the thoughtless lies of childhood, and she was grateful for the dim light and the distress she felt to cover the deception she was certain must show. She hadn't lied as much as misrepresented, in a cause just enough to excuse her. So she hoped and prayed with all the fervor of her young heart.

Stanley had been restless and unhappy since last evening; this business with Percy hadn't been as easy for him to do as he had thought it would be. The young girl's response awakened some need in him. He didn't want to admit that monstrous need again, but as long as the girl had come here: he need not *hope*, but he could *indulge* just a little.

"When can I see you again?" Perhaps he could snatch her away from this evil, redeem the loss, the miserable failure. "You have obviously slipped away without permission to come here today. Could you do so again?"

"I believe I can."

"Tonight?"

Allison panicked. That was too soon. "Tonight is a bad time. Would tomorrow night do?"

"Yes, here. No—" The house was a tomb, he wanted to court her a bit, show her his power. She was young, she was impressionable, he could mold her—

He rose, dropping the frail hand. He must not walk back into this trap.

"Are you in love with my brother?"

"No, sir." She was grateful his back was turned. "I'm a little afraid of him now. I don't want him to take me—"

"Of course you don't." He turned back to her.

"You are a man of position, sir. Can I put my faith in you?"

Stanley's eyes seemed to bore holes in her. "We shall trust in each other and hope the devil stays out of it." He laughed brusquely. "Tomorrow. Do you know where the Prince's Lair is?"

Her eyes widened. "I believe so."

"You will be safe with me there. No one of your acquaintance will happen upon us." He drew near again, he knelt down on the stool. His face was close, exuding a power that seemed to sap hers.

"Meet me at seven, Allison. We will enjoy good food and soft music and privacy there." He reached out and touched her hair with his fingers.

She said, looking straight ahead: "I will be expected to visit your brother, to comfort him. If you should see me there, please pretend you do not know me. It would go hard with me if my father discovered—"

She swallowed against the dryness in her throat. She didn't need to go on. He bent so that his lips nearly touched her cheek.

"I am a master at that. Your secret is safe with me."

She took the hands he offered; they were warm, strong hands. With his aid she rose. With his arm encircling her waist he guided her out of the room. She was aware of the fact that he enjoyed the touch of her.

"Are you well enough to ride, or will you swoon on your pony? Shall I send my man along?"

"No! The night air will restore me, I'll go slowly."

"Go carefully."

He helped her mount the gray pony. "Seven o'clock, the Prince's Lair." He held her bridle. "Don't fail me, Allison."

He stood back and folded his arms across his broad chest as she started down the long lane. This time she was sure of the eyes that were watching her.

What have I done? What have I done? A weakening excitement ran through her. She forced all thoughts, all fears from her mind. She would do what had to be done, heaven willing. She would not think beyond that. At the end of the lane she gave the pony his head and let him take them both home.

10

*A*llison was concerned about seeing Percy that evening. She feared he might sense something strange, see what she had done when he looked at her. But there was good news to discuss that overshadowed his interest in the activities of her day.

Bail had been set: seventy-five pounds. It seemed a fortune, but at least they knew what they were up against. Percy seemed hopeful, and Allison left it that way. She talked only a little of her day, told tidbits of her visit to Louisa, but not of her request — even the lesser request that she come visit him. Louisa had not arrived yet: how would it help to raise his expectations? They wondered together when Randall would show up with Mildred: if she even would come, and if seventy-five pounds would be out of her range or her willingness.

"Don't leave me so long tomorrow, Allison," he chided her gently when she was preparing to leave. So he was more aware of her than she had realized. What did he think?

She made light promises, she kissed his wan cheek, he watched after her. *What is afoot?* Percy couldn't convince himself that Allison was capable of doing anything dangerous or foolhardy, but he was beginning to wonder a bit. There had been a look on her face, something guarded, something unsettled that he had never seen there before. And he realized that she had spoken little of how she had filled the hours of their parting.

He did not sleep well. He wanted to hope for what tomorrow would bring, but he didn't dare. Disappointment and failure would undo him unless he steeled himself for them. Of that he was sure.

When he thought of Stanley a great sadness came over him, a sadness worse than his rage. Brother against brother. He knew such things happened in wartime, or in the dividing of large family fortunes. But cold-blooded like this, and for what purpose? His whole mind screamed to know.

He didn't dare let himself think of his mother, though she seemed never far from his thoughts and feelings. Awareness of her increased the great sadness he felt. *I have failed him. I'm sorry, Mother. I didn't want to cause you this pain.* How he could use Claire's gentle, yet firm, hand now! How he had longed for her over these past days. He didn't feel grown up at all. He felt young and in need of comfort and guidance.

What would the world be like without women? That was the last thought he had as he fell into a fitful and dreamless sleep.

They came in the night. Percy woke to their voices.

"You've got yourself in a fix!" Mildred blustering; Mildred ready to go to battle for him. And so she did. She stood before the magistrate the next morning with President Clark at her elbow, but she didn't really need him.

"I'm here to post bail for the boy," she stated.

When the judge peered over his glasses at her she glared right back.

"No, I am not one of his Mormon compatriots, so don't get any ideas. I hail from Liverpool and, for your information, I come from a long line of magistrates; my own father was a magistrate." He sat back at that.

"Seventy-five pounds is a bit stiff," she complained.

"I won't lower it." There was stubbornness in the judge's voice.

Mildred didn't have that much. She had been hoping to bargain. "If I were you, sir, with all due respect, I'd think that over again. It's a smudge on any man's record, any man of integrity, to set bail for such a crime as young Graham is accused of at such a ridiculous sum."

Magistrate's daughter or no, she had piqued him. He stuck out his chin and remained silent.

"I quite agree."

Allison, sitting on one of the benches beside Randall, looked up in amazement. The person who had spoken was a slight, thin woman who was making her way to the bench, holding herself like a ramrod.

"It's the vicar's wife!" Randall whispered. "What is she doing here?"

She walked right up to the judge and addressed him without permission. "I am Vicar John Evans's wife," she explained. "You know my husband well, sir."

The magistrate gave a short nod of his head in acknowledgment. "What can I do for you?"

"I am here to help post bail for Percy Graham."

A sudden hush filled the room. Allison looked at Randall; his face was drenched in amazement.

"Ma'am, are you aware of his crime?"

"I am aware of the crime he is accused of." She drew herself up even straighter. "I happen to believe in his innocence." She turned to Mildred and addressed her. "What sum are you in need of?"

Mildred met her eyes squarely. "Twenty pounds will do."

"I can manage that." She drew the money out of her large black purse and set it up on the bench.

"I believe it a shame what has happened to this fine boy. I expect to see his name cleared." She cleared her own narrow throat. "Good day, sir." She nodded to the judge. "Good day, ma'am." She nodded to Mildred.

Mildred winked back. "It has been a pleasure," she said.

Jane Evans smiled. The smile lingered at the corners of her mouth and carried her all the way down the long aisle and out of the chamber.

Mildred broke the silence. "Well, that is that." She slapped her own money up by the vicar's wife's offering. "I think this should do it. Good Liverpool pounds and Church of England money. There ought to come some good of that."

It was a scene Allison wouldn't have missed for a fortune. When she described it for Percy tears came to his eyes. When they released him that afternoon he walked slowly, very slowly, out of the cell, seeming to grow more withdrawn with each step, rather than happier.

"I'll never go back."

He spoke so softly that Allison had to lean close to hear him. "Allison, I'll never go back! I'll die before I'll let other men lock me up again that way."

She knew how deeply he meant what he said. She squeezed his arm. "With God's help we won't have to face that, Percy."

She hoped he believed her. She wasn't sure she believed herself. She had an appointment to keep at seven. If she were to make it through that she would need all the help heaven could spare her.

They all went quietly to the Clark house and ate Dorothy's good food and conferred upon the best course of action. The first thing they agreed upon readily was to keep Randall free.

"We may have need of him at some point in the future. No one should know he is here, not even Louisa."

Randall drained his cup of cider to that. "And the longer it takes Stanley to learn that Percy's out on bail, the better," he suggested.

"I don't know about that. If I confront him tonight at the mansion, beat him to within an inch of his life, I might discover some things of interest—"

The rest ignored Percy's outburst.

"I wonder what Stanley is up to, if anything," Randall mused.

Allison cast down her eyes. She had to tell them, she knew she must tell them, but what if they interfered? What if they foiled the careful plans she had laid?

They went on talking around and above her. But she had been thinking all day. Ever since the arrival of Randall and Mildred, she had been revising her plans. She felt confident of the decision she had come to. At last she broke in, with the almost apologetic air they expected from her.

"You don't have to wonder where Stanley will be tonight or what he'll be doing," she said softly. "He'll be at the Prince's Lair having dinner—with me."

All talk ceased, all eyes stared at her. "Allison, my dear," her mother said. Randall attempted a laugh. Percy had been watching her very closely.

"The devil he will. No way on earth will I let you go meet him." He grabbed her arm a little roughly and turned her to face him. "What are you up to, Allison? Have you already spoken with Stanley?"

She nodded her head and sat patient and still, waiting for his uproar to wear itself out.

"Let's hear what the girl has to say." Mildred Boswell had been watching her, too. Her face wore a speculative air. "I'd put my money on this dark horse," she said. "Go on, honey, tell us your plan."

There was no way to fault her, there was no flaw to her reason. It was brilliant, but sure. There was almost no way it could cause danger to Allison. At last they agreed. Allison encouraged, Mildred bullied them into it. Dorothy served up the last plate of cookies, resigned and pale. Allison's father was quiet, too. "I don't like it," he had said, "but I feel it is the best, perhaps the only chance we have."

"Can you do it?" That was Percy's concern. Allison boasted no false confidence, yet she gave him a coy smile.

"If you could see what I've done already. Your brother's quite taken with me."

She grew sorry when she saw Percy's reaction. She wished the hours would pass. It would be better for everyone, especially for Percy, when he had something to do. She was anxious to face the night, to get it over with, no matter how things fell apart or together. Anything was better than this.

The Prince's Lair nestled back from the road in a small hollow or dip, camouflaged by nature's abandoned tangle of tree, bush, and hedge; there was no landscaping here. One would have to know the existence of the place to discover it. Allison had never had cause to go close to it. She hired a coach to take her there and was happy she had done so. The approach was eerie and dark. She didn't like the feel of the place. She didn't like the feel of the people, many of whom looked at her as an obvious outsider.

She was barely inside the door when Stanley came up—from nowhere, it seemed—and assisted her with her light wrap.

"I have a table with a view of the river," he said. He guided her there through a maze of rooms, some lavish with gilt and gaudy fashion, some more tasteful, subdued. To her relief he stopped in one of the latter.

He had indeed found a spot to please the sensitivities of anyone with an eye for beauty. She told him so. He seemed pleased. He seemed nervous as well as he pulled out her chair and fussed about her. By the smell of his breath she could tell he'd been drinking already. Percy had said: *He'll be uncertain about this meeting with you, so he'll go well fortified. And that means more than one snifter of brandy, I can assure you.*

A waiter brought drinks to the table as soon as they were seated, but she waved hers aside. "I am not used to strong drink," she apologized, pushing the glass closer to him. "You may have both if you'd like."

He tilted his head, but gave no other answer. "Did you have any trouble?" he asked. "Getting away?"

"A little." She put her hand to her throat.

"Does your father suspect you?"

She laughed with sincerity. "No, he'd never dream that I'd have the courage to do what I'm doing."

That seemed to please Stanley. He leaned close. "Have you changed your mind?" he asked softly. "Do you still want what you wanted yesterday?"

"Oh, yes!" she replied with conviction.

There was a small scuffle at the table beside them. They were seating a rather large, rather boisterous woman and her thin, sparse companion. Stanley swore under his breath.

"I'll get them out of here—I gave instructions!" he hissed. He started to rise. Allison placed a hand on his arm.

"Oh, don't—they won't bother me."

He paused and glared at her.

"I rather like the idea of a loud, busy neighbor. We can talk more privately that way. No need to whisper. They'll not mind us at all."

Stanley hesitated. She pushed her drink a little closer to him. "Drink that and don't worry about them."

He eased himself into the chair. Allison said something vague about moonlight on the water. A waiter came and they ordered their food. A small trickle of panic, like ice water, slid down her backbone. *I'm getting nowhere*, she thought. At least the large and thin ladies were safely in place.

"What will you do," Stanley asked, "once you refuse to wed Percy? Will your father turn you out?"

"I hope not." She appeared distressed. "I hadn't thought about that."

"I have a large home," he said, watching her carefully. "I could prepare apartments for you. Not only a room, but a suite of rooms with your own maids and servants—"

He was bribing her! She hoped that she appeared interested, that her smile looked sincere.

"I cannot imagine that," she said very honestly. "But if Percy is safe behind bars, if my father is convinced he is unworthy of me—"

Stanley reached for her hand. "More drinks here," he cried to a passing waiter, who took a bottle from its tray without missing a step. Stanley bent over her, smoothing the skin on her hand. "You wear no rings," he said. "No jewels to adorn your white skin." Malice gleamed in his eyes now. "Mormons keep their women plain, they take pains to cover their beauty. Why, my young Mormon, is that?"

"I do not know, sir." She shifted uneasily. "Probably because most Mormons are poor."

He liked her answer. He threw back his head and laughed at her. But he didn't let go of her hand. "That may seem a proper reason, but it isn't. It goes deeper than that. Mormons are niggardly, they don't believe in the things of this world, they don't believe pleasure can serve men . . . and women . . ." His voice had a honeyed tone.

How does he do that? Allison wondered. A chill passed over her. A tall waiter in evening dress brought their soup. Stanley released her hand now and poured himself a drink from the bottle.

"Get something lime and refreshing for the girl here, no liquor," he said.

The waiter nodded and vanished. Allison addressed her attention to her soup. She was grateful that it was liquid and would go smoothly down. She didn't know how she would tackle anything more solid. She was nervous: she didn't want to make her move too soon, but she didn't want to make it too late. And she didn't see how she could sit through the entire meal. Stanley saw her distress.

"What is the matter?" he demanded. "Something is bothering you."

She shook her head. "No, it's nothing," she protested.

"You've been fidgety all night. You're not being straightforward with me, Allison. I warned you about that."

His words were like cold stones hurled against her.

"It's probably nothing. I am afraid, sir, to mention it." There was a side of truth to most of the statements she made and that lent them sincerity.

"Out with it!" he snarled. He snatched her hand again. "Not one more bite, one more moment until you have told me."

She looked into his eyes. The fear and unhappiness in hers moved him, spread over his hardness the way water streams over stone.

"It will not be as easy as I had hoped," she said shakily. "I have heard rumors today that my father and his friends are on to something—" She pushed a loose hair back from her cheek with trembling fingers. "They seemed much encouraged—"

"Lies!" Stanley hissed. "Wishful thinking."

"I do hope so, sir, but I overheard my father say something about a man who had been found, a low sort of a man, who is boasting that he did the deed and you paid him well—" she leaned a little closer, her fingers winding around his in her tension— "and that he would get more from you yet. That he could bleed you for a—"

"Curse him! I told Bobby he was too stupid—"

Who was too stupid? Who?

"It cannot be true, sir! If it is I have no chance!"

"Tom Bede will wish he was never born." Stanley's eyes were on fire. He raised his glass to his lips and drained it. The large woman leaned so close Allison feared she might lose her balance and tumble into his lap.

"Tom Bede is a dead man," he repeated through clenched teeth.

"Squire, what do you mean?" Allison blinked back stinging tears. He saw. With a gentle finger he wiped the corner of her eye.

"You're too pretty to cry," he growled. "Stop this minute."

"But what does this mean? Is it true that your brother is innocent? If he is released, what will become of me?"

She leaned close, for his comfort. The large woman slipped past, out to the lavatory, presumably. The thin woman bent over her food.

"I will take care of you," Stanley said fiercely. "You have nothing to fear. Percy and his end are incidental to your happiness, if you want it that way."

She was trembling. He saw and moved his chair so that he sat close by her side. He smoothed back her hair. "You are so young," he murmured, "so fair." He bent until his lips touched her cheek, then the lobe of her ear. "I will take care of you," he repeated. "Percy will be ruined one way or another. Let that miserable Bede foul my schemes — he shall pay for it dearly! But as far as your twisted, greedy young suitor is concerned, I have not played my hand. I have it in my power to crush him, Allison! Do not fear."

With a low moan she dropped her head on his shoulder. She was unwinding his reason; emotion seeped through his battered defenses like water through a sieve. The waiter came, she lifted her face, red with crying and embarrassment. Stanley took the fold of a linen napkin and dried her wet eyes.

"Courage, my dear, you are in my hands."

The food was savory, succulent. He coaxed her to eat a few bites. Her presence bewitched him; he didn't want to take his eyes off her face or be out of the range of her voice. This new desire fought a bitter contest against his fierce, angry need to find Tom Bede and punish him, punish him well.

The horses were drawn up well back in the shadows behind a long, rambling building. A stream ran nearby; its low singing kept Percy occupied for nearly half an hour before Officer Graff arrived. Burke Graff was the bigger of the two policemen who had assailed him three days ago and politely taken him in. Percy breathed a sigh of relief when he saw him.

"I hope you're not wastin' my time," the officer grumbled.

"I share that hope most fervently, sir."

Burke Graff gave him a short laugh. "I suppose a little excitement to stir my blood can't hurt any."

They waited long minutes still. It was damp and chilly in the low bottoms; it had rained well that afternoon. Even the trees dripped cold rivulets to run under their collars.

At last Percy heard the vague sound: light wheels crunching over wet leaves and pebbles. He inched his horse forward. The gray buggy slid into view. Mildred Boswell stuck her large, bonneted head out the window.

"Tom Bede," she hissed, "the man's name is Tom Bede."

Burke Graff spit into the bushes. "Yeah, I know him. I could have guessed him if that's what I'd been thinking. Come on, lad, follow me."

Percy brushed close to the buggy and planted a kiss on Mildred's rouged cheek. "Bless you," he cried. "Watch Allison for me."

Graff was already moving. Percy bent low in the saddle to avoid the heavy, hanging branches, and spurred his horse to follow.

Tom Bede lived in a hut by the water; the approach to it made the approach to the Prince's Lair seem open and pleasant. Percy heard the muffled baying of dogs and the hairs along his neck rose. They pulled off the path to where the thick shadows swallowed them and tied their mounts there.

"Mark this spot," Graff whispered. "You may need to know it."

They moved forward by foot now, at a slow, cautious pace. Graff carried a small pistol and a short, thick stick, which he handed to Percy. They had no other weapons. The door pushed open at their touch. Like a shadow Graff slipped inside, despite the bulk of him. Percy followed more awkwardly.

Surprise was clearly on their side. Bede sat at a table alone, drinking from a bottle of cheap whiskey. He looked up with bloodshot eyes as they came in.

"The boys are comin' for a game of cards later," he slurred.

"There will be no cards tonight." Graff jerked the man up by his limp coat collar. "Do you know who I am, Bede?"

"I know ye well enough," Bede growled.

"Good. The jig's up. We've got the goods on you, you and the good Squire."

At his words Bede woke up a bit, tried to squirm from the big hand that held him.

"I don't believe ye! Who squealed?"

"Frankie for one—the rest's none of your business. Shall we take you in now, let the citizens set a date for your hanging?" He leaned close to the sour-faced man, and made his eyes go mean and little. "We've got a list of stinking things a mile long we can pin on you, Bede, and you know it." He tugged at the man's collar. "Let's go."

Bede clung to the edge of the table and stiffened his legs. Graff pulled man and table a few feet, then stopped. "You want mercy? You can buy a little, Tom." He jerked Tom back by his hair. "Are you interested?"

"I'm interested. What do you want?"

"We want a confession from the Squire. Very simple. He'll be here in a while—here for your hide."

Percy watched Tom Bede visibly pale and shrink where he sat. Burke Graff grinned at his squirmings. "We two will be in the back." He jerked his head. "Right behind that door, Tom, so as we can hear every word."

"You just get yourselves out here in time to save my neck, Graff! What if he's carryin' a knife?"

"Then it's your tough luck, isn't it?" The two men glared at each other. Percy, watching them both, was consumed with one thought and one thought only: *Come, Stanley, come! Take the bait and come after him, Stanley!*

They both calmed down a bit; the meal began going nicely. Stanley ordered brandy for himself and ices for the lady. He was loath to leave Allison. Tom Bede could wait. He'd be drunk in his cabin be it nine o'clock or midnight. Stanley may as well take his pleasure here and have it later as well.

Ten o'clock came. He could see Allison tiring, she even yawned once or twice. "I am not used to late hours," she apologized.

"You're delicate," he replied, "you need taking care of." He called a carriage for her himself. He handed her into it, but before he did so he turned her around in his arms. She was his prisoner, she had no strength against his strength. He had covered her mouth with his lips before she could stop him. Her struggles were no more than the flutterings of a caged bird.

"You have fired me for the work I must do, lass," he breathed.

"Please!" She twisted out of his hold and sank gratefully into the coach, felt it move, lurch away from him. She did not look behind. Nor did Stanley stay to watch after her. He had ordered his black horse brought up; it was ready and waiting. Halfway down the dark road, as the coach leaned to take a twist in the path, he shot past it. In a moment more man and horse were blotted out by the dark hand of night.

Tom Bede snoozed; he was too drunk to do otherwise. Even Officer Graff drifted off a time or two, but Percy stood, wide-eyed, straining for the first movement, the first sound that would release him.

Burke Graff heard the first sound. He yanked Bede up to attention and made all ready. Percy couldn't see the black horse, didn't know where horse or man was. He heard Stanley enter the room: heard the chair kicked out from under Tom Bede, heard the thud and the curses toppling over each other. He heard the little man whine.

"It ain't true! I ain't been talking," he sputtered.

"You're a coward and a liar," Stanley roared. "And you'll never cross me again."

"Who's callin' who scum? It was your own brother you framed, man, I wouldn't do that."

"You'd sell your mother for the price of a bottle, Bede," Stanley slurred back.

Graff stood closest to the door, where he could glimpse what was happening; Percy had mainly to guess. But he sensed the tightening in Burke Graff's body, felt him lean slightly forward, tensed.

"It was a simple job, you've done many like it. I paid you well."

Percy heard the scuffle, the panting: Tom Bede was pleading, but Stanley paid him no mind.

"You chose the wrong job to botch up, Tom. Too bad! I'm calling in your number, you worthless —"

Burke Graff moved like a shadow, with that same efficient speed Percy had witnessed earlier. Men must be trained to do that! He was on top of Stanley; the struggle was short; he had the knife from his hands and Stanley to his feet with his arms bound behind him before Percy could grasp what was happening.

Stanley cursed like a demon, but Graff stood unmoved. "You'll have to come with me, sir," he said firmly. He glanced back toward the door.

"There's no reason for this, Graff," Stanley growled. "Don't make a mistake — you know I can have your job, you know I can break you."

Burke Graff twisted the rough rope that held his prisoner. "Don't threaten me, Squire. You're coming with me, one way or another."

Percy watched the two men leave the house. It sounded as if they both climbed up on the back of the black horse. He pushed the door and walked slowly out into the room where Tom Bede lay sprawled.

You can show yourself or not, as it suits you, Graff had said earlier. Percy took the rope from his back pocket and bound Bede's hands behind him. He hoped the policeman would understand. "On your feet," he said. "You can ride the officer's horse back. They'll be waiting for you."

When it came to it, he couldn't do that to Stanley, couldn't face him that way. During his long hours in the cell Percy had pictured just such a triumph, had reveled in it, in fact. But in the end he couldn't break Stanley in such a manner, face him and leave him no out, no last shred of dignity to pull over his nakedness.

He dragged the drunk man along, out to the bushes where the horses were waiting. He breathed in the moist, fragrant air of the night and everything, even Stanley, was forgotten in gratitude for the freedom he had to walk here, unhampered—the freedom that was no longer threatened, thanks to the courage of a very beautiful, very amazing young girl.

11

*T*hey had a key to the house and a legal warrant to be here, but Percy still felt like an intruder.

"She must be in the house," Allison assured him, "he must have hidden her here. He told me himself that there are countless apartments he could fix up for me—"

Percy raised an eyebrow. "You didn't tell me that," he answered. "You didn't tell me very much, actually."

She dropped her eyes. "It's over," she said. "We have to find Rose now."

Percy nodded and let things drop. The whole experience had been trying for both of them, but he was a little disturbed at Allison's reticence to talk about her part in it.

"Leave the girl alone," Mildred told him. "She can't face it all over again by talking about it. Give her time, lad."

He had seen Stanley at last: in reverse roles, with his younger brother behind bars now.

"He's got friends in high places," Officer Graff reminded him, "and some of them owe him. He'll be out in no time. It would help if you pressed charges."

Percy would not, despite Stanley's hostile refusal to even talk to him.

"Do what you can while I'm in your power, Percy. It won't be for long. When I hold the trump again I will show you no mercy, you can be certain of that."

That was the only thing Percy could get out of him.

"I just want to know where my sister is; that's all I want from you."

"I know nothing about Rose," Stanley persisted. "You can die and rot before I'd tell you a thing."

"Stanley entertains a hatred for Mormons that goes beyond any reasons we know of," Randall kept insisting. "That's the key to what's happened to Rose."

So they wandered through Stanley's house, feeling vaguely foolish, looking in closets, wardrobes, storage bins, calling up stairwells; the whole process had an eerie feel to it. The longer they looked, the more restless Percy grew. Something was gnawing at him, something he couldn't quite put his finger on.

It took hours of searching, and when the futility of it struck, a feeling of gloom, almost of desperation, beset them.

"If Rose isn't here, she could be anywhere." Allison stated what everyone feared. "He could own a house in any part of England or Wales or Scotland where he has taken her; we have no way to find out."

What was it that had been gnawing at Percy all day? He closed his eyes, tried to remember the dream. Was there something there he was missing? He had seen Rose by the tree, reading, content; then he had seen her rise up in fear and run—and the running had shifted, she was fleeing down corridors, *dark, narrow corridors!* Of course, that had to be it! Dark corridors: Stanley's halls were wide and papered in bright patterns and lit by tall, mullioned windows.

"A hidden passageway! There's a hidden passage, hidden rooms. Such things are common in houses this old. That is where Stanley is keeping Rose."

Allison and Randall looked at each other. "This isn't a romantic novel, Percy," Allison responded.

Percy didn't reply. He was on his feet. "There lies our answer," he insisted. He recalled the dream for them. Allison grew enthusiastic, Randall grew thoughtful. They both agreed.

"But how to find such a passage?" Allison lamented. "We could search for weeks, we could search for—"

"We won't search at all. I have a better plan. It's a bit farfetched, but it may do the job. And if it doesn't, no harm will be done."

He glanced around him with sudden attention. "Where is Stanley's man? What's his name?"

"Stanley called him Winston the night I was here," Allison answered. "I haven't seen him around. Perhaps he ran off once he learned Stanley was in prison."

"That may be, but he'll be looking behind his back if he did, and he won't be gone long. He must know the chances of Stanley obtaining his freedom and calling him to account."

"That's true, and Stanley would probably keep in touch with him and expect him to take care of things here."

Percy still acted uncomfortable. "You don't think he has seen us?"

"No," Allison said.

"Then let's get out of here, let's get Randall out of here, as fast as we can." He was moving even as he spoke. "I'll explain when we're safely home."

But by the time they reached their horses he had thought the thing through more carefully. "You two go back to Allison's house, I'll meet you there," he instructed.

"Where are you off to?" Randall asked.

"I have one last favor to ask of Officer Graff. Without his assistance my plan is useless."

That was all he would say. They parted ways. Allison rode beside the big, silent Randall and nursed her curiosity with a patience that proved quite unsatisfactory and gave an edge of irritation to the weariness the long day had brought.

Percy was grateful to reach the Clarks' home and pleased at the outcome of his interview with Burke Graff. He was surprised to see Allison at the door to meet him.

"Your sister is inside," she said without any other preface. "She came to see you."

"Not Randall?"

"Not Randall. Oh, she's met the surprise of him as well. But it's you she seeks. She has need of you."

He followed her, puzzled, to the back parlor where Louisa sat, straight and alone, her hands lying like stones in her lap. She turned when she saw him. He watched hope flare in her eyes, but her face reflected uncertainty.

"Thank heaven you're here!" She didn't rise, but looked up at him with an appealing gesture uncommon to her. "There still is time. Victor isn't due to return for another two hours."

"What is it, Louisa?" He sat down beside her.

"You must help me, despite what that girl says." She glanced over her shoulder to where Allison had graciously vanished and left them alone. "She thinks ill of me for coming in my need after deserting you in yours."

Percy wished he could have heard what Allison said to get across such a strong impression!

"I hold no ill feelings toward you. I think I understand, as much as I—"

"Then help me, please!" She reached for his hand. Her own was shaking and cold.

"What is it, Louisa?"

"There is a sick man in my house. Could you come and do what you do, whatever it is called—"

"You want me to place my hands on his head and to heal him. Who is this man?"

"My husband's brother." She looked at her lap as she said it.

"The one for whom your son is named?" She nodded. "But why are you afraid?"

"Because Victor would never allow you to touch him, and I believe you are the only one who can save his life now."

Allison's words came back to him, the description she had given him that day in the jail, another world ago, when she had told of her visit to Louisa, describing the man Percy had not even met yet.

He's much older than Louisa and so severe. She seemed ill at ease with him; I sensed no love between them, I felt only coolness from him.

"I'll come with you right now."

She rose, she half dragged him in her eagerness. Dorothy Clark appeared at the doorway and nodded when he explained his intentions.

"I'll warm your supper for you later," she said. "We'll all be waiting."

She meant Allison! He smiled gratefully.

"I have a carriage," Louisa was saying. "We can be there in no time at all."

The house felt of sickness. It seemed dark and too quiet, as if holding its breath. Louisa had been vague about what was the matter with this Ian; he had a terrible fever and spots on his skin. The doctors complained that he showed conflicting symptoms and so were not sure how to treat him, and he was not getting well.

"We have been caring for him," she explained, "since Victor's mother is dead and he has no wife of his own. But Victor is tiring of the strain on my time and resources; he fears his son may become infected. If he turns Ian out—"

"You're in love with Ian, aren't you?"

It was only a guess, but he knew it was true as soon as he had the words out and saw her reaction.

"Oh, Louisa."

"It is no matter. I made my choice."

"Did you love him before?"

She hesitated. The lines of her face seemed to go limp, to reveal the dark struggle that was normally hidden.

"I met him before I met Victor. I fell in love with him then. But when I learned he was the younger son, in all ways unfavored, and so would get nothing, I determined to set my sights on his brother. I wanted no more truck with poverty, struggle and uncertainty. I closed my mind to the demands that my heart made, and it was a simple enough thing to win Victor."

She spread her hands. They were trembling. "So, you see, I have all this—" Her face crumpled, like that of a wax doll left too near the fire. "I have all this, but I have nothing, because I do not have the man that I love."

He followed her into the sickroom. He was praying most fervently. Many times he had been blessed to know the will of God concerning a person, blessed to pronounce that fair will, and to be accredited for it somehow. He knew where the credit lay, and also the power. It was not his to say yea or nay. How could he make Louisa see that, if her desires failed to be granted?

He closed his eyes. He placed his hands on the sick man's head. He stood a long time without speaking. He knew Louisa had opened her eyes and was fidgeting in her chair. He stood entreating heaven until he knew that he could pronounce a blessing for recovery on the head of this young man who had been robbed of joy by the fears and insecurities of the woman he loved.

"She was lucky," Allison said as she watched Percy eat his warmed-over venison and dumplings and listened to his recital of his experience. "Some people would have refused to even try to help her after the way she's acted."

"One in this room in particular," Dorothy said to her daughter.

"She is not lucky," Percy said softly. "She's to be pitied. But when I put my hands on his head I felt that young man—well, I don't know, I'm not sure—but I felt something. We'll wait and see."

He was tired. Almost too tired to be hungry. Dorothy shooed him back to the inn and a good night's rest before Allison could "entangle" him, as she put it.

"There'll be time tomorrow," she said. "What's good today will be better the next day."

When he got to his room he found Randall snoring soundly on the bed that had been brought in for him. *Let him rest well. He's got important work to do tomorrow.*

Percy climbed into the sheets and closed his own eyes. He was too tired to wonder or worry. Let tomorrow take care of itself. Sleep was all he could think or care about now.

The note was written in the hand of the bailiff. Only the signature was a forgery of Stanley's name, very nicely done by Mildred Boswell, who had a flair for such things. She had taken a room at the inn and declared she would stay the duration, until Rose had been found.

"No one needs me at home," she had stated. "As long as you need me, I'll stay."

Percy was delighted. Mildred had proved invaluable so far; she may again. The sheer overwhelming enthusiasm and confidence of the woman was a strength to him. He felt driven and torn, insecure and betrayed, and in need of all the strength he could get.

The note was delivered early the next afternoon. Winston, the servant, was there to receive it. He read simply:

I am to be released. Expect me early
evening. Get out my best whiskey. We
have plans to set. Be ready for me
by seven. Master Stanley Beal [Esq.]

When seven came there was no black horse clattering noisily down the gravel drive and being tied hastily at the house front, no master bursting in with his usual bluster. Seven-twenty came, seven-thirty; still no one arrived. But the whiskey was ready on the table. Winston poured one glass for himself, then another. By quarter to eight he had drunk two or three more. At last he heard the horse, the muffled curses, and the master blew in the door with his cape billowing out behind him. Winston hurried to light more candles.

"Leave it," the master slurred. "The light hurts my eyes after that hole I've been in."

Randall was dressed in Stanley's clothing. Mildred had trimmed his dark beard to resemble Stanley's. He had even practiced Stanley's voice, under the tutelage of the officers who knew the Squire's voice well. "He should do," Graff had pronounced.

Randall was the least apprehensive of any of them; he looked upon it as an adventure. He had nothing to lose. And he knew he had the sheer bulk and experience to handle the smaller, slighter Winston should worse come to worst and the game be found out. His calm was good for them all.

Percy and Allison, entering through a back door left unlocked, waiting in shadows, straining and listening, had the less enviable task.

"This is a miserable business," Randall growled. "Pour me a tall one, and one for yourself. We've a long night ahead."

Winston did as he was told. Randall stood with his back to the light, shoulder hunched slightly, and gulped the drink down.

"I want to move her. There'll be no peace from that brother of mine till I do."

"That may not be so easy, sir. She's been a bit spunky of late. You let her out into the night air—"

"Spunky or no, what I have here will make her sleep like a baby." Randall patted his pocket. "Now, do as you're told. I've got some papers and things I must gather. You bring her down. I'll take things from there."

Winston turned. He did not head through the double doors to the library, nor yet to the long fireplace set in wood with a picture above it—not to any of the natural places where a button might be concealed, a trick panel in place. At the end of the room in a dark, shadowed alcove hung a portrait of the last squire, Sir Geoffrey Beal. The painter had done justice to the man, but he did not flatter him and the dark presence scowled with a quiet menace from its voiceless spot. Winston approached it now.

He tilted the portrait with an indifferent irreverence, his hand reached in, touched something, then he took a step back and the entire curve of the wall shifted with a groan of protest. Randall had walked from the room; he dared not linger to observe what was a customary proceeding, but with a sharp wave of his hand he signaled Percy and Allison forward from their hiding place.

They had discarded their shoes and moved as silently as they could toward the empty room and then through it to the curve of wall that jutted into the chamber and left a gaping black doorway revealed.

The servant had already disappeared into the blackness; Percy reached for a light. "You should stay here," he said to Allison.

She nodded. "I'm sure you're right, but I'm coming anyway."

It would be tricky to follow at a close enough distance, and yet not too close. They didn't want to warn him, but what if they lost him? They could have waited outside, but Percy feared that Winston might somehow harm Rose if she chose to resist him, if she grew frightened. So it was agreed Percy would go. Randall would wait and listen and play his cards as he found them before following after the two.

The corridor they entered was narrow and dark, as it had been in his dream. They could barely make out the dim glow from Winston's candle somewhere ahead. Allison was nothing more than a shadow, a wisp of movement trailing in Percy's wake. All at once the light ahead of them blinked and seemed to go out entirely.

"He's turned a corner," Percy whispered.

They followed more cautiously. It wasn't a corner he turned, but rather into the entrance of a room. He had turned a key in the lock and left the door partway open behind him. He did not hear their approach. He was arguing with the girl in the room.

"I'll not tell ye again. Anything you want here, you take it with you right now."

"But why? Where is my brother?"

"He's waiting outside."

"Where is he taking me?"

"I know nothing, lass, you know that. I just follow my orders. But I'll dare say you'll not see the inside of this room again."

"I ought to be glad for that," the girl replied in a low voice.

Allison put her mouth to Percy's ear. "It is Suzanne—Rose—I can tell by her voice."

Percy felt himself tremble. He wished Randall were here. His overwhelming desire was to rush forward and take Rose into his arms. They should have waited outside. A struggle here would shock and disturb her all the more.

He felt something touch his arm lightly, then grow firm. "Go in, you ninny, I'm here to back ye." It was Randall. When Percy still hesitated he squeezed past and walked boldly into the chamber.

"Hurry yourself, Winston. Go out and see to my bags, I'll get Rose out of here."

Winston turned and ran right into Percy. Randall grabbed his arms from behind and bound them with the length of rope he had carried slung round his neck. Winston blinked, more confused than anything.

"What goes, Stanley? What do you think yer doing?" He swore

a time or two for emphasis, but Randall just grinned, and turned to take a good look at his sister.

"She did grow into a beauty, Percy, just as I said. I'll take this gentleman outside and wait for ye there, but don't be too long."

Rose had recognized Allison; they stood with their arms round each other. There were tears in her eyes.

"This is what people call a miracle, isn't it?" she said uncertainly. There was something in her voice that sounded painfully familiar to Percy. "Who are you?" she asked. "You are my deliverer—"

He walked until he stood right before her. He watched recognition come over her the way the sun back home, trapped behind the high mountain peaks, suddenly spills across them and floods the valley with golden light.

"You are my brother! Percy!" She cried his name. Before he could open his arms she was in them. She smelled like Rosie; although grown, she felt like Rosie. He buried his face in her hair.

"I knew you would find me, I knew you would find me," she whispered. He raised his eyes above her head. The room they stood in was large and well furnished, warm and dry.

"Has it been awful for you?" he asked.

"I have not wanted for food or heat, or even entertainment. Stanley would always bring books, even writing materials." He could feel her tremble against him. "But it was a cell, shut up from the world, from the light of day—"

She raised her head. Her eyes, though tear-filled, were shining. Without turning to face her she said to Allison, "See, my dear friend. It was important for you to wear my locket. I knew it! Wasn't it Mother's locket that led you here, Percy?"

"Yes it was, Rose."

She moved in Percy's arms. "I do hope this is not a dream. I couldn't bear that—"

"It was a dream in the first place that led me to you, Rosie."

"A dream?" she repeated. "I think I have much to hear."

"And much to tell, we hope," Allison responded. "We have so many unanswered questions."

"My Percy is here, so nothing else matters," Rose said, and suddenly Percy knew.

"It is Mother!" he breathed softly. "Your voice is like Mother's—the way you just said my name—" He realized that his words had begun to slur. He looked with misted eyes at the two women he loved, and he knew that beyond them was the presence of a third one; he felt it strongly. Rose must have felt it, too.

"She loved you dearly," she said, "even as a small child I knew that. Mama loves you still, Percy, I know she does. I know she is proud of you."

He turned, even from Rose's eyes. The release, the joy was too much for him. He walked a few steps away, fighting the tears, though they were sweet, cleansing tears that swelled his full heart.

CHAPTER

12

*T*he three walked back down the cool, dark corridor together, ducking their heads, brushing against each other and indistinct cobwebbed walls; then they were out into the room, a bright, normal room lit by tall windows, and he was there. The servant, Winston, had been disposed of in some vague way that did not concern them. Rose blinked her eyes, and smiled as a little girl might who had been led blindfolded, and then shown the tree, the Christmas Eve tree hung with lights and tinsel and half-concealed gifts.

"It has been so long." The words reflected feeling more than sound.

The man who was waiting moved closer to her; Rose drew back with a gasp.

"Don't be frightened," Percy soothed. "You have one more brother yet to meet." He nodded. "Speak to her, Randall. Your resemblance to Stanley is frightening her. We'll have to explain."

He moved close to Rose, he took up both her hands, she struggled and twisted as he tightened his hold on her.

"Rosie—"

"Tell them, Rose. Tell them who I am."

The voice sent a little shiver along Allison's backbone. She drew away.

"Stanley, please!" Rose's eyes grew wide. "Someone, tell me what's happening—"

"You brute, let her go!" Allison darted forward with the grace of a young fawn, she tugged at his hands. "You've hurt her enough. I don't care how you got here, but it's over now, can't you see?"

Stanley let go of Rose and pushed her roughly away from him. "Yes, you little vixen, it is you I should be dealing with—"

He lunged toward Allison, but she had already moved. Percy's tall, slender bulk stood between them. "Don't lay a finger on her." They stood facing each other; the ragged drag of their breathing was the only sound in the room.

"You are mad, Stanley!" Percy spoke without moving.

Stanley lowered his head like an enraged bull preparing to charge. "Call me whatever you like. *I had my reasons.*"

"He was so in love with her, Percy, that's what it was."

Still without moving Percy let his eyes shift and flicker and find Rose's face. "What are you talking about?"

"He loved Annie Christy, and she loved him. He was happy then, he was different—"

"Shut up, Rose."

"No, let her alone. Let her tell us." Percy took a step forward. Stanley moved to oppose him, but then he froze. His eyes had gone beyond Percy to the big man framed in the doorway. He held a gun, and the long barrel of it pointed at Stanley's head.

"I can use it," Randall assured him. "I've felled many a border deer, and grouse stirring under the bushes."

Stanley stood still.

"Sit down, both of you," Randall said. "Rosie was talking."

Percy backed away until his arm found Allison. He sat with her beside him. Stanley stood where he was. Randall perched on the edge of a wing-backed chair, the rifle over his knee. Rose looked uncertain; she sank onto a small, overstuffed sofa.

"I don't know where to start—"

"Take your time, however you'd like," Randall assured her.

"I first became interested in Mormonism because May told me that Percy was a Mormon, that was why he went to America, why he left me. I was curious. I went to one of their churches and asked questions, I read their materials and I began going to meetings. But I knew my interest distressed the old doctor, and I didn't want that. He had been so kind to me. I agreed to use another name, Mother's name; that way I didn't involve him—"

"That's what I knew her by," Allison broke in. "Suzanne Miller."

"That's right. My study of Mormonism helped me through the death of Dr. Davies, through the insecurity and change when May married John. And there was another girl, a young wife when I first became acquainted with her. Her name was Annabelle Jones. She was newly married to one of the six Jones boys. Do you remember the family, Allison?"

"Yes." Allison glanced over at Stanley. "Yes, I remember them well. She died in childbirth—"

"She died because she was a Mormon, because her father made her marry a—" Stanley swore in his best form.

Randall lifted his gun. "That will do, Squire."

"This is my house," Stanley growled back at him. "If I must die in it, I shall yet have my voice."

"Only if you keep it civil," Randall warned.

"The devil take you! Annie wanted to marry me. She became a Mormon because of her parents, she married the man of their choice. And he let her die because he wouldn't fetch a doctor, said all he needed was to pray over her—"

"That isn't true," Allison murmured. "Annie was happy—she loved young Andrew—"

"Mormonism killed her!"

Their arguments were lost on Percy; he saw only the pain. He understood now. *Some other reason why Stanley hates Mormons . . .*

"An ignorant man allowed her to die, Stanley, Mormon or otherwise." Randall's calm maddened Stanley.

"Shut up!" he cried. "It was I who lost Annie, and I know full well why!"

"When John became determined to go to Australia and I knew he could not be dissuaded," Rose broke in softly, "I could think of only one thing: I had to stay. I went to Stanley. He was amazingly helpful, he was kind to me. He said he would offer me a haven as long as I wasn't a Mormon. As soon as I joined the Church he would kick me out on the street and let me die there if he had to."

"I had a chance with you, Rosie!" Stanley turned on her viciously. "Why didn't you listen to me? Why did you want to throw your life away, like my Annie did?"

"It's true," Rose said, swallowing with difficulty, casting her eyes about, as if to make sure of support around her. "I can see it as Stanley meant it now. He lavished affection and presents on me, hoping to woo me away. When nothing worked, I think he truly believed I lacked the wisdom to know—"

She shuddered. Percy could see her shudder, see the change settle down with the abruptness of his dream that reflected it. He touched Allison's hand and went over to sit beside Rosie. "Go on, dear," he said.

"You talk of me as if I am addled, or not present among you," Stanley shouted. "I'll tell, I'll tell what I did! I tried to get Rose to come to her senses. I knew she was young and could be easily influenced. If I made life wretched for her until she gave up these strange notions—I didn't think it could take long—"

"Rose is as stubborn as any one of us, Stanley," Randall quipped at him. "You should have known."

"You made life miserable for her," Percy prompted. "Just what does that mean?"

Stanley glared; the fine edge of his malice began to show for the first time. "I would think you could guess. You've seen enough of my ways and my methods, brother."

"You hurt her."

"You might say that. It's all in how you look at it: a little pain now to save a life of pain later, a life of unhappiness—perhaps even a painful death. If you hadn't shown up, if you hadn't persisted, she'd be free from it now."

Percy ground his teeth against his growing impatience, against the familiar rage building inside him. "What did you do?"

"I took away things she wanted: books, pretty dresses, sweets. When that did no good, no good at all, I locked her inside her room, let her weep there, let her go without supper."

"And then?"

Stanley cocked his head, like a fox who hears the faint bay of the hounds in the far distance. "What matter is it?"

Percy leaned forward; his hands were clenched into tight, hardened fists. "It is obvious that nothing worked, Stanley. What else did you do, before you took to locking her up in the darkness?"

Rose shuddered at his side and buried her face in her hands. Randall swore softly.

Percy rose. "Never mind," he said, "that's enough. You're right, Stanley, I shouldn't have pressed you." His eyes, with great weariness, searched for Randall. "Let's get him out of here."

Stanley moved low to the ground, with the speed and cunning of a fox cornered by mad dogs with their teeth bared. He was beside Allison, he yanked her to her feet with her arm twisted behind her. "Out of my way," he growled, "all of you!"

He dragged Allison a few feet with him. "Empty the gun and then slide it to me, Randall. Quick with you!" A low sound rose from Stanley's throat. "You do resemble me, brother. Did you have poor Winston convinced?"

"I believe we did," Randall replied. He was bent over the gun. Stanley saw his move before he had made it. He thrust Allison in front of him. "Don't try something foolish, Randall, I'm more than one step ahead of you."

With a scowl Randall pushed the gun along the soft rug; Stanley bent to retrieve it. "There's a good boy. What are you doing here, anyway?"

"Let's just say I got tired of Scotland."

"Let's just say you're a fool if you mean to get mixed up with the likes of him." He threw a dark look at Percy, whose angry eyes clashed with his.

"Your hackles are up, brother." He ran his fingers through Allison's hair. "She and I got along well during your absence." He caressed her with his eyes. "She hasn't said otherwise, has she?"

Rose's hand on Percy's arm restrained him. Stanley laughed low in his throat.

"I'm taking Allison out to my horse. Once I'm mounted and ready I'll turn her loose — unharmed." His scowl slowly took in the whole room and then rested on Percy. "If I even suspect I'm being followed — if I hear a sound, see a shadow —" He wound his hand around Allison's long hair and yanked her head back. "She'll pay the price."

"How did you get here?" Randall asked, ignoring his threats.

"We thought we were safe to carry out our little charade without interference."

"There are ways, and there are ways. Threats speak, and money speaks even better." He shrugged his shoulders. "I am safe in my own world. All I need now is for you to get out of it, stop interfering. I want no part of you!"

Rose had tears in her eyes. "He is so unhappy, Percy," she whispered.

Stanley turned, pushing Allison in front of him. They heard the squeak and scrape of the big front door opening. Percy began to move. Rose checked him again. "He means what he said—"

"He'll hurt her anyway—"

"No, in his way he plays fair. He'll only hurt her if you force his hand, Percy."

Outside a wind was rising. Its fingers tore through Allison's hair, its breath plastered her dress to her legs, forcing her weight back against Stanley. He turned her in his arms to face him.

"You betrayed me!" he spat at her like an angry alley cat. She could feel his venom.

"I'm sorry," she shouted against the wind.

He tightened his grip on her arms until he knew he was hurting her. "The devil you are."

"I was sorry almost from the beginning," she managed through teeth clenched against the pain.

"You had nothing but disdain for me—loathing!"

"That isn't true!" She looked into his face, met his eyes at last, saw the raw pain there, the terrible need. She did not have to lie to help him, only to stretch truth to the point of kindness.

"I found things in you that were attractive to me, that drew me to you against my own judgment and will—"

The pain flickered. "You lied to me!"

"I was fighting for what I love!" she cried, twisting until his hold loosened. "That is fair—I was playing your own game—you would do the same thing—"

"Yes, I have done, and I would do again." There was satisfaction in his eyes as he ran them over her face for the last time. "Farewell, little Allison. I could have made you happy, now be happy if you can—"

He drew her close and kissed her, at the same time releasing her hands. In the next breath he had sprung on top of the stallion. The black horse reared. Stanley turned him expertly and headed down the dark lane and into the wind.

Allison stood watching after him. Tears stung in her eyes. Shivering, she wiped them away with the back of her hand. She turned and walked back into the house. Percy was there at the door to meet her. His eyes were thoughtful, his face guarded.

"Did he hurt you?"

She stared at him and shook her head slowly. "No. No, he didn't hurt me. Hold me, Percy, please."

He stood quiet with his arms around her. He felt like an instrument that a brilliant madman had played upon, leaving his strings bruised and sprung, his soundboard quivering with a passion he could not understand.

There are some things in life we won't ever understand — who had said that? Way back in some childhood centuries removed from today's reality he remembered mistily: *Mother.* What else did she say? How did she end it? *That's where faith comes in.* Yes, of course. He should know that.

"I love you, Allison," he whispered. She was so dear to him. How could he ever tell her?

"I love you, Percy," she replied, lifting her face to his. "I have always loved you, I believe, and I always will."

It was a while before they turned to join the others, and by that time the black horse and its rider were moving rapidly down a far stretch of dark, lonely road.

There was time now, there was freedom. It seemed that in an instant the whole world had changed. Percy was with Rose now, he had Allison beside him. There was no more to search for and no more to fear. His thoughts began turning to home. Rose would go back with him, and Allison would return as his bride. Foremost in his mind was the joy it would be to see Claire again, to bring into her sure arms these people he loved, to mingle happiness with happiness.

Percy spent long hours with Randall walking beside the river or curled up in Dorothy Clark's quiet parlor. Randall read slowly, but he read carefully, and the questions he came up with taxed Percy's patience and persuasion. He would not be easily won.

"This is weighty, Percy," he would protest, "too weighty for me."

"Pray about it," was always Percy's instruction. And Randall did.

"I don't understand this. It makes no sense, Percy."

"Take it up in your prayers, then."

What Randall didn't realize was the fact that Percy was praying, too. Praying fervently, night after night, exercising his faith. And he was rewarded by seeing confidence and light replace the fears and uncertainties Randall had shown.

"You're taking the prettiest girl back with you," Randall complained during one of their sessions. "Where does that leave me? What of this Emmeline you threw over for Allison?" He was teasing, yet half in earnest.

"She's most probably married by now. But she would be no better for you than she would be for me." He closed the book they had been studying. "However, there is a girl . . ." The possibility was just formulating in his mind.

"Go on."

"Her name is Melissa. I've loved her myself since she was a child."

Randall frowned until Percy explained. His eyes grew warm as he listened. "Your adopted sister of sorts," he mused. "This is worth looking into."

"There's only one way to do that."

"You're right, brother." The slow smile came, and then Percy knew. "I told you I'd come to Zion if you'd have me."

"Does Mildred know that?"

"I've already told her to book my passage." The slow grin spread.

What a bountiful harvest! Percy thought. He dropped his eyes, blinking back the warm tears he didn't want Randall to see.

*　　　　　*　　　　　*

There were still loose ends to tie. Percy went to the vicarage one cool August morning when the gray skies were dripping, squeezing out only an occasional shower of halfhearted tears. With the overbrightness of the sun's glare removed he noticed how green the color of the grass was, how deep the shades of the last full summer roses. He knocked at the door. Jane Evans answered it. When she saw him she smiled. They walked out and sat under the shade of a catalpa tree on a low stone bench.

"My faith was justified, my stand vindicated," she stated in her smug, crisp way.

He took her small, slender hand. "Did the vicar ever know what you did?"

She drew herself up a little straighter. "He is burdened with many concerns; I chose not to burden him with one more."

"As you did when six orphaned children were thrust upon you," Percy said quietly.

She fidgeted a bit. "We all do our duties, do the best that we can."

"No, Jane Evans, some people don't. And some make of duty a shriveled-up, distasteful old prune the way Aunt Judith does—"

She raised her eyebrows in accustomed disapproval, but he smiled away her reaction. "There is more of a foolhardy spirit to you than shows, ma'am," he teased. "You finished off your show of faith with quite a wild venture."

"You mean our night at the Prince's Lair?" she replied, unblinking. "I've never enjoyed such an excellent meal."

"I shall never forget you," he said simply. "If it is duty as you call it, you have made of duty a benediction, as I suppose the Savior himself would have."

He leaned over and kissed her thin cheek. She blinked unwanted tears from her eyes.

"Good-bye," he called, walking away from her. "I shall write now and then and keep track of you and the good vicar."

"I should like that," she cried back at him. "Take care of yourself, Percy Graham. Don't let any red Indian with a tomahawk catch you off guard."

He turned back and waved. "I've no mind to do that."

"God bless," she called.

He turned. There were tears stinging his eyes, too. He paused by the quiet green grave and went down on his knees. *God bless you, Mother and Father, for being what you were, for giving me life—all this, all that life holds for me.*

When he walked away he left the last shadow of the orphan boy beneath the trees in the graveyard, to whisper his way among the unnumbered leavings of generations: he walked away a free man.

Mildred took over, in her way. No one minded.

"Write a letter to Claire," she instructed Percy.

"I've already done that."

"Have you written that son-in-law of mine? You'd better. Give him plenty of time to get used to the idea, time to get ready for me."

"There would never be enough time to get ready for you," Percy teased. "It's quite a menagerie I'll be trailing along to Zion with me."

Happiness was in the very air they breathed at such moments. But still, it was not easy to leave.

I will probably never see England again, Percy thought. President Clark was already making plans to join them in five years or less. Allison would have her mother and father, there would be no reason to come back; there would probably be no means. The city, the green fields, the river: he would never see them again. Laura and her border lord, Louisa and her Ian, Master Beal—what would become of them?

"You can't hold everyone's happiness in the palm of your hand," Rosie told him. "You have to let go," she said, with a wisdom past her years.

She was a new person to him and he marveled every time he looked at her. The child she had been seemed beautifully incorporated into the emerging young woman. Despite her sensitivity—or perhaps because of it—the things she had suffered had left no ugly marks. Rather than bitterness, her discerning spirit chose compassion instead. She and Allison were inseparable. Percy in jest complained that it was impossible for him to get either alone, and there surely were times when he wanted Allison to himself, as well as those moments when his tenderness for Rose overcame him, when the years fell away and she was again the small child who had pleaded, *Don't forget me.*

They spoke of those times only once. One dark night when he was brooding over Stanley she came to him, curled up at his feet like a kitten, and reached for his hand.

"Grieve over his unhappiness, Percy, but don't hate him," she said. "I don't. He isn't as wicked as he wants you to believe."

"How can you forgive him that way?"

"Because I love him. Because I've watched what life's done to him. Because I know how he suffers—" She hung her small head as though the weight of it was too much for her. Percy lifted her up.

"You're more Saint than I am," he cried. "I forgive him, but the anger is there still—"

"You're a man," she said softly. "It's different with men. You judge yourself harshly, Percy. That isn't right."

She placed her fingers against his chest until she felt where his heart was. "How strong your heart beats," she smiled. Her eyes were alive now. She placed her other hand over her own heart. "I was only a child," she began, "but I remember, I remember still what I said."

Her fingers stirred, touched the locket she wore now, moved over it gently. "*Don't forget me*, you said." Her voice had tears in it—sweet, soothing tears. "*I'll never forget you*, I said. *I have you here in my heart, Percy.*"

She looked up and smiled. "I gave the locket to Allison. I didn't really need it. I carried *you* here, inside." She rested her head against his shoulder and he held her.

"Did you ever doubt, Rosie?"

"No. I felt you would come for me, I always felt you would come."

Percy was aware of a weakness rushing through him. *What if I hadn't come? What if my own weaknesses, my lack of faith, of perception, had prevented me?* A sudden swift awareness of the influence of the Spirit in his life pierced into his mind with an almost overwhelming force.

"Don't ever let me take you for granted, Rose," he whispered fiercely.

She smiled coyly. "There's no danger of that. Allison and I, each in our own way, will keep you in line."

He smiled back, but his thoughts were still serious. What if Claire hadn't run into the vicar that afternoon? What if she and Benjamin had not come for him? What if he had not been raised up a Mormon, if he didn't know what he knew, if he didn't hold the priesthood power he had felt moving through him, blessing so many lives?

Why me? he thought, trembling. *Why have I been so blessed?*

There was much to be done in a very short time. Mildred preceded them to Liverpool to take care of her own affairs and the details of departure. It was much like his first departure from England; the days slipped through their hands and brought things to a close of their own accord. At last it was time to say good-bye to Louisa, to break the last tie.

She surprised him. "I've been thinking, Percy," she said. "I believe it was important for you to come—important for each one of us, not just Randall and Rose. You've touched each of our lives in some way, you've changed us—"

Not as much as I would have liked to, he thought sadly. *But I kept my promise. I did keep my promise!*

"Ian isn't mine, but he is alive, and I'm grateful for that. And I've faced some realities I refused to look at before. Perhaps things can change. Perhaps people can change and make things better."

"What makes you say that?" Percy thought she had a strange look about her.

"There's somebody here—who wants to meet you." The words twisted her mouth. She inclined her head and called his name, but before she had spoken it, Percy knew.

"Ian," she said.

The young man walked into the room. He looked thin and colorless, but his eyes were shining. He held out his hand.

"I'm honored, Percy," he said. "The last time you were here I didn't see you—of course. I've been anxious to meet you." His voice sounded tense.

"What is it?" Percy asked. "Did it distress you, the fact that Louisa called me, the fact that I administered to you—"

"Oh no, please don't think that. You saved my life. I know that you did." He moved to a chair and sat down rather shakily. Percy drew his own chair close. Louisa stood behind Ian, her own face white, her slender hand on his shoulder.

"I heard your voice. I didn't see you, I didn't know who you were, but I heard. I felt something—it must have been when you touched me. The sound of your voice spread over my body like a cool, soothing water. You made me well. How did you do it?" He leaned forward a little. "I want to know."

"It was not by my power, Ian."

"There was power, though. I felt the power."

"I felt it, too." Percy's heart was racing. The impression he'd had—the impression about this young man!

Percy liked the look of him. "Why do you want to know?" he asked. "Are you curious?"

"No, it's not that. I feel something inside. Some longing, some sensation that will give me no peace." He glanced up at Louisa. "She said you would help."

Percy looked past him to his sister. "Do you know what this means?"

"Yes," she answered.

"You love him that much."

She trembled at his words, but made no reply.

"There isn't much time."

"I'll go with you to Liverpool." Ian's voice was pitched high with excitement. "I'm well enough for the trip, but I can't work yet, so I've nothing to stop me." He said the words, but his fingers felt until they touched and held tight Louisa's limp hand.

"We'll be a few days in Liverpool. Yes, that might work. We leave tomorrow."

"I know. I'll be ready."

"Will you come, too?" Percy hadn't meant to say the words. Once they were out, he was sorry. He glanced guiltily at Louisa. Her eyes were wet.

"Not yet. Not this time," she whispered.

"You wish me to teach you, Ian?"

"Yes," the young man replied firmly. "I want to know about this power that healed me. I want to know what it is that I'm feeling inside."

Percy nodded. "I'll send Randall over later with details of time and departure point, Louisa." His head was reeling with possibilities. "Will that be all right?"

"That will be fine, Percy." She released herself gently and, leaving Ian sitting there, moved to her brother's side. She put out her arms and he held her so tightly that his own arms ached. His head and throat hurt with holding the tears back.

It was hard to let go, so wrenchingly hard to leave her.

An English night was drawing the color from the sky as she walked him out to the porch. His last Birmingham sunset, and it was already fading. How gentle the pale light was—not sharp like the light of day. He liked the light of the gloaming, he liked the feelings it harbored, the sensations it drew from him.

Another parting; another little death. Another new challenge ahead. That was what life was made up of, he guessed.

He kissed her good-bye, he left her watching behind him. There was no way he could change the tide, the destined movement and pattern of each wave in its turn. There was no way he wanted to try.

England bore me, Zion holds my future, he thought. *But it really goes deeper than that. I hold my own future within me. No matter what comes to me, I can make my own happiness or make my own woe.*

He turned the horse's head; the beast knew where to go now. *I'm a Mormon and I'm going back to Zion, and whatever happens I'll never face life alone. I know who to go to for help if I need help. That's perhaps the crux of the whole difference between Stanley and me.*

As though the very thought had power to call him forth in some strange way, Stanley appeared suddenly in the road before him. Percy drew on the reins. The horse slowed reluctantly. The black figure drew close, very close, before stopping. His horse pranced and blew out his breath. Percy gazed into two black eyes that held no meanness in them. The pain was still there. But the brittle glaze no longer covered it.

"I've been waiting for you. You leave tomorrow."

Percy swallowed and nodded.

Stanley leaned closer. "I can't let you go. Not like this. This will be the last time."

"Yes, I think it will."

Stanley moved abruptly to lean back in the saddle, lean away from him. "Do you remember the first time you left, when you came to tell me? How jealous I was. How miserably, wretchedly jealous!" He shook his dark head. "Life was too hard with the Squire, too hard. Do you recall what I said?"

Percy's mouth was dry. "I remember. You said you might stow away with me—you said you were the one, anyway, who ought to be going." He attempted a smile. "I hate to admit it, but I watched for you, Stanley. I even prayed. I prayed that somehow you'd do just that, you'd manage to—"

"Huh! What a blowhard I was!" Stanley growled out the words, needing to stop him. Percy felt himself trembling.

"Whistling in the dark. That's all I've ever done, Percy." Stanley's words were unsteady. His gloved hands clutched the pommel of the saddle as if for dear life. "Pity, isn't it?"

"Yes."

"I might have been better. The Squire, then Annie—" He shrugged his big shoulders. "It makes no difference now."

"It makes all the difference. You still have a long life ahead of you."

Stanley laughed gruffly, ignoring his comment. "You ran me a merry race. But then, I should have known that you would."

"It's in the blood."

"There's something to that after all, isn't there?" Stanley mused.

"I don't know why you came, but I'm glad of the sight of you," Percy said. "This makes no sense at all, but I shall miss you, Stanley, miss—"

"I'll have none of that!" One hand withdrew from the pommel and dug deep into a large leather pocket. "I've come for this—"

He tossed it and Percy lunged, grabbing air, his fingers touching, then closing around the cool hardness. It lay safe on his open hand. "The button from the greatcoat, *your* button—" Percy's words were scarcely audible.

"It belongs rightly with you. I lied when I told you I tossed it into the pond." He ground his teeth. "I wanted to hurt you."

Percy nodded his head slowly. "I know. It doesn't matter. It never mattered. This makes up for—everything—"

"I wouldn't go that far. You're a rare one, Percy." This was not easy for Stanley. He drew his breath in sharply. "I'm sorry about Rose. I was wrong. I couldn't help myself." He threw his head back as though in pain and sat stiff and erect. "I've come to make peace. What peace I can."

Their eyes met and held until the pain grew too much for both of them. Percy threw his arm out and reached for his brother. Their hands touched and locked. Percy was loath to let go. It was as though he had severed a part of himself when Stanley's grip loosened and lifted.

"Take care." Stanley pulled the black horse up and turned him sharply. "As the children come, write and tell me," he called out. "The marriages, the deaths—you know where I am."

He was moving. He lifted his hat in farewell and waved it. The black horse sprayed the fine dust and spread a burning red path behind them in the sunset.

Percy sat still and watched, his eyes burning like the red dust. He sat that way for a very long time. When the painful emotions quivered through him and settled, when he could breathe freely at last, he was left with one remaining feeling. *Gratitude.* He knew he didn't deserve all he had. He didn't deserve this much happiness—but he intended to make the best of it.

At last he moved slowly out. He drew in the fragrance of the rich English air. In just a few minutes' time he would reach Brother Clark's house. Randall was there, playing his mouth organ off in the corner. Rosie was waiting, too. And Allison. She would be with him tonight and for the rest of his life.